THE ESCALATOR

Andrew Budden

editstream
press

First Published in 2023 by Editstream Press

ISBN 978-1-7397391-0-2 (paperback)
ISBN 978-1-7397391-1-9 (hardcover, large print)
ISBN 978-1-7397391-2-6 (ebook)
ISBN 978-1-7397391-3-3 (audiobook)

A CIP catalogue record for this book is available from the British Library.

Cover design and typesetting: Averill Buchanan

for Margaret, Mark and Jill

1

The polyester and cotton navy uniforms were hanging up for each new working day. Lois pulled on the trousers and pushed her head and arms through the tunic, smoothing the white piping around the short sleeves and collar. As a teenager she had dressed sure-footedly too, though more quickly. She could be up and out of the house in minutes then to hang out with Kal and Maidie. She remembered the shoulder pads, the purple, orange and green colours, and the clashes with her mother. Mostly, adulthood had been a continuation from childhood for her, with Jack alongside. He was still muscular. She was still thin. He was reflected in the dressing table mirror as she brushed her hair. He was lying on the bed, comfortable in his skin, spreadeagled on his back, naked from his shower.

*

William was dead and Cas had moved south from Birmingham to the sea. It was a seedy place with a Tesco neon sign visible from the Victorian terrace but with a sea view over the mostly new town. Brexit, in name at least, had taken place, but William had died beforehand and they had cremated him. He had known nothing of the pandemic, but it might have been more fitting for the virus to have killed him. He had always embraced every culture, China and Europe especially, but life and death were rarely as accommodating. They had last seen the sea together some years ago. She had loved him for all his faults, and there were many of those. He was a remainer, for one, and he was often deluded, for another. She had gone there for the sea and to escape her family and her friends. She could not watch the sea in Birmingham. Her children, James and Lois, for all their support, knew nothing. She could cope. She always had. But the sea helped to keep it all in perspective. She had things to say, though no one to hear them. Some things mattered and other things did not. Most things were bullshit. From the shabby terrace, she could see mist over the sea and Lundy Island was rubbed out. At low tide, the glass-like sand continued to the headland several miles away, crossing the estuary, a strip of grey barely noticeable. The headland held distant wind turbines, partly obscured by rain.

*

Cas had suggested the cruise from Genoa to Shanghai because, she said, *everyone was at it*. And as they weren't at it themselves, they might as well go on a cruise. To cruise with Cas would be no holiday but, like every other couple he knew, they had found ways to navigate their relationship. William had worked hard with Cas to live in retirement like any other couple. There was no advantage in feeling guilty for having fallen apart in middle age. In many ways, they were just another pair of baby-boomers voyaging in the autumn of their years.

The idea of a cruise had appealed to William too. In hospital, some years ago, he had woken one morning feeling happier. He had thought he was on an ocean liner, and so a ship at sea symbolised his recovery and return to a measure of normality. They had been on a journey together and this subsequent journey could be thought of as a maquette for their life's larger sculptural journey that had chipped away everything other than the *David*, so to speak. He acknowledged that this idea could only work if, in a post-Einsteinian world, the maquette could follow the main sculpture.

This was an opportunity to take stock. In music, this would be called the last movement or section, when the chords and tunes of the earlier movements could be reinterpreted and, with any luck, a new tone or harmony could be found. Who was he kidding? Of course, he did not have to be on a ship to do this. In rural Worcestershire, where Maria from college and her husband Stephen lived, he could simply look up to the sky as the clouds scudded by or lingered above him, with perhaps the sweet scent of burning wood on the air. Alternatively, in Birmingham he could watch the clouds through the glass dome of New Street Station or the cars, buses, trams or trains, moving or stationary, petrol or diesel fumes lending context to the philosophical moment. But he hoped that by being away he might discern more clearly the patterns, sounds and smells that distinguished his life – or any life – at this time. This was not a heroic age and the most he could hope for was a measure of truth and completion to take back home with him to Birmingham.

Also, he thought, on a cruise, he might get a better sense of the distance travelled; more time perhaps to get used to not being where he started. He had never been on Concorde, and Concorde no longer flew, but he imagined that he would have no sense of journeying on Concorde, whereas on a cruise there was a greater possibility of comprehending where he had been, wherever that was. It no longer mattered greatly where he was. He could still be in touch through the cloud with family and friends – his daughter Lois, and her husband Jack, his son James, and wife Ioanela, his brother Paul married to Ruth, and Maria and Stephen too. At the same time he could keep his feet on the deck. Even when wet, the compound deck rooted him to the ship and to reality. It was still a comfort to him that the physical world seemed largely unaffected by his thoughts.

So they had set out together with their wheeled suitcases from Gatwick, flying to Genoa and catching the cruise there. After a tedious three-hour wait to board, they had started to enjoy themselves, in as much as an elderly couple could enjoy anything. Their cabin had an obstructed view, with a lifeboat blocking the porthole – a picture frame without the picture. This had suited William, if not Cas. To have had an ocean view would have been too indulgent, or so his father would have thought. As it was, William had never been so well looked after, and he felt the disapproval that his father would have felt at the sense of entitlement and rudeness of some of his fellow passengers. On board ship, rudeness was as much life as the ocean.

He had been swimming in one of the deck pools each morning. He was thin now and so the seawater had felt particularly cold at first, though it had warmed up during the journey. He remembered how, many years earlier, James with armbands used to hold tightly to him in the swimming pool, kicking fit to burst, and he remembered the smell of Bovril on the swimming pool balcony afterwards.

The breakfasts on board were an education to William. There was always fresh fruit, yoghurt, muesli, pastries, cheese, sausages, bacon, scrambled egg and fried potatoes. Then there was juice and endless cups of coffee. William didn't like using the linen serviettes as someone would have to wash and iron them afterwards.

'Aren't we allowed some pleasure in our old age?' Cas said. William would have been happier, were he young or well enough, scrubbing the decks or toiling in the laundry. He had taken to making porridge for Cas in retirement, so he took an interest in the ship's breakfast spreads as someone who at least knew what was involved in making breakfast. Cas had once attempted cooked breakfasts herself on Saturdays when Lois and James were teenagers, but they had never been like this. In fact, the breakfasts had rather got the better of her. He had never held this against her because he had married her for other reasons. He had married her because hatred was strong in her, including a hatred of God. This had made her stand out for him. Whether or not she could make breakfast had been neither here nor there.

In Naples, they had resisted the hawkers and taken the cable car up to the palace for a view of Vesuvius in the haze. The cable car had intrigued William as the tunnel had widened midway to allow the descending car to pass their ascending one. His mind was not scientific but he was nevertheless appreciative that the cable cars hadn't crashed halfway up. He was indebted to science, and the scientific method, even though he rarely understood it. The idea that rolling a ball down a slope on Monday was the same as rolling a ball down a slope on Tuesday appealed to him. The cable car also seemed to be akin to the web where, he was told, packets of information were transported, cable-car-like. It was also similar to an escalator, in that it went up and down, and also perhaps to the medieval concept of a heaven and hell as distinct cable cars either ascended or descended, with the added charm of Vesuvius waiting to encase him in lava, in whichever direction he was heading.

At Heraklion, they had been reminded of Greek myth and how, bull-like, the gods had been at it too, but the lack of passion between himself and Cas wasn't going to ruin their holiday. They had always been all right together, even in abstinence which, in truth, had been most of the time. They hadn't stopped in Egypt, but it had looked Pharaonic from the Suez Canal, with sand, palm trees and tiny boats fishing, if not carrying the dead into the underworld, or was he mixing that up with Greek mythology? A reference to Tutankhamun might have been more apt here. He had never been a stickler for the facts.

On the Silk Road bus from Aqaba to Petra, their Jordanian guide talked about the Syrian refugee camps in the north, reminding William of Syria's devastation and making him think that he had no right to be on a cruise at all with so much suffering in among this voyage. The guide also dwelt on Abdullah II's benevolence and descent from an uncle of Muhammad. Sitting next to him by the coach window, Cas gazed at the horizon with unbending dark eyes. This was her desert. William was fascinated by all the stones and olive trees he saw from the coach window, associating them with the biblical references from his childhood and his father's sermons. Petra meant 'rock', the guide said. In spite of their frailty, or at least *his* frailty, the bond between Cas and himself felt rock-like too, William thought.

They walked over wet stones through the gorge into the city lost to all but local Bedouin until the nineteenth century. There were ponies, pony and traps and camels climbing and descending, and tousled Jordanian boys trying to sell trinkets and souvenirs among the cathedral of Nabatean, Greek, Roman, Byzantine and Christian carvings intertwined with the natural carvings of time and water.

'It might be a wonder of the world,' Cas said, 'but it's more like Clapham Junction. Give me Dudley's Wren's Nest any day.'

'Cas says Petra's like Clapham Junction,' William texted to Lois.

'Look after yourselves,' Lois replied. 'It's raining here. Callie's home for the weekend so we're in McDonald's!'

William smiled. You wouldn't find Callie cooking.

After five days at sea, they docked at Muscat and visited Nizwa. William could still smell the fly-ridden tuna from the fish market when Cas bought saffron from the spice market for Lois, Ruth and Ioanela.

'They've nothing better to do than cook,' she said. 'Callie has more sense. She's got a mind. She never cooks. She takes after me.'

But Oman, like Jordan, made an impression on them. The Sultan appeared to have used oil and his Sandhurst training to good effect, at least for Omanis. This, combined with Ibadi tolerance and the lack of skyscrapers, was something to celebrate, William felt, among the empty values of some Gulf States and the devastation in Syria, Iraq, Afghanistan and Tunisia. And approaching Khor al Fakkan early the next morning, the sun from behind the ship had caught the twin minarets and houses of the white town and the wings of small waders swirling low over the water. It had also picked out in relief the red and blue hues of the mountains behind so that the picture frame was filled and nicely balanced.

In Dubai, he had gone down with a fever and hadn't eaten for two days.

'A good reaction to Dubai,' Cas said. 'Palm-tree islands, my arse.'

William was more interested in how wealth could distort judgement. From personal experience, he knew all about distorted judgements. Since the monetary crisis, Dubai had run out of money, but there was little evidence that any good sense had replaced the hubris. How did anyone back down from an insane project like Dubai? Only with Cas and Lois's help had he come to terms with his own insanity. William appreciated Dubai's difficulty. Dubai too, at some point, would have to wake from the bad dream.

Goa was lush. Their trip started in Old Goa with a baroque church containing the tomb of St Francis Xavier, the *other* St Francis. There had been more than one St Francis, just as there were now two popes. Their guide had then taken them further into the forested hills to the Mangueshi Temple dedicated to Manguesh, an incarnation of Shiva. Reincarnation had been an idea that William, as a small boy, had stumbled on for himself. It had not been a concept talked about at home. In other ways, he had been an unexceptional child. Now, nearing the end of his life, he felt that reincarnation had merit as well as a long pedigree. The idea was familiar to the ancient Greeks, as Leopold Bloom explains to Molly in *Ulysses*. There were so many things he would still like to do. Removing their shoes, they had entered the temple to experience the devotion of the Brahmin, young and old, at the temple's heart. And the stallholders leading to and from the temple opened William's senses to sacred India. Garlands, music, flower fragrance, gentle cows, friendly haggling, incense and ripening fruit contributed to this sensory experience.

In old Kochi, the cantilever fishing nets smelt of fish and were still lifting and dropping to catch fish as they had done for generations. These ancient timepieces were of Chinese design and had been described by Marco Polo. Did wheelbarrows come first? William wondered. And they had stumbled on the synagogue, an oasis of calm with a blue hand-painted porcelain tiled floor. The building's simplicity would not have been out of place in the Congregational churches his father had preached in. He touched Cas on the shoulder in the synagogue and felt close to her in other ways at that moment.

'They would have been better off in India,' she said, meaning her German family.

In Colombo, they had seen some fine Buddhas, including Buddhas with haloes. It was good to see the iconography shared, even if, having no god, Buddhism was more philosophy than religion, their guide said. She also explained that the impressive reclining Buddha at Kelaniya could be seen to be at the point of death because the feet were slightly out of alignment. And on the way back to the ship, their guide had sung to them about yesterday, today and tomorrow. In William's case, there was more yesterday than tomorrow to sing about, he felt. And, from the ship, the crescent moon now faced upwards like a pewter plate.

During the days at sea after this, they spent many hours together watching the wide wake of the ship stretching behind. On one occasion they had seen several dolphins swimming across the wake as if trying to stitch the water furrow back together. The wake was red, brown and green in the evening sun like gros point needlework and Ioanela's braided hair on her wedding day. But mostly they were content to simply stare at where the ship was coming from, wherever that was.

The ship had anchored several days later at the Phuket deep-sea port where they took a lifeboat to the Thai mainland. They had then taken a tuk-tuk to the old town in among the young on scooters, rather than motorbikes, and ate a pad thai meal as they looked over the coast. Yes, it was trite. But just how much could they ask of a holiday in the autumn of their years?

The next day in Georgetown, Penang, they had searched in the heat of the day for a restaurant serving sea bass and failed to find one. Just as valuable, Cas said, as searching for it and finding it, but she was mocking his puritan upbringing, of course. Instead, they found steamed dim sum, which were delicious, and had returned to the ship well satisfied with their failures and successes in the Penang heat.

At the Negara Museum in Kuala Lumpur the next day, there had been some stone Buddhas and, by way of contrast, a picture of Queen Elizabeth at the Independence Ceremony wearing long, white gloves. He remembered his mother wearing gloves like that on one or two occasions in his childhood, though she had been in no way pretentious. After the museum, they had taken one of the lifts up to the viewing platform of the KL Tower to view other towers in the hazy heat. William said that he felt nearer to heaven. Cas told him to pull himself together and that no one should pay good money to go in a lift.

And it was at this point in the cruise that William's Dubai fever spread from family to family and cabin to cabin as if rehearsing for a global pandemic. It made no distinction between crew members and passengers, but he identified those he considered heroes of this voyage, albeit of a non-heroic kind.

In particular, two dancers, Leonardo from Cuba and Fernanda from Brazil, who had a remarkable work ethic, like his father, and continued to dance throughout, lifting everyone's spirits with dance instead of war.

William had never taken much interest in politics, but this cruise showed him that politics made a difference. Singapore with no resources seemed to be built on strong government, high fines and immigrant labour. In another incarnation, he might have taken more interest in politics. His political judgements – perhaps most of his judgements – had always been poor. He had always thought, for instance, that the Berlin Wall was there to stay. And now, he could not fathom the Brexit vote, though Cas was a Brexiteer to her fingertips, nor Donald Trump's election. This world was no longer for him.

During his illness, he had embraced absolutism. Now that he was recovering, politics seemed to have taken on the mantle of his own madness and populism was everywhere. He was recovering, but the world had gone crazy! Nietzsche may have been onto something when he said that it was not doubt but certainty that drives you mad.

Visiting Raffles, they had, of course, like little Englanders, taken the Singapore Sling in the Long Bar and thrown the peanut shells onto the floor in colonial fashion, the only littering that Singapore tolerated. The light-and-sound show in Marina Bay afterwards might have made anything that Birmingham offered seem provincial and of little consequence. But Birmingham had Mirga, by way of Lithuania, a worthy successor to Simon Rattle and a match for any light-and-sound show. Also, Birmingham was where he was from and no one could argue with where they were from. William wondered why, in this internet age, he could not be in both Birmingham and Singapore simultaneously, for the sake of comparison. But having a unique location was in the nature of what a place was. Even on a privileged cruise that his father would have disapproved of, in spite of the obscured view and where most things were at his service, he still could not occupy more than one place at a time, even on board ship. But then places had always puzzled William and it didn't do to think about them too closely.

In Ho Chi Minh City, the old Saigon, they had both been moved by the photography from the Vietnam War at the War Museum, including the consequences of Agent Orange. What times they had both lived through, and without suffering to the extent that others had. His own small suffering seemed trivial. But the city's people were also touchingly welcoming and William had felt intrusive when their taxi driver had shown them into his home in the back streets, where each dwelling opened onto the street with dogs, cockerels or cats for company and smiling faces curious to see them. In Birmingham, William's family had not deserved to do so well financially. Mostly this was down to Cas, as he had had no gainful employment, or employment of any kind, after the age of forty.

'We should downsize,' he said to Cas, as they looked into a one-room home facing the street, with a smiling mother and two children and no more than a curtain for privacy. This family might well have a more meaningful life than his own family, William thought.

'I might as well have married your father,' Cas said. He knew what she meant. It was a bit late in the day to feel squeamish about his financial acumen or their life of accumulation, at least up to when he was forty. His father had never owned his own house, always living in the church manse, and had always lived frugally.

They had not gone far from the ferry terminal in Hong Kong, only as far as Nathan Road, when it started raining heavily. The colourful umbrellas had uncoiled as if a Chinese parasol dance had begun. With Cas, he descended the stairs into McDonald's to shelter from the rain, an elderly English couple surrounded mostly by young, cool Chinese with gentle smiles, the women with colourful tops, shorts or skimpy dresses, a life-affirming sight to William's old eyes. McDonald's, like other brands such as Quality Street, had become a kind of certainty in William's life. Wherever he might be, even in Hong Kong, and at whatever stage in his life – this must be the last stage or movement – brands brought continuity and a kind of stability, even though he liked to think that he usually disapproved of brands. He also realised that he had not been into a McDonald's for many years, in fact since his illness, and he sobbed quietly, remembering how Lois used to meet with him every Sunday in McDonald's by the ramp down to New Street and how he had refused to accept that she was his daughter.

'You sentimental old git!' Cas said. She didn't always complete her sentences. They sipped quietly at their eighteen-Hong-Kong-dollar espressos, William mopping his eyes with an off-white paper towel that for some reason reminded him of Diana's wedding dress.

William had difficulty in reading the signals in Japan. Was Abenomics working or not? Arriving in Fukuoka City on Shōwa Day, Cas and William were taken by their guide to Dazaifu and the Shintu Tenmangu Shrine. As they walked to the temple, there were three students collecting for the Kumamoto earthquake, a precursor of the Fukushima earthquake some years earlier – assuming once again, Einstein permitting, that the prequel could follow the main event – when the sea, terrifyingly, had receded before it advanced. Cas donated willingly. The guide told her that the sun was always watching her, implying that Cas's generosity would not go unseen.

'I've more time for the sun than for my bastard god!' Cas said, and she took her hat off so that the sun could get a better view of her. Her grey hair had bleached some more during the cruise so that it might now be described as off-white, but to William she was still as dark and striking as ever. Each of us is here, beautiful: like sushi, William thought, and then gone in a mouthful. Their guide also explained the level of the bow required for colleagues, the boss and the emperor. And she explained that, as workaholics, many Japanese workers would not take company holidays, and so national holidays, such as Shōwa Day, were a lifeline. But was there enough hunger for change yet in this ageing society? Was there enough willingness not to accept what was said, as Lois and James had quite rightly never accepted what he said and had gone entirely their own way? William did not know. Japanese cars seemed to be on the streets and Japanese cars had been everywhere in the other countries they had visited. The Japanese must be doing something right. At one time – up to the age of forty – William had had a proper job and had had to know all about Total Quality Management, and he still very much approved of continuous improvement, whether in engineering or in life.

At the Kyushu National Museum, there was no Staffordshire Hoard or folded cross as in Birmingham, but they had stood quietly in front of the stone sculpture of the child Prince Shōtoku, the founder of Japanese Buddhism.

'He's just like James,' William said.

'Not any more he isn't!' Cas said. 'Not the way Ioanela feeds him. And anyway, James would be looking down.'

Arriving in Shanghai in the evening, they had seen the Chinese acrobat show at the Central Theatre. William had called to mind Rilke's acrobats in the *Duino Elegies*, whose bored routine was compared unfavourably with children and angels. But acrobats were less of a brand than Quality Street. The acrobats of Rilke's 1920s Germany were not the same acrobats of China's twenty-first-century transformation, or of their Han-dynasty predecessors, who might have known all about newly invented wheelbarrows. William's reaction to these young acrobats was wholly one of awe and admiration, though he acknowledged something complex in their demeanour. There was also a feeling that, as a viewer, he was complicit in some sort of exploitation that his father might not have approved of. In the final act, a girl of possibly no more than sixteen, standing on one end of a see-saw – were the Chinese first to see-saws as they were first to wheelbarrows and cantilever fishing nets? – was thrown into the air by two young men that were a study in concentration, jumping from a high platform together, the girl landing in a chair at the top of a pole held by a man standing on another man's shoulders. There was true danger and apprehension, clearly visible in the acrobats' expressions, the danger not exactly akin to flying Concorde, where safety was at least partly in the pilot's hands, but in both cases the consequences of error did not bear thinking about.

'I wouldn't have let Lois do that,' Cas said.

For once, William agreed with her. 'Even with life insurance,' he said.

2

Lois boarded the slow train to the hospital. Wearing a surgical mask on the journey was a new variant. She had loved taking the train with her father as a child, holding his hand to climb up from the platform. Later, she had been there for him too as far as possible, trying to steady him, her own feet on the ground instead. He always had ideas but he never knew how far to take them. It was hard to say where he had gone astray. Perhaps he had not gone wrong at all. He would never stop thinking. Those long train journeys were always happy. There was a golden chair at the end of one train journey with him. Her dolls would have loved to sit on that chair. Now he was absent, and there was only time to arrange herself carefully in the seat before this shorter journey ended.

*

Cas watched the sea from her high window. It did not understand humour, or anything else. With William, she had been able to open her mouth and say whatever came into her head, however outrageous. He would smile sometimes, or at least understand what she was driving at, even in his madness and even when he disagreed with her, as on Brexit. With William dead, everything was clearer. She could dance over it all now, like Fernanda, the Brazilian dancer on their cruise ship, erotically never touching her Cuban partner as if the virus had already arrived. She was in a different place now, and the world was in a different place too. She would have loved to talk with William about the virus – make him feel responsible for it even, Donald Trump fashion. Were the virus to have killed him, they would both have appreciated the irony together. There would have been endless possibilities to tease William over his love for every culture and religion. She would have told him that this was virally unsound. He was the only person who had always listened to her and understood her jokes. Through his final illness they had continued to talk, just as, through her window, the waves at the seashore continued to roll, with the herring gulls above flying north and the sun catching their wings, white against the purple sea.

*

He had come some way with Cas in retirement since he had been in hospital. And he didn't mean only that they had reached Shanghai together. William remembered his stay in hospital in the old century. Dr Derrington, like an ancient alchemist mixing compounds, had eventually told William that he was recovering. The series of magic potions had worked. William was engaging with people again. He felt better too. He had noticed the witch-hazel's yellow flowers and musty smell in the hospital garden and the snowdrops on the bank behind the car park. He was a man at peace again.

Emerging from this treatment, he knew where he had gone wrong and what he had learned. He had come through all this and what was left of him seemed spare and uncluttered. It was a puritan idea that through difficulty he had found truth. But it wasn't necessarily wrong for being puritan! He was wasted. But what was left felt true. Now he could discern the essentials.

There had been a winter thunderstorm when he had woken that morning to a relative normality. He had briefly thought that the hospital building was an ocean liner with waves at the portholes. It had felt like the storm in *King Lear* bringing him back to sanity after a long journey ... and to the smell of cabbage from the hospital canteen.

It was almost as if the years before this had been in order to make him more human again. He had no personal ambition any longer; no axe to grind. But as Rilke had said, being here was wonderful; participating in his old age was all that he asked for, and to be an observer of his family and of this rich moment in history was privilege enough. He was already elderly but he was seeing things with a child's eyes, as if for the first time. He had spent his youth not knowing what he was about. As a young man, he had had his head in his books before marrying and getting an industrial job, having two children and acquiring other stuff on the way. After forty, he had experienced years of floundering through which he had explored many things. So in his recovery and beginning the last stage of his life it was good to be grounded again.

He recognised how lucky he was. Lois had stuck by him through thick and thin, always his dependable nurse. She had been there for him in the depths of his illness. She had never flinched. He was talking to James again – when James wasn't too taken up with Ioanela's dark smile and fierce temper. Lois, James and Callie were his family. He would be able to watch Callie growing up; she was an outward-facing girl, almost American – or as Americans used to be – in her sureness of herself.

He had become curious too about the other patients. Marjorie had always been kind to him during his stay, aware of his every mood and small improvement and, when he was sad, showing him well-thumbed photographs of all the dogs she had cared for. And then she had killed herself, saving up and hiding her medication over several weeks. The tenderest people often suffered the most. He missed her, but not as much as he missed Cas.

Cas was still the love of his life and he hadn't seen her in years. Love of this kind was not delusion. Why was she so essential to him? One reason perhaps was that she had confronted him and refused to accept his nonsense. She wasn't tender or sentimental, but his insanity must have been intolerable to her. He had believed for a time that she had taken someone else to be her lover. This was not the case, Lois had assured him. But Cas must have found it increasingly difficult to argue with his irrationality and argument was pivotal to her Jewish soul. She could either accept his madness, or have nothing to do with it. Lois had helped him to survive by tolerating his idiocy, by nurturing him as one of her patients. Cas might have washed her hands of his incoherence, but could she evade his love? Love worked on a different plane. His love for her had remained. Would she ever come back to him? Had she indeed stayed put for him?

William was back with life. And Callie, his granddaughter, would rush up to him and fling her arms round his waist, gripping on to him in the same way that James once used to hold onto him in the swimming pool. James now, rightly, embraced

Ioanela. Callie would also run around the hospital and say 'hello' to all the patients and nurses, apparently unconcerned whether or not they were too distracted to reply. Lois had been about Callie's age when, with Cas, he had taken her and James by train to see Tutankhamun at the British Museum. Lois said that she could only remember a small chair with gold painting on it from that exhibition – the first exhibition he had ever taken her to. But it was such things as small gold chairs that defined a childhood: blue was the defining colour from his own childhood; the same blue he noticed on police cars now – that mix of speed, rhythm, blueness and apprehension. He remembered the colour of the childhood blue, but not the exact object. China's Terracotta Army had not even been unearthed then but China was now on the march.

Lois had taken him shopping to Marks and Spencer last week for new clothes. The store had been dull. These were hard times. But he had imagined himself flirting with one of the shop assistants like a man without shame. How beautiful the city had seemed! The women, men and children of different races, shapes and sizes were wondrous. Had there ever been so much beauty in his life? The girls in hijabs or low-rise jeans gave him joy and hope. He had noticed that the shoppers, contrary to what he had been led to believe, did not seem fat, lazy or uncaring. They were just getting on with their lives. They shopped mostly in pairs or with young children and they carried more paper carrier bags than plastic ones, filling them with fresh soup in plastic cartons, among other purchases. They were not looking for trouble or fame. They appeared to be mostly happy with their lot and with their companionships or families. He had noticed the smiles and the hand-holding. The ordinary had at that moment seemed entirely honourable. Lois had had to cajole him back to the car. He was more comfortable with others again and he could smile sympathetically when Ava, the nun, rolled on the floor and kicked her legs in the air, calling out in anguish as if for the poise of her youth or the wind in her hair. This could have been a cormorant's courtship display, her black habit in disarray. It was a comfort, in a way, that a nun also needed psychiatric help, the confessional not always adequate. He knew her plight. He had been there too. In fact, he could have made love to her on the hospital floor, their wings beating together and his new eyes taking everything in.

He had written to Cas and told her that he still loved her. Was it really so many years since all this had started? He couldn't remember much. But love wasn't subject to time. He would always love her.

Paul and Ruth had come to see him in the hospital several times recently. They had sat with him in the lounge where the television was always on. They talked about Darren who lived in North Carolina now, with his American wife. 'It makes you think,' Ruth had said. 'His legs once didn't touch the floor when he sat in a chair.' And William had been surprised to learn that Paul with Ruth had tried to talk with him constantly between the two weekends, even at the end when William was living on the streets. And he found it hard to believe it when they said that Cas had been with him almost every day during this period – accountancy permitting – and that her unfaithfulness and rejection of him must therefore have been only in his own head. William could not remember having seen any of them since that first weekend a long time ago. Maria came yesterday too from Worcestershire with Stephen, holding Stephen's hand in the hospital, her faith unaltered by circumstances or surroundings. She had been talking with Cas, she said with a half-smile, as if she had access to a larger proposition than words could convey. This reminded him of how his parents used to talk when he was a child, leaving William reassured that everything was in hand.

He was piecing together the beginning and end of the episode, if something that spanned many years could be called an 'episode'. He did not remember much of those years. But the period certainly had a beginning and an end in two weekends.

Another patient had taken out the picture from its frame on the wall beside his bed, leaving the empty wooden frame still hanging. This empty square provided both fixity and comfort. He pictured a round Chinese coin with a square hole in it, as if he held the cold metal in his still soft hand. In Chinese cosmology, the Earth was thought to be square when the coins were first minted and the heavens domed, like a Wagenfeld lamp. He too had squared the circle, circled the square. Each weekend related to the other: the first seeming to lead inextricably to the second; the second concluding the first. This frame seemed to enclose his craziness and he could examine that empty picture; the first weekend at the bottom, the second weekend at the top, and the intervening period a bare wall lost to his memory, an outline to wonder at and share with others from the safety of his recovery where he could draw a circle round it.

Philosophical analysis had taught him to view a problem in different ways, and an alternative rendering of the period was as an escalator: he remembered stepping on at the bottom on the earlier weekend and stepping off with the more recent weekend – nearer to paradise perhaps – but not the moving steps carrying him upwards through time, and on which Cas had often held hands with him, though he remembered nothing of this. There was no escalator in the hospital for him to examine, other than the one with angels on it moving up and down in his mind's eye occasionally.

An empty picture frame and a moving escalator could only go so far in explaining the period between those two weekends. The empty picture frame before his rounded childlike eyes on the square hospital wall did not show the change in him between the two weekends, whereas an escalator could encompass change, though it was too mechanical for what had happened to him and therefore also an imperfect analogy.

The closing weekend was separated further for him by the smell of cabbage and hospital corridors. He had woken on that Saturday in November at the top of the escalator to recall the earlier weekend when he had been trapped in the claustrophobic world of family and possessions. He had not been as content then as he was now. On the weekend that his long journey had begun, at the bottom of the escalator, he had woken cold, the chill of self-doubt in his heart.

*

It had been a cold morning, but he liked the excitement of winter. He liked to wake up cold. He sat on the edge of the bed and rubbed a hand over his forehead, round his cheekbones and under his chin. It felt as if a team of spiders had been at work, traversing every crevice. He wasn't a fresh-faced boy, but he was handsome enough in spite of the nooks and crannies up the neck, round the cheeks and over the forehead. And with a day's growth of stubble, the spiders would have a field day.

Uncomfortable about the unfortunate association of 'stubble' with 'field', he felt for his slippers with his feet. He would not put the Wagenfeld lamp on. He knew from her heave and sigh that she was sleeping. She was a light sleeper, often catching her only solid sleep in the early hours as he was waking. Was this a carry-over from her Jewish ancestry: the long, cold nights in the desert with Abraham, sleep only possible when the sun got up? Besides, it wasn't good to be always pulling at the lamp's cord switch. And it was on her side of the bed in any case. He leaned down and lifted the scuffed backs of the slippers over his heels. How expensive they had been and they were ruined already – quite flattened along the back. He would buy a cheaper pair next time. It wasn't worth the extra if they still got scuffed.

Was it Puritanism that made him avoid the landing light switch too, or an older instinct seeking out the winter light, the morning mist? He drew back the curtains at the top of the main stairs. Lois and James would be sleeping. He liked the thought of them asleep in the two attic rooms at the top of the stairs. It was good to be up before the family, nice to have them still asleep while he was up and about. It reminded him of the fishing trip with his father. They had had to be up while his mother and young Paul slept. He saw his father's dog collar and those searching, Congregational eyes behind the tortoiseshell specs. It had been a good feeling to be up with him then. Now it was a rather different contentment. Now he, in his turn, was the father. The family was as secure as a man could hope, mainly because Cas had always earned more than him. But he liked to think that he had also been alert financially – bought the house in the late sixties, borrowed excessively, invested in antiques, gold (he had sold the gold at $850 an ounce), granny savings. Then he had switched into Gilts and National Savings twelve months ago, before interest rates fell – 'Noah's sense of timing', Cas had called that move, though this compliment, from an accountant, a lapsed Jew and God-hater, had not been without a certain irony of tone. As he crept down the stairs, steadying himself on the banisters, he remembered those curiously unbending dark eyes of hers. Banisters! What a quaint old word that was. Banisters were for an age when the downstairs connected with the upstairs, when one area of life could be expected to bear some relationship to another area. Now the connections were all askew; father to son, husband to wife, land to sea, work to home, life to death, and there was no certainty that the Higgs boson existed at all. The last banister generation was already gone. *Goodbye last banister generation!* he thought.

He ran the tap full pelt and filled the kettle. The water rang against its metal sides. The tea was better with fresh water. But his father had taken this too far, making William empty a kettle of boiled water because it had boiled too long. 'You've boiled out the oxygen,' he had said, huskily. His father had been dying and he was stooped slightly by then, but he had held on grimly to that gentle authority of his. This had saddened William; his father always so careful not to waste anything: eating cold potatoes, scraping the mould off bread, soaking stamps off envelopes; sticking the old slither of soap onto the new bar. Watchful his father had been, and almost as white as the sink itself; the son tipped the water away as if it were his father's lifeblood.

Still, the new kettles had a cut-out switch and he could not over-boil. He warmed the brown china pot, took a teaspoon of red label tea from the tea caddy and poured on the water. The caddy was decorated with filigree paper and, at the front, the picture of a chubby boy painted in blue on yellowing silk. It had a keyhole at the front too, but the lady he had bought it from had said that her grandmother had lost the key on an outing to Brighton. The story seemed unlikely enough to be true. He ran his finger over the top of the caddy's mellow wood, feeling that it was really rather too good to use for tea. It dated back to before the close of the eighteenth century. Jane Austen would have been a girl at the time.

His mother had always allowed one spoon for each person and one for the pot. By that reckoning, it would require three spoons. But that was afternoon tea: she had conjured up cup after cup of the stuff, and wholesome chat to go with it. Her secret, she had said, was never to let the pot run dry. She would add hot water from the kettle after each pouring. She had had a way with tea. And she had spent her life in the kitchen. There were always scones or a cake for visitors. And the smell of her fruit cakes pervaded every corner of the house as they were baking, as had her love for her family. With Paul, he would scrape the bowls while she wrapped the cake tin using string and brown paper.

'It's as if you don't want it to cook!' their father would say, but she would only smile and carry on. And it was the same with her children: they were wrapped in brown paper. Cas, as a mother, was poles apart.

Even the short flight of stairs with the two cups of tea made him breathe slightly faster but he was middle-aged and this was to be expected. 'Here we are!' he said quietly and he put down the cup on the stand beside Cas, next to the lamp. This was all that it would take to wake her. She used to wake up almost before the babies started crying. The children could now look after themselves. Nevertheless, seeing their youth made him still feel necessary.

He took his cup to the washbasin. It was a comfort to have it there although the prospect of drinking it was perhaps better than the fulfilment, as with reductions in the interest rate.

However, such anticipation had to be grounded in fact. The tea, shimmering and murky in its cup, needed to be there – its stiff aroma at the back of the throat, the steam rising – concrete evidence of what was in store. Poetry was like that. It needed the object to nail down the idea. Indeed, without the object, he could hardly think at all. Words depended on objects as much as objects required words. Neither could be understood without the other. Like man and wife, perhaps.

3

Lois took care of life and death as a matter of course. She had not been involved with the virus especially, but geriatric wards had patients not in the first flush of youth. She liked to have a mug of tea before ward duty, always arriving early and sidestepping the smokers – nurses, visitors and patients – outside the glass hospital doors. Her father had loved such contrasts; *boundaries are where things happen*, he would say. Patients did not always know that they were dying, another boundary. It was not for her to tell them unless they asked. She never took her job for granted. She respected her patients. Her staff usually followed her lead, holding their hands if their family could not be there, which was often the case now. Alternatively, if they wished to be left alone, they were left alone. Her mother wished to be alone at the moment. Lois was no priest, rabbi, imam or pujari, but she could hold a patient's hand if this was what they wished for.

*

Cas held the mug of tea in her hand and watched a luminous fog over the sea, outlined by the oak window frame. The headland was blotted out. The virus did not reside in the fog. William no longer resided anywhere that she knew of. The nature of place had always been of concern to him. She had no idea why this was one of his madnesses but it need trouble her or him no longer. William had been flawed in so many ways but he had also always seemed to contain all the kindnesses that she had known as a young girl. Marrying him had been like marrying the rabbi. He was always rabbinic while she was nothing of the kind. It had been her choice to be with the sea eventually. She had chosen to be here without anyone else, though Lois, God bless her, phoned each day. Unlike William, she welcomed her country's approaching self-government. She held Parliament dear. But she was also an observer of the pandemic's fracture. How could you not hug each other even in old age, or especially in old age? Now, with lockdown, everyone else seemed to be without anyone else too. There was a low murmuring from the breaking waves stretching out along the beach, with a gull's sequential call above as it circled in the sunlight, though the sun was only visible at dawn and dusk from this north-facing terrace window.

*

The hospital canteen had neon lights and a visitor might have expected it to be without soul, but he had found solace there, in spite of the fact that the vegetables were always boiled too long. Perhaps this was part of the treatment. Cabbage aromatherapy. The seating was informal but he usually felt welcome whichever table he sat at. There was little room for antagonism and the nurses were the salt of the earth; the salt the cabbage needed. They were as patient with him as Lois had always been.

My papacy is nearing an end, he remembered thinking, running a finger across the top of the picture frame as if checking for dust. The dampness was in his body, particularly at the back of his neck where the papal vestments, *pontificalia*, never kept the winter out. This discomfort had been for a purpose, of course. Through such difficulties he came to understand what mattered more fully.

His soul had not always been so much at peace. Before the cardinals had made him their pope, he remembered waking on a similar morning; then, as now, with the first signs of light. He had woken in more physical comfort then, but in greater confusion. It was only now, at the end of his life, that he had found clarity of mind to bestow on the Church.

It became particularly important as his body declined – the body of the Church, he might say – that he should keep up appearances. Today, therefore, he would shave. It would enable him to build a bridge to that weekend when his mission had begun. He still had some money from his *Big Issue* savings. Tony's Tenth Anniversary Issue – 'Grin & Blair it' – had sold well. Some of his colleagues selling *The Big Issue* had not kept their heads above water. To be blunt, some of them should have been in a psychiatric hospital. Certainly, few of them had his inner strength or were as firmly rooted in the real world. He intended to shave today if he could find a razor. New Street Station would be the place of his anointing. When he was on the streets, he could not put his coat on to go outside. His coat was always on, summer and winter. Without it he did not feel dressed. His coat was his home. He climbed the ramp from New Street past McDonald's, where the night before he had paid for the nuggets with his *Big Issue* salary. There was still the smell of fries and the certainty of low wages that a pope might campaign against. There was a camera trained on him even at this time in the morning. Out of habit, he glanced in the bins for discarded beefburgers. The plastic sacks had recently been emptied but he decided that he wasn't hungry any more. In fact, he felt sick as he went down the escalator on the left-hand side. *They would not get away with that in London*, he thought, *or indeed in Rome*. Birmingham people did not observe London ways, or European ways. It was still a provincial city.

He remembered going up an escalator like this on his own as a boy. A woman had been coming down, and she had laughed at him continuously, loudly, rudely, so that everyone else on the escalator could hear and knew him to be the centre of her attention. Had that woman been mad? he had often wondered. Or had she seen something: the boy in short trousers on his way up; the old man on his way down, feeling sick? He could not blame her for her amusement. Had she seen the structure of his life, of any life, and laughed at its futility? But he would still shave if he could find a razor.

The people waiting outside the station were mostly young. *It was such a privilege to be young*, William thought; a privilege the young rarely valued until, like him, they were no longer young, perhaps even sick. Sickness was like entering another country, and he acknowledged, with Heidegger, that boundaries were interesting. He gently lifted a hand to them and blessed them pontifically. The station had open access. No one needed a platform ticket. This was just as well because a pontiff, like members of the royal family, rarely carried money. He needed twenty pence for the toilet. He could not find the twenty pence that he had carefully put aside after purchasing the chicken nuggets, but he was thin enough to squeeze through the turning barrier without paying. No one would have expected the pope to pay in any case. The royal family had been through the mill too since that weekend many years ago when life had started for him. There had been no royal yacht for the Queen recently; hardly any public interest at all. And even royalty could not walk on water. *The Big Issue* certainly hadn't mentioned her. And yet, since Diana's death there was perhaps the sense of order restored, as at the end of a Shakespearean tragedy. Peter Townsend's example that Christian marriage was indissoluble had been left hanging in the wind, and perhaps this family was ready to be modern and to embrace Hollywood as well as divorce. This was the decree absolute that mattered and all romance must come to this, William thought obscurely.

There were no discarded razors to be found, but he had shaved earlier in the week. If he had found a razor, he would have shaved. He would pray instead of shaving. The reason for not shaving might be revealed to him in due course as he prayed.

He lifted his head weakly from the washbasin and blinked. His own vomit was almost as bad as someone else's and there was the added sadness of knowing that it was he who was sick. He had not noticed anything wrong with the discarded curry he had eaten on Friday night after the chicken nuggets, but even a sage could not be sure how long it had been there. The Diwali fireworks had kept him awake, so he had combed the pavements around St Chad's for something to eat, just as his parents had always given him a banana when he'd had difficulty sleeping as a child. It was no surprise to him that this portentous time in his life should coincide with Diwali, with Eid at the end of Ramadan, and with Armistice Day. Wearing a poppy – as well as the grinning Blair cartoon on the front of *The Big Issue* – may also have helped to boost his earnings last week, although it was hardly a controlled experiment. Perhaps the contributors surmised wrongly that he was an ex-soldier down on his luck. Still, a prophet, by definition, was concerned with the future rather than the past. Illness was merely a part of his present trial. Such suffering was ennobling: it enabled him to comprehend the world and his place in it. And after being sick, the shakiness was soon counteracted by a sense of relief.

William, well-schooled in humility, would not leave the mess for the next man. He pushed up the ornately embroidered drapery around his coat sleeves and put both hands into the mixture, moving them around expertly while running the tap to clean the basin. As he did this he looked in the mirror above. He was unrecognisable as the man who had looked in the mirror in his bedroom that November weekend in 1982, when he had been shaving and had begun to see the reflected light. But perhaps this was what was meant by supersymmetry. He remembered the year because it had been the last year that he had had what might be thought of as 'a mundane job'. He had vision and fulfilment now, but his body had wasted. It was better to keep his eyes on the basin. Vomit was more cheering. He had been in the thick of family life then. At the bottom of the escalator, he had woken to realise, as if for the first time, that he was not a fresh-faced boy any more. He had known then that he must take charge of his life, take himself seriously and, true to this revelation, this was just what he had achieved. He had learned the way that mattered. He knew the value of love.

*

If he squinted in the shaving mirror, he could see her ruffled dark hair above the roses of the continental quilt. She was quiet enough now. Not that they talked much at the best of times;

not as much as Lois talked with Jack, or just stared into his eyes. There was a resoluteness between Lois and Jack that he still had with Cas too, a circle around them in the sand. Lois drew other circles. She talked to her mother, and to Kal and Maidie, of course; red head to green head; earring to nose-ring; chatter, giggle, chatter. They should talk. They talked about Michael Jackson, whoever he was. And they practised something they called *moonwalking*, hamming up all the movements as William felt sure they were ordained to do. Talk and dance might not come so easily to them when they grew older. Such frivolity wasn't for Cas and him any more, he felt. Nevertheless, the quietness between them seemed healthy enough: it was out of alertness to each other and out of long association rather than from any tiredness or lack of contention between them.

He washed his face, content with this thought and dabbed on soap from the can. As he did so, he caught sight of his back view reflected in the swing-frame dressing mirror on top of the chest of drawers. That mirror, unlike the scabby one above the sink where he now shaved, was valuable. He noted its bow-fronted base in gleaming mahogany. At least he wasn't bow-fronted, nor were his buttocks unsightly. Nevertheless, it was unsettling to catch himself like that; the two mirrors passing his shape back and forth to each other into posterity.

Punning was not for the twentieth century, he felt, as he scraped off the foam in the way that his father had scraped the mould off bread. Metaphor was more likely to do justice to the complexity and confusion that he, for one, felt. But then again, metaphor had probably had its day too. He squinted at Cas again. He could tell from the crinkles on her forehead and the deliberate scowl in the pursed lips that she was wide awake now. She was watching him with derision. It was East Europeans, with names like Svetlana or Ioanela or Mirga, who were meant to scowl like that. They had less to hope for, arguably.

He had noticed a similar expression directed at the children yesterday evening. She had said to them: 'God help me, I love you – acne, earrings, feet on the table – and to think the best years of my life went into creating slobs!' She did not always complete a sentence. She did not need to. 'Look at me!' she had said. 'No lorry driver would pick me up, more's the pity. Seventeen years of my life and nothing to show for it! Not even a lorry driver. It's as well my plot is paid for in Witton. I won't have to look at you there!' In fact, Lois, if not James, took great care over her appearance. But Cas was right not to give the children credit for anything. It was her duty to keep up the offensive.

He continued to glance in the mirror at her as he shaved off the remaining soap on his left cheek. She sat up in bed and reached clumsily for the tea. He had the advantage over her at this time in the morning.

'What have you done to this?' she said, pulling a face. He dabbed himself with the flannel, smiling. He knew his wife. 'Tastes like you're shaving with the milk!' she added.

This was feeble for Cas but it was early in the day. He had married her because she could surprise him, keep him guessing. 'Will you still love me when I'm sixty-four?' This had been a good question. He had taken the song seriously at the time. He had taken everything seriously then. Now, he felt more strongly life's uncertainty, so that sixty-four seemed more than he should contemplate. But he had thought to himself then that no girl would love a man who had lost interest. Love cut both ways. He thought of the other girls in their tight-knit, ribbed cardigans and piled-up beehive hair. They had liked him too. At least, he remembered it that way. It was not only he who was liked: everyone had liked everyone, such was the unreality of student life then.

The happiness had perhaps been a kind of delusion or, at least, a diversion from what really mattered, like the fairground in Rilke's *Duino Elegies*. The pressures came later. It was as if the moth mothers, in their buns and tweeds, had given birth to smiling butterflies, quite lacking in austerity and resolution. Never before or since had he met so much absurd goodwill. But Cas had been different and he had married her. She had hated just about everyone, God included. Hatred was very strong in her and this had pleased him. It still did. He never quite knew where hatred would end up. Love, on the other hand, was predictable.

Cas had always seemed amused at how seriously he had taken his essays in literature, philosophy, theology and art. She had eventually become an accountant to support the family, but she had always matched, if not surpassed him. Unusually for students of the time, he had taken care over every word. The essays had become a part of his soul, whatever his soul was, were the soul to exist. He had completed his doctorate through conscientiousness alone; talent had had no part in this. Although Cas had mocked his painstaking troubles, she may also have been attracted by the seriousness of his nature. She was a serious student too and always a step ahead of him. At forty, William could still recite every word from those essays and from his dissertation. He tried not to do this in bed any longer as Cas did not seem to find this as interesting any more. In fact, he had few regrets about the moderations of his behaviour that middle age, fatherhood and marriage had brought with them.

The way he dressed was now predictable too – clean, white underwear, a checked shirt, the salt and pepper suit; a puritan distrust of flamboyance. If Marks and Spencer were ever in difficulties then he would be also, he felt. But Marks and Spencer was at least as solid as England. He sat down for the socks and shoes on the rosewood chair. The legs and backrest were carved rather too heavily for his taste. It was more cumbersome than Chippendale. This chair was a century or so after Chippendale, smack in the middle of solid Regency. He did not care for Regency any more than he cared for art nouveau. But a collector must cast aside personal taste. He did not care for the painted armchair that they kept in the attic: its cane back and seat were not pleasing to his eye but it was valuable – *designed*, he had been told, for George III. Even kings could have bad taste – and be mad for that matter too. The hessian protection on the seat of the chair on which he sat pricked him occasionally. It protected the original gros point needlework – red, brown and green. He had always covered his emotions in much the same way.

But with his shoes tied, he could stand up and, for the moment, he watched over his wife. She lolled against the headboard, her angular chin cutting into his morning. That uncompromising Jewish disfavour was always appealing to him.

'Honest,' she said, 'the ears just fell off. I didn't pull them.' He had not expected this mock defensiveness. And the idea was far-fetched but he knew what she meant. She had been telling him lately that he was developing a moral stare and that he was beginning to look like his father. In her book, this was a harsh accusation. It was probably also true. He had noticed this trend himself: a growing impatience with tolerance, with anything boring or inconsiderate or harmful. Yes, morality. But unlike his wife, he did not view the development with any great alarm. The moral sense was just a necessary part of middle age.

It was true, however, that there was an uncomfortable side to the process. Cas was exploiting this admirably: his moral stare was clear evidence that he had not, after all, broken away. He was still his father's son, but William liked to think that he had never quite been able to fit into his father's trousers.

4

It was good for Lois to chat with Shane, the duty nurse, on their red plastic chairs outside the ward before they started work. This was not always possible when the shift handovers were more fraught. Shane was one of the best, with a huge smile.

'With all your memories, you will still be sad,' she said. This was exactly so. Between them, in the course of a week, they expected to meet death several times, but your own father's death was more difficult. Lois had loved him. They put down their empty mugs beside the water cooler, arranged the elastic of their surgical masks around their ears, lowered their visors, washed their hands at the sink and walked carefully onto the ward together.

*

Cas looked through the rectangular oak window frame, an easel or visor onto the seascape, as the light strengthened over the charcoal headland. She had returned to bed after pouring the tea, the steam rising from the mug, warm in her hands. In recent months, in Birmingham, with William bedridden before his death, she had made the tea herself, except when Lois came round. Lois had been a wonder, but she wasn't William. Not that she would be venerating him. He had been a fool. He had believed all the lies; that Russia, America and China were different now; that goodness would prevail; that harmony mattered above principle. He had never had a backbone. He had never seen the need for a sovereign Parliament that could argue all the way, or that confrontation had to precede accommodation. It was the same with Lois and James. She had had to love them by confronting them. To be willing to be walked over was no asset. Nevertheless, she had loved him. He had been a good man for all this, always there to engage with her, to accommodate her every thought. The sky above the headland was grey with pink clouds over the estuary. The estuary formed a bright streak, dulling as it merged with the sea. Above the sea, there were three diagonal clouds as if placed for balance by an artist's brush. The sea, to the west, away from the sunrise, was a dark blue, with the sky above slightly lighter. As the dawn rose, occasional dark herring gulls swam in the still air above her head. The sea, on its way out, had waves so calm that they barely broke the surface. It was almost as still as the strip of glassy water left on the beach as the tide drew back below the dark band of rocks.

*

The streets had taught William to value himself. They had taught him to be resilient in the face of hostility and above all, they had enabled him to see the truth. Now, from the top of the escalator, truth mattered. He might not have become a fellow of the Royal Society or the Master of a Cambridge College. He did not speak twenty-four languages. He did not speak his own language much. Polish wasn't understood very well in Birmingham in any case. He did not spend winter holidays skiing with his teenage daughters and taking photo calls. And his brother hadn't played cricket for England. Nevertheless, and unreasonably perhaps, he believed in his own worth. It helped to picture those captains of industry and high-fliers on their deathbeds. Death was the same for everyone, and the more expensive coffin or the more lavish funeral service counted for little beside the fact of death. Everyone was in the same boat at death. Even the pope had to die. Indeed the pope's life was especially a preparation for death. The pope might be more prepared for death than the next man, his funeral might also be more elaborate and ornate than some funerals, but it was still death.

For William, the splendour and pomp of the Vatican was its least endearing quality; it was apt to protect a pope from the suffering of humanity. He had sought to engage more fully with street life not for the sake of appearances, but because this seemed to him the right approach. Given the size of the Vatican's publicity department, it was inevitable that word would get out that the pope was engaging with his flock in innovative ways. Feature articles would be written about this not only in the dry theological journals, but also in popular newspapers all over the world. The cameras were always on him, after all. One was tracking him in the forecourt as he walked out of the station towards the escalators again. Never in his long papacy, however, had he done anything merely for show.

That weekend many years ago – the concrete floor at the bottom of the escalator – had been the time when he had first begun to stand on solid ground. He could recognise this now, retrospectively, although that weekend had started much like any other.

*

When he had opened the dining room door into the hall after washing up the cups in the kitchen, he had heard Cas bawling at Lois. By way of distraction, there were two letters and a card on the mat. He leaned forward like an old man and picked them up in his right hand, taking them with him into the study. He did not get many letters. This was probably because he didn't write many either, only run-of-the-mill ones, to do with investments mostly. People kept letters. What anyone wrote was there for good. He couldn't think under the pressure of posterity. He remembered his reflection in the mirrors again.

He knew what one of the letters was immediately. The half-yearly report on the unit-linked life insurance was always in a vivid green envelope. It was as if they wanted him sick. In fact, William had a strong stomach and was never ill. But he had been pleased with the trust's performance. It had outstripped the FT Index. The card was from his brother, from the Pembrokeshire coast: 'We've all had diarrhoea and Darren was sick in the car! Mackerel only ten pence each if you gut them yourself. There's some in the post!' William smiled.

The other letter had a local postmark and had been sent first class. He opened it and read the contents. Now this was something. How calmly he took the big event! It was as if he saw it from a distance, from years away even: a play within a play. He was acting the emotions too. He felt nothing. So, he had been sacked and Sidney had signed it! In fact, the letter said very little. He was being asked to attend a meeting, but redundancy was the only explanation. He felt nothing. How would he manage this?

Cas. He needed time. This would be quite something to her. She earned more than him but he needed work too. This was like crossing the Atlantic. He never felt as if he were in the States for quite some time after he had arrived – if ever. In the same way, he did not feel redundant yet. Perhaps one day everyone would be able to travel without leaving home; they would be able to connect with anywhere in the world from their home or office for negligible cost. Pigs might be able to fly by then. Perhaps cases would have wheels then too. But it was only by foot or boat that he could truly arrive anywhere else.

Emotions were like this: they needed to get used to not being where they started. He was the same person who had made the tea this morning and washed up the cups. He could not tell her. He wasn't even used to this himself. Besides, it was breakfast. The children would be there. She had been shouting at Lois. He could not change the tone so easily. He wasn't a Modernist. Eliot or Pound might report a redundancy at breakfast – they could switch tone with each mouthful – but it was bad taste. It took an Englishman to understand taste. He could smell the toast burning: breakfast must be ready. He liked his toast lightly done, nearer bread than toast – virginal and pubescent. He left the study and met James bounding down the stairs, three steps – or was it four? – at a time. Three or four, what the hell! He wasn't a stickler for detail. There was only one fact now: his lost job.

Nor was he someone to say that stairs were to be walked down. The energy of a fourteen-year-old could not be dissipated so easily. If the attic were in the clouds, that would be different. Then his kangaroo son might use up all his energy in getting to bed and coming down to breakfast again; a foolish idea. Once the imagination started to predominate, irrationality was near to hand. He still thought of himself as an artist, in spite of many years in industry – even, perhaps, because of those years at the coalface. Was he born with art or was it wrought out of him? Industry would know that a bedroom could not be in the clouds and that no one could work in the clouds. It would not entertain the idea even.

Or was this distinction between art and science too naive? Was Indonesian dancing so very different from technical drawing? In both were not the patterns and forms rigidly defined? And in both was there not room for individual variation at the same time? Where exactly was the difference? But he must be off his nut already: any damn fool could see that dancing bore no relation to technical drawing. He was wasting his time. A man without common sense, a man who prevaricated, was a liability in a steelworks. To sack such a man was wholly logical.

Their Saturday breakfast was a quite unreasonable test so soon after waking. There were the shiny spoons, the bowls, the milk and sugar, the cereal in packets. Then the children had a cooked breakfast. That meant a fry-up, brown sauce, salt and pepper to go with the salt and pepper suit, plates to warm, knives and forks. The process seemed almost endless. There was the toast to burn, the butter hard from the fridge, marmalade, honey and coffee. The coffee required hot milk, a strainer that could not be found, cups, saucers and teaspoons. All this was breakfast.

He was glad that Cas was not methodical and that she did not take all this in her stride. It was breakfast that was at fault, not Cas, and anyway it was about time he helped out with breakfast for a change. Such breakfasts, like banisters, were outworn. Their family must be one of the last still to attempt such a thing, even if only on a Saturday. Cas still insisted on such a weekend breakfast, he felt, mainly because she was so bad at it. She would not let it triumph over her. She fought it tooth and nail and he supported her in the struggle. He had a soft spot for the underdog.

Did the lost job make him an underdog now? The letter was against his heart, safe and slightly stiff in his inside jacket pocket. His heart, meanwhile, felt as if it was on his sleeve. Could they not see that something momentous had happened to him? Maria would have noticed a change in him. And yet he was presenting a calm exterior. What was there for them to see? This was a state of mind that allowed for quite useless thoughts – the sort of thoughts he should be sacked for: how, for instance, the dusky brown card from James had been left on the rococo desk in the study, incongruent beside the insurance report's garish green envelope, the grandfather clock, with only one hand, watching over the scene and tut-tutting, lending it dignity even.

'Sit up too fast and you'll get the bends,' Cas said to James casually.

James grinned foolishly, coloured slightly and left his face more or less in the cornflakes. James had changed considerably lately. He still clumped down the stairs, but he talked less and was easily embarrassed. And he spent too long alone in his room. This was the same child who, grinning, used to hurl himself at William in the swimming pool. William could now almost smell the Bovril on the swimming pool balcony where it mixed with the smell of chlorine from the almost blue water below.

Lois opened the door and sidled in, thin as a teenager. Her mother, in the kitchen, transferred the sausage and fried bread onto two plates, examined Lois briefly and put the plates in the oven.

'You can't wear that sweater,' she said. 'We used to throw them away when they got like that.'

It was an old jersey. Lois had dyed it pink and green and taped it up so that the back piece was triangular in shape; it did justice to Johnny Rotten.

'Oh, Mum!' Lois whined. She alternated nowadays between the little girl and the reserved adult.

William kept quiet. He was a slack father. James smirked and kicked her under the table.

'The other girls wear much worse at weekends,' Lois added, kicking James back.

'You aren't the other girls, fat face,' Cas said. 'And what have weekends to do with it? Saturday you wear your best.'

Lois said nothing, but William suspected that she valued her mother's hostility more than his own unerring affection.

'Are you still with us?' Cas asked, turning on James. James cowered. 'It's in the oven. The square thing for heating food. You know ... food?'

Knock it on the head! James might well have said, William thought. But James just grinned again and, head down, fetched his plate.

'You look full of beans,' she said, handing William the cup of coffee, some of which was in the saucer, 'the executive of my dreams.'

He smiled. It did not seem to matter particularly that this smiling man had lost his job.

5

Lois could see the hospital and campus stretching on in the mist as she walked back to the station. Darren, Ros and Carmi had visited from Raleigh over a year ago before her father's death. She had shown them round the campus, including The Barber Institute, and the hospital. Darren had said that it was all rather small.

'Size isn't everything,' she had said. She had teased him when they were children too. He had been a serious little boy. He had not changed much. Neither had she.

Carmi had worn ripped jeans and a T-shirt reading: *The planet is getting hotter than my imaginary boyfriend.*

'It's quaint here. I love it,' Ros had said. 'And Stratford is only down the road.'

'Down the road we will all be burning!' Carmi had said.

Lois had not tried to explain to them why she liked it in Birmingham. There was no God, but other things mattered to her.

*

Cas was looking out in the morning dark and the sea was already whispering. There was no family life for her but a good view of the sea once dawn broke. She could view the shape of the world. There was not much leadership or vision any more, but there might be a way through when the virus subsided. She was already aside from the centre, an observer. As with her approach to both art criticism and accountancy, she had a steady gaze. She noticed a few lights on the headland. Then there was a horizontal lightness in the sky between the darknesses. As the whole sky lightened slightly, she could make out the headland with a lighter streak of sky above it that extended over the sea as well. The sea was not only audible but visible, the tide against the pebble ridge. She heard far off an occasional three-stage bleat from a herring gull followed by a string of sounds in a lighter register, so familiar at the seaside, if not in Birmingham. With rain clouds, the dawn was slow to break. But soon the whole scene was lighter and the clouds less ominous as the waves stroked the shoreline rocks. From time to time, herring gulls flew north, wings pushing up and down against the air stream, or glided south with the air current. She was only a small part of what she heard and saw.

*

When he reached the top of the escalator again – or the straight top of the picture frame – after making his way out of the station, he was a little out of breath. He paused at a travel agent's window. One of the displays had a picture of a Concorde on it. Concorde's commercial life was over. Commercial flights had only recently started when he had been appointed as their chief test pilot. The travel agent could hardly have been expected to understand what a poignant sight this photograph would have been for him. How could they have known that Concorde's chief test pilot would have viewed the display? The work had been exacting, but it was over. All good things come to an end. He was still held in high esteem by his colleagues as he had never put a foot wrong during his flying days – consistency had been his hallmark – and there was little margin for error at those speeds, needless to say. He could recall the golden sun on the trailing edge of the curved wing in the early morning above the melting off-white clouds above the grey sea. Concorde had flown faster than the speed of sound. The speed of light would be the next challenge.

Faith was like flying. Trust was essential; trust in your own judgement. Without this trust, no one would ever believe, would ever leave the ground. Faith was swinging about on a trapeze in a big tent and daring to let go. With Concorde, the pilot pushed the right buttons at the right time and they reached their destination safely. The passengers might be in technology's hands but they were in the pilot's hands too. He had made their luck, determined their fate. He was earthbound again, tramping the streets, but his imagination soared to the stars. Even in Birmingham, that most pedestrian of cities, he could reach beyond his circumstances. When he used his imagination, he was not limited by the material facts faced daily; the world was his oyster, to use a shoreline saying. When a swami fasted, he was freed from his immediate circumstances – from tramping the streets of Birmingham, so to speak – to engage with the divine. His holy centre was no longer his hunger, but his flying the skies with British Airways, the imagination set free, time compressed, distances shortened and the senses alert.

William was the Son of Man in an Aramaic sense, meaning that he was close to man, or so his father had argued in a sermon on Mark's gospel many years ago. In the scriptures, Israel was often referred to as a bride or wife and when she turned from God she was adulterous. It would not be correct to say that Cas had never known God. But she had slapped God in the face right from the start and therefore could not be described as adulterous in this sense. She had never got into bed with God in the first place. She had made up for not being adulterous to God by being adulterous to William. Although strict chronology was important at the controls of Concorde, this was not so important in daily life and he was not quite sure when Cas had first been unfaithful. As in the gospels, rather than at the controls of Concorde, it was the message that mattered, not the precision of the information. The message was that Cas had turned from William while keeping their possessions intact. She could not have turned from God as she had never given God any encouragement, other than slap his face.

On Concorde, he did not need to link his instructions with phrases like 'for whosoever,' 'for what' and 'whosoever therefore'. Flying Concorde was not writing Mark's gospel. On Concorde, he did not need these devices to reach his destination safely or to convey unity and movement, because a flight's success spoke for itself and depended on making the right decisions at the right time rather than on blending one instruction with another.

To write a gospel was therefore a different kettle of fish from flying Concorde and it was not quite the same thing as Cas's flightiness either. When it had been flying, Concorde had been as much science as art. Now that it was grounded, it had more in common with a gospel: poetry more than science, myth rather than history. Cas had no time for myth. She looked to the future – in the sweat of another man's arms as it had turned out, but surrounded by the possessions that William had bought with her.

At the risk of losing a sense of proportion with regard to these verses, his father had said that the problem in Mark 8:35 was one of language. The verse contained a paradox – if you want to live, die. The language of paradox needed to be recognised as such. Zeno's arrow in fact still flew, unlike Concorde, even if it was always in a now. You got into trouble if you tried to interpret such paradoxical language literally. The following verses served as a comment on the human search for power, or so his father had said. Most people had difficulty with the idea of a soul because they considered the soul something apart from themselves. But in the Jewish tradition, the soul referred to the whole person, both body and soul. So the following verses were saying, don't swap yourself for success – or at least, this had been the gist of his father's sermon. Was it acceptable to become the pope even? Did Mark's gospel make allowances for someone who had been elected to power by the cardinals in front of Michelangelo's frescoes?

It was hard for William to reach any conclusion here in the light of Mark's gospel. It was just as well, therefore, that he was now planning his search with Sunday night in mind. There were not many weekends with so much to look forward to, not even weekends away with wheels on your suitcase.

That weekend when he had visited Maria, his only other love, his senses, even his soul, had been alert. But he had hardly known at the time, from the bottom of the escalator, the bottom of the cliff face, where he was heading or whether it was upwards or downwards.

*

Reversing the car, gravel under the wheels, William was going anywhere, he felt. Soon there was a patterned mist on the screen and the fog almost shone on the car's yellow bonnet and on the bonnets of the cars that passed him in the other direction. Was the car really a decadent yellow? Cars were never yellow. But switching on the rear-screen demister, he noticed that the two side mirrors were misted too. He could not see where he had been any more than he knew where he was going. This was twentieth-century man, he thought, unhelpfully. Still, there was a certain renaissance in him that morning – he was for life, for the Earth circling the sun, for the gleaming lights on the yellow bonnet of this speeding car as bold and subtle as Michelangelo's sun in the Sistine Chapel. At the same time, his spirit went even further back – back to somewhere in the Dark Ages, the Brome mystery plays, heaven and hell, dark thoughts of revenge. Would he ever look back on this captured moment, he wondered, and give it meaning? As he joined the motorway, flat and dull, a solitary black crow wheeled overhead and plunged into the mist.

Here were grey and dullness and persistent crash barriers; here and there cars, lorries and vans; futile they seemed, some travelling one way, others the other way. Against this dull backdrop, William became consumed by the thought that his life was changing. Could the M5 south be his road to Damascus, the pivot of his life? Would he look back at this moment and imbue it with meaning? The grey road curved ahead in the mist almost like the curve of an ivory tusk. Indeed he was faced almost entirely, it seemed, by such misty curves – curved grass verges, curving bridges, a flock of wood pigeons flapping and curving away – and now this curving imagination. He noticed that there was more road than green and more sky than road, the sky a slightly lighter shade of grey. Bridges loomed out of the green fields, each one casting a shadow like that of a giant kestrel. Each time, he was the mouse, the vole. He froze as each new form lurched over his head.

Later, there was Worcester, its early Christmas traffic, its cricket ground and foolish roundabouts. Then out into the wide roll of valley and hill. He opened the window. Cold air rushed in.

On the road, he was aware of broken and double white lines, big, white arrows and a rumbling sound under the tyres when the car strayed over the cat's eyes. A green verge swept past while the wood behind travelled more slowly. The wires looped between poles. He passed two yellow tractors, black and white road-marking posts, a flat-topped 1960s Esso petrol station, its oval blue sign and red lettering a period piece. Scattered lime on a green field was not quite regular enough to be frost, nor was it cold enough for that matter. He saw larches together, a strong oak, sheep here and there, a horned bull, then a roadwork sign and traffic lights.

The hedges were tall and tidy, a mixture of brown, green and yellow. The line of red-washed cottages seemed to complete his journey's texture.

6

Lois was in her dressing gown watching TV with Jack before he left for work; he was on nights this month. The phone rang.

'Hello, sis!' James said. 'They've taken out the leaded windows and tarmacked the front garden. The gravel path too.'

'What do I care?' Lois said. 'They can do what they want.' 'Mum sold it. All the tat too. The money's for the children. You know that. What do the windows matter, or the garden?'

'I know, it's just they were a part of us.'

'Bollocks to all that! It's who we are now!'

'I guess so. Who's that?'

'Fuck off, James! Stop thinking. You sound like Dad. It doesn't matter. We've all we need. How's Dorin, the little peach? Maidie says Lottie and Stela love Billie Eilish. That's what matters. Not windows, little bro! Open the wine with Ioanela. She's the best! Move on! What colour's her hair today?'

'It's sort of mauve,' he said proudly.

Lois knew that he would be looking at the carpet.

*

Cas knew that to be in Devon was not the same as to be in Birmingham. This was why she had come here to look over the sea and the brown, green and yellow of the headland and the burrows. She had loved her husband. Even accountants could be in love. She had been a good accountant, supporting her family with her work. Someone had to. In the days of pounds, shillings and pence and before spreadsheets, she could look down a column of entries and add them up in her head. William never took her for granted. At university, they had fallen in love over ideas. She was always a match for him. Unlike her, he wasn't for the real world, however. She could handle anything ... other than cooking. They had been good for each other because there had always been friction between them. They had disagreed on the fundamentals. She could not find reassurance in the people around her. He had found it in every blemish and wart. How absurd! The world was hard; Darwinian; red in tooth and claw. Just to look around was to see that people did wrong. Everything was askew: climate, morals, actions. Nothing would change under William's acquiescence. She had loved him totally, but from her own trajectory, which now faced the gradations of silver in the sea and sky.

*

Having recovered his breath – few would have known from his posture that he had been Concorde's chief test pilot – he shuffled back down the ramp past McDonald's. He was already looking forward to meeting someone at McDonald's tomorrow. Tomorrow was Sunday, a holiday. Instead, for today, he turned right into New Street past HSBC, Lloyds TSB, Bradford and Bingley, Vodafone and Pizza Hut towards the new Bullring. When he walked along the street like this, there was never any confusion about where he was. This could only be Birmingham. It was not Genoa – no one looked stylish in the misty rain – and there were no throngs of young people as there might be in Shanghai. At the end of New Street there was a huge advert that changed from one display to another. At the time of the earlier weekend, he had noted then a small display that altered from time to time. Leopold Bloom, restricted to paper ads, would have been impressed by that too. If William had not been so much rooted in the real world then as now, these moving ads might even have made him question his own sanity. Marketing seemed to have taken over the world even more since then, and since *Ulysses*, entering every sphere of existence. Marketeers knew, for instance, that one tenor was less than a third of the value of three tenors, with James Joyce, a fine tenor too, that would make four: they were growing their empire from small adverts that moved to large adverts that moved, and that no doubt would soon contain video, shifting from small Mars Bars to snack-sized Mars Bars to frozen Mars Bars to giant Mars Bars. They might be giving ground on giant Mars Bars, and larger portions generally, but they would find other ways to over-egg the pudding, he felt sure. Once a product sold, it was dressed up in as many different guises as possible. There were so many different ways to sell your soul to the devil. Selling *The Big Issue* was a marketing skill too and even communion wafers had the crucifix logo now. Thankfully, today was more than marketing; his life's work spoke for itself.

Continuing along the pedestrianised New Street, he avoided the cracks between the paving slabs as he used to do as a child. They said that no one was ever more than a few yards from a rat in Birmingham. He was fairly sure that he wasn't searching for a rat but for some confirmation that his life was on track. To reach this state of grace had not been easy. There had been hurdles to overcome, not just cracks between paving slabs. The others in the street, early to their Saturday shopping, had no comprehension of the trials to which he had succumbed. He could love them all unconditionally, but only because of everything that he had been through. To paraphrase Nietzsche, love, like music, had to be learned. His loyalty and commitment had been tested to breaking point, to the point at which only love remained. He was wasted. He was without power and influence. He walked along the street a broken man, a man who was rarely spoken to and yet in whom was this great redemptive melody.

*

Then, his long journey had been just beginning. He remembered a fern growing out of the red wall and there were bulbs in red pots on the windowsill. The holly beside the door had one or two berries, the colour of Maria's hair. There had been a chill in the damp wind. The winters had been colder then. There had been the chill of the disbeliever in his heart.

Cas did not bother much with either spirituality or plants. She avoided anything that smacked of sentiment and yet she had studied art history. Cas was sharp, worldly wise, financially strong; Maria quietly resilient. He had knocked on the door, his knuckles against the painted door. Maria had opened the door to him. In retrospect, he could see that moment as an entry to his new life, perhaps.

Her light brown eyes were steady and she held herself straight. Then her eyes seemed to laugh. But he could not surprise Maria. She accepted life, whatever it brought her. She led him in. Their cottage was tiny. There was no hallway. He was immediately in the front room. It was cosy. Logs burned

57

on the fire, giving the room a sweet smell. The walls were papal white. There was a red armchair on each side of the fire and a solid table facing it. It wasn't a special table – in the sixties you could buy such a table for thirty bob – just an oak table with extension sides that slid under the square top. In this small room, the extensions would probably never be used. What a waste of the extensions! But they were there nevertheless, and they could be called upon if required. Nor could he talk about the table as if the extensions did not exist. There was possibly a moral somewhere, though he couldn't, at that moment, quite put his finger on it. Did it perhaps link up in some not easily definable way with his thoughts on the cup of tea and on the nature of poetry that he had had while shaving this morning?

Maria used to write poetry. She used to type her poems on that same black Imperial typewriter that now stood clumsily on the table. It wasn't quite the IBM PC they had at work, the machine that Sidney said had no future, but it was good enough for bad poetry. Of course, everyone wrote poetry then – not Cas, but everyone else. And it was bad poetry too. Maria's wasn't as bad as some, but it was bad enough: indulgent, self-conscious, absurdly confident. He could still vaguely remember a piece she had shown him about a flower shop. She had tried to show how flowers were a vehicle of corruption in the city. Needless to say, the poem hadn't worked. He had found it embarrassing even then, though he hadn't said so. He had been dishonest at that time too. Dishonesty, he had found, was necessary, at least for him. Cas didn't seem to need either dishonesty or poetry – not that accountancy was all that she was about. Her first love, well before her love for him, had been art.

Fifteen years after their student days, this other girl, the converse of Cas, was sentimental still, but possessed a tranquil strength and a steady, hazel gaze with which she had obstinately caressed him when he told her that he was marrying Cas. Now she was married herself. He looked again at the old Imperial. It was hefty and unyielding, a relic of the mechanical age before the chip. And it was unlike Maria, her flowers, her poetry, her relationships! He took all this in slowly before seating himself in the red armchair to the right of the fire and to the right of Maria, who was now kneeling in the hearth like a pope at prayer and carefully positioning a log at the back of the flames. She had taken the log from a brass-bound mahogany bucket. He felt brass-bound too – by his salt and pepper suit in particular. The bucket was old. He would have liked to buy it from her if she hadn't been a friend. As a rule, people didn't know the value of things. Maria especially treated things with nonchalance. She wore a crumpled brown sweater, a long tweed skirt, sensible brown lace-up shoes and brown socks. It was, he supposed, an early seventies look, though the orange short-cropped hair, a match for the flames, was more like today.

The task completed, she sat back in the other red armchair to the left of the fire: red and orange together. The hue should have been blue, not red. It was blue that was associated with the divine on the skin and face of Egyptian statues. There were no words from her and she was calm. 'I've lost my job,' he said. He stumbled slightly with the words. Her gaze was steady. 'They sent me this letter,' he continued, pulling it from the inside pocket of his jacket.

It would have been nice to wear a made-to-measure suit; the linings would have been smoother. The tips of his fingers were quivering slightly. He watched them with interest and not without a certain self-indulgence. She accepted the letter. He had been steady before, in his own home, at breakfast. He remembered saying, 'Good morning, James!' He had said this crisply – the authoritative father. And here, his hands shook. He was even unsure what his next words were to be.

But she forestalled him. 'There's not much in it,' she said. 'I'll get some coffee.'

She stood up and opened the wooden door into the kitchen. He could hear her filling the kettle, the ringing of the water again, and he watched her setting out cups and saucers and a chocolate cake. With the kitchen door open there was a little more light in the dark front room. The darkness and the wooden table reminded him of the cabin in the fishing boat he had been in with his father on holiday. They had got up early before anyone else was awake. He had felt grown-up with just his father, eating their cornflakes and the others asleep – more grown-up than he felt now! And this had happened on three mornings in a row. The first two mornings had held a black sky and a strong wind, and the old fisherman, respecting these, had decided not to leave harbour. Instead, between them, they had cooked laver and fried bread for Paul and his mother – the waking family. On the third morning, however, it was cold but the sky was clear, the stars out. The fishing boat had been cast off from the jetty, the smell of fish on board, father and son on deck. He had seen a lot that cold morning. William had been given the wheel and had watched the curving furrow in the water over his shoulder. He had gasped as the fish flapped on the deck. He had seen the brittle filled-up sea urchins thrown back into the sea, the fish gutted – one quick flick of the knife – and dropped into trays. Thank goodness there would always be fish in the sea, he had thought, though his father had said that cod were once so plentiful that you could hardly row a boat through them. On this occasion his father had refrained from mentioning loaves and fishes. William remembered the hot, sweet tea down in the cabin. It was dark, beams overhead, a table. Maria's front room, he might say. Now, he could smell the coffee and vaguely remembered the marigold-covered tea cosy. It was less than marigold now. Tea, coffee, what did it matter? Were Maria and he not above such distinctions? She leaned over the table, the shock of hair staring at him. She said nothing. 'Lost your tongue?' Cas might have said. That wasn't Maria's way. She absorbed a situation anemone-like. Cas was perhaps more advanced, more cerebral – she pounced. But with Maria, he could swim around, choose his moment to be swallowed up.

Her eyes watched him. Was there laughter there? Or weeping? He remembered how infuriating he had found her during their one and only brief romance, when Cas was pregnant with James. He had found her luscious silences too much for him then; too strange. He had fled back to Cas, to her insults, to her no-nonsense. And it had been good to hold the baby, of course.

And then, soon after Maria had married Stephen, ten years ago, they had met up again. William's father had just died. William had been alarmed that he had felt no immediate remorse – the remorse had come later – and he had gone to talk to her. Stephen, tactfully, had busied himself with the roof of their garden shed; no seeping damp allowed into their lives. William was left to himself with those almost laughing, almost tearful, almost brown eyes. He had told Maria about his father's stroke – his father's left arm made helpless. He had told her how, with Paul, he had helped bathe his father. On one evening, as the bath was run, his father's arm had dropped down into the too hot water and his father had yelped. He told her how brave and sweet his father had been and how, later, his father's left leg had weakened too and he had bumped into things on his left-hand side. Once, he had wanted James to fetch his watch and drew it without any digits on its left side – a watch his condition could comprehend. Now that his father was dead, William had told her that he didn't miss his father, only his father's questioning – the one thing that William had always objected to. The last time his father had questioned him, he could remember thinking: 'I'm a man and I'm thirty. Can't I live my own life?' But without the questions, he had felt far from liberated. He missed conflict more than he missed friendship. Who would read a novel about friendship?

Maria was all friendship. There would be no circumstances in which she could ever hurt anyone. She had none of Cas's murderous nature. She had listened to him and consoled him as she always would, as his mother used to do. And after unburdening himself to her, he had felt happier. He had returned to the solid children and to Cas. Indeed, Cas became in time a true consolation for the lost father. At least she wasn't a friend. She fought him: not his father's deep questioning about the direction of his life but another challenge, something to wrestle against.

With Maria, he never hit rock bottom. She was quite unshakeable. This, admittedly, was what he needed now. In her presence, this matter of the lost job seemed as if it was nothing, and he was grateful for this. But would she still not have batted an eyelid if there had been some great horror to relate? What if he had administered poison to his family and put them in the freezer? Would she have made him coffee then? Tolerance! Good old tolerance! It was what he had striven for when he was younger. But his wife was right: there was a change coming on.

Still, he was sipping at Maria's coffee and warming himself at her fire. He had no right to wonder at her acceptance of him. He felt tired. 'Look Maria,' he felt like saying, 'I can't talk now. I've had it.'

'You look done in!' Maria said, leaning her spiky, orange hair sideways in the red chair. She knew his thoughts. 'Look!' she added, 'Stephen will be back any minute. He's refereeing the football. But there's a church bazaar at twelve and he's picking me up. Why not stop? You can doze in the chair, go for a walk, take yourself off to bed even. The spare bed's made up.'

He consented gratefully to staying behind, and when Stephen rattled the front door and pushed it open, William had to blink himself awake. Stephen's dark, lanky appearance had none of Maria's visual flare, but there was no question that they were man and wife. William watched as Maria and Stephen watched each other steadily. They had the same deliberation too, thinking before each movement. And as he shook hands with Stephen, William felt a slight twinge of envy. But envy did not become him at all.

'Don't let me keep you,' William said.

Stephen smiled. It was the smile of a man of faith. 'All is all right,' it said. 'Life, death – it's taken care of.'

7

The bell rang and Lois went to the door in her dressing gown. Kal and Jane were there with their new puppy – a brown, white and black mongrel, wagging its tail and smelling one of the flower pots. They had married last summer. Jack had dressed in his firefighter uniform.

'Sorry! You're ready for bed,' Kal said.

'No. It's good to see you. I'm often in my dressing gown ... in case Scottie drops by! I wish I could invite you in. What are you calling him?'

'Tiger,' Jane said.

'Good name!' Lois said.

'Maidie says your mother's in Devon,' Kal said. 'She's a tiger too. I loved hanging out at your place as teens. Your mother shouted at us all the time but I knew she was on our side.'

Lois smiled. 'She says there's no sea in Birmingham. She says the sea doesn't care about her or the state of the world. She wants to be alone with the sea. You know what she's like. You can't argue with her. She's grieving.'

*

The scene in front of Cas was wide and breathtaking. It was difficult to know where to concentrate. As in life, it was all for the taking, but where to start? Her grandchildren, for instance, wanted to go everywhere all at once. And why not? With global warming and the pandemic, their dreams might be curtailed.

Her generation, after a bumpy start for her, had had everything. Her one and only cruise with William a few years ago could never happen now. Cruise ships were as vulnerable as nursing homes and prisons. William would have relished the comparison between a cruise and incarceration in a prison or nursing home. Unlike him, she never felt guilty about their good fortune. She had helped to make their luck. Nevertheless, she acknowledged that her working life had been privileged and straightforward. With accountancy, she could just start at the beginning and work her way through. It fitted her nature and it had kept them all afloat.

Faced with choice, where did she start? – a grain of sand, the cold water, a seal off Baggy Point? She was not as incapable of decision-making as William. She knew where she was and what was right. He could never make jokes because he could not take a position. A joke was anarchic. It shook things up. To make a joke, she had to know where she was heading, however unacceptable this was. Maria couldn't make jokes either, the tart. It had always been a comfort to Cas that William had appreciated everything she had said, including her jokes. Now, without him, there was less opportunity to talk or to be funny. She missed him.

There were dark rain clouds above her head but, over the sea, layers of lighter grey cloud. She could hear the sea too. It had a relentless, comforting murmur. *This is where you came from and will return to*, it was saying. Occasionally, a herring gull was consumed by a staccato flight mirroring its call. She was on her own in front of all this.

*

As he continued his journey along New Street, he was trying to work out what he still searched for beneath his feet, within the shops to his left and right, and in the buildings above, easily overlooked – or underlooked. He had not been idle since that first weekend. He had found resolution through application and hard work. Only a few days after losing his job, he had been head-hunted to work on the new Channel 4 soap, *Brookside*, eventually becoming their main scriptwriter. The pithy dialogue and cutting-edge themes were his responsibility. But *Brookside*, like Concorde and his papacy, could not last for ever. Such achievements had a natural time span and he had to be willing to let go of the helm at the appropriate time. The curving wake was over his shoulder as New Street stretched behind him to the *Iron:Man*, tethering him to the factory and the city he loved. Indeed, with time, he had learned that achievement counted for nothing. Stephen and Maria, many years ago, had had the right idea. It was love that mattered; nothing else.

He walked slowly, in keeping with the dignity of his office, past the heavy but animated sculpture of a bull with one hoof lifted – a relic of the early Roman Empire no doubt, where Rome and the Church had their roots. The weight of history and of Christendom were on his shoulders. Those carefree days when he had played in goal in his home village in Poland were over. He had known then that to save a goal was like catching a waitress's eye – he needed to mean business. Nor could he see the papacy in isolation. The lineage could be traced from St Peter. He liked to think that he had been a solid, reliable and holy successor to St Peter. He passed Café Rouge and Starbucks on the right and Miss Sixty on the left. An effete Nelson was on a pillar. Was Nelson an anchoress, perhaps? Below were square water sculptures in pink, yellow and blue, the blue suggesting divine regeneration and endurance. The markets and a Birmingham skyline were in the distance. To the left was the bulbous form of Selfridge and Co. covered with dustbin lid-sized, disc-shaped alloy forms on a blue background. St Martin's filled most of his vision as he leant on the glass and stainless-steel balcony. Would Selfridges or the Church last the longer? He was touched to see that so many of his spiritual children had turned out to hear the Holy Father's words. These might be the dying embers of a papacy, but he still had much to say. He told them quietly, barely audibly, that love mattered; that nothing mattered but love, and he blessed them from the bottom of his heart.

He surveyed the square below, the sleeves of his vestments catching an early morning breeze. The believer did not have to wear his heart on his sleeve. He did not have to affirm his faith from the rooftops. He was aware of his calling. Every sinew of his body responded to God's will. But he was content to go about his life without declaring to all and sundry that he was anchored, like Nelson too perhaps, both to a heavy bull and an iron man. How did he explain to others that this love could be their love too if only they were prepared to accept it into their hearts?

*

Many years ago, before the cardinals had elected him, he had been faithless. It had been foggy and November then too. The adze-cut beams, the wood smoke and the deal floorboards were an opportunity to assess his position. His friend Maria and her husband were at a bazaar and William had been sacked. His wife knew nothing of this. He had fled there with his lips sealed to her. There was a sense, nevertheless, in which he was still back with his wife, her red lips and his worries.

This was the trouble, perhaps, with modern transport. He had no time to get used to not being where he set out from. It was only by foot or boat that he could truly arrive, truly get used to not being where he'd started. If he had had to walk all the way, for instance, it would have taken him days. He would have known the mist on his face. The frost would have numbed his toes. By foot, he would have known the distance that he had travelled. And it wasn't as if suitcases had wheels. The next technological progress might be even more unsettling. He had read about a plan in the States to link universities and labs to a network – the ARPANET, it was called – so that communication could be made within seconds; you might be in Massachusetts one minute, Wisconsin the next. How would humanity manage that; barely time to put your coat on! And how would it feel to travel without leaving? This making travel easier had started with the horse, and progressed to the horse and cart and beyond. It was part of a continuum. The article had even speculated that one day all this might be done from our own homes. One of the technicians had mentioned this possibility to Sidney.

'What a load of bollocks!' Sidney had said.

But today's transport was enough for William to get his head round. The point being that there had only been the hum of the car in his ears and, through the glass, the white road and the green fields. But he had had this same thought already today. It wasn't as if it was years ago. What a long way off the morning seemed! It had to wave at him now for attention! Yes. He had had this thought in his study under the Matisse print that reminded him of Cas. Was the eye always charged with thought, as Proust had said? Could he never escape? He had been holding the letter in his hand then, the letter that was now in his jacket pocket that could have been smoother. And the news hadn't got to him – like flying to the States, he had thought. And here he was, in Worcestershire, thinking along identical lines. One day, he might even look back on these thoughts and reassess them.

But if the repetitions only occurred within his head, perhaps there was no harm in them. Indeed had he been a preacher, perish the thought, or the pope or a great orator, repetition would have been a necessary part of his armoury. At least he was relaxed now, able to laugh at his pedantry, comfortable enough to reflect upon, but without any great anguish, whatever his life back there still held for him. There was Cas, of course, and there were the children and there was the big house. All these things were quite something. But his job was quite something too: a man really could do with a job even though Cas had a better one. And it was his fault that he had lost it. He had been a poor director of late: he had put ideas before billets. Who wanted to buy components that had cracked on the presses? This was why Sidney had sacked him. Sidney had served his country in the war and could not now be blamed for doing his job.

And, as if in an effort to show that he no longer wanted to let things slip, he opened his eyes and, noticing that Maria's fire was dying, he knelt down in the hearth and used the tongs to lift a log onto the embers. And for good measure he bashed at the remains of the fire. It would not do to let it die on him. He was not a man to do nothing about dying embers. So he could still get down to brass tacks when he chose to, the sort of brass tacks that held in place the brass band round Maria's mahogany bucket that held the logs. And that was what he had been hired to do. It was no use looking for meanings in a steelworks: there weren't any. Wasn't it enough that so many adequate components were loaded onto the lorries each shift? His responsibilities as a director went no further than that. If he had concerned himself with this alone, his job would have still been his. If he had stuck to jolly old steel, he could still have boasted a jolly old job. He watched the flames lapping the new log again. There was pleasure in a burning fire. Was there not pleasure in being a good director too?

He thought of the others on the board. They had had to claw their way up too, and they valued their achievement. They liked the staff canteen, the possibility that a labourer might sometimes call them 'sir', the company car, the staff pension. It was a limited ambition, perhaps, but not a foolish one. William – no-job William – was the fool. Anyone who had carved out a ledge somewhere up the cliff face would be well advised to hang onto it. Even looking out to sea was not to be recommended.

It had been an error of judgement to regard the steelworks in the same way as the Romantics regarded the Alps, Monet a sunset or Bacon the open mouth – as a catalyst for the inner life and imagination.

It wasn't even as if he had a novel to write. Take the car journey that morning: he could not have written about that even though his senses had been alert, shocked into alertness, perhaps. He remembered the sweet smell of petrol at the filling station. He had heard a dog bark, and then a postman had lounged up the street with a grey bag over his shoulder. At least the post office wasn't for privatisation. There had been a credit card advertisement on the pavement outside the petrol station; one of those new displays behind a transparent panel, suddenly shifting to another display so that he wondered at his sanity. 'I am your flexible friend', the poster read. *No friend of mine*, he had thought. But he had to acknowledge that the financial system was sound, even if he did not wish to befriend it. He had noticed then how the sharp outlines of the television aerials had disappeared into the morning fog, and how the streets themselves had followed after.

But there had been no ideas connected with these observations. He would not have known what to do with them. Now a novelist could make something of the most mundane happening. A novelist on the same journey could come up with something noteworthy or poetic. He would say something like, 'The red in a car's rear lights is not the red of the morning sun,' and the reader would be taken by the imaginative verve. Or a novelist might latch onto particular images: for instance, cows – black and white – on a motorway bridge, one of those more exhilarating bridges perhaps, arching concrete with the green fields around. And then this image would be used as a symbol of the hero's inner state or of the human condition in general. A simile, even, might be wedged in: 'Like cows on a motorway bridge,' the novelist might say, 'William's life was disjointed.' That was the kind of effect that had to be sustained in a novel. After all, a novel was not life. And poetry, of course, was that much harder: a poem was a novel with all but a few of the words left out. Sitting there in that red armchair in Worcestershire, William knew that this was merely his life and that he could never have written a novel, let alone poetry, about it.

In an attempt to halt this line of enquiry, he stood up and walked a pace or two to the rectangular leaded window to the right of the front door. He could feel the cold air creeping in around the window, but there were also hyacinths on the window ledge to warm his heart. They would be flowering by Christmas. Already the crisp, green leaves were parting to show a tinge of yellow. He never saw such things in a steelworks. They reminded him of corn on the cob. His mother would cut the cob in half and there would be half each for Paul and himself, little boys in short trousers. They would push a fork into each end, and they would be allowed a knob of butter too. They would look up and grin at each other – then gnaw like rabbits. But his mind was wandering. He looked at bulbs and he saw corn. He looked at steel and he wondered, 'Why all this steel?'

Looking up across the road and above the fields, he saw that the hills were still in mist, though there was a slight radiance now where the sun should have been. The mist was unlikely to lift today, especially down here among the clustered farmhouses at the base of the valley. Across the road, an old gentleman in a duffel coat waited at the bus stop. He was carrying plastic shopping bags and when he stamped his feet, they waved around. What was the man doing there? What did his life mean? He could even have been that man himself one day.

These were the questions that a production director should never ask. A director did not say: 'Look here! Why are we doing all this?' These were questions for dramatists or philosophers. He could ask other questions: 'How many components per press per day? How many broken dies? How many absentees?' But not: 'Look guys, what's the point?' Such questions were both anarchic and irresponsible. Industry had to carry on irrespective of the meaning of life.

He sighed, moved away from the window and glanced around the room again. Yes, the room might well be a boat.

If he half-closed his eyes, he could even imagine the misty sea stretching out beyond the windows. But it was a liability, this drawing of comparisons. So he sat down again by the fire. What exactly had got into his head of late?

Last week, for instance, he had considered, in his lunch hour, the new pickling plant from West Germany. His company sent components to East Germany. Would they keep the trade without the Berlin Wall? Speculation again – the Berlin Wall was here to stay. The pickling plant was so complicated that none of the maintenance department could possibly repair it. The company had to fly West German contractors in. As production director, he was right to have been thinking about the pickling plant, but his thoughts were not a production director's thoughts. He did not give consideration to how the maintenance department might be given the incentive to learn from the contractors, or how the operators might be encouraged not to press the wrong buttons.

No. He had spent his lunch hour on the philosophy of the situation: a plant that could not be comprehended by those who used it. William Morris wouldn't have stood for that, he had thought, nor the Bauhaus. He was not actually sure what William Morris or the Bauhaus had stood for. He did not clutter his mind with detail. But they had William Morris wallpaper in the sitting room. He rather liked it. And it was a certainty that a man who could design wallpaper so fine would have been opposed to a machine that baffled its operators. Wouldn't anyone? He had been sure, also, that this would have been true of the Bauhaus too, though he hadn't been able to explain exactly why he had been so sure of this. He had then recalled a question asked by his philosophy tutor at college: 'Is man a machine?' the tutor had asked. At times, philosophy could be a little foolish. In such situations, William had inclined towards a common-sense philosophy of his own, although he would have said nothing about this to his tutor. In his own mind, he did not really know whether man was a machine, but he couldn't help feeling that man probably was not one. Some questions were just asked to be skirted around. By this time, his lunch hour was over. His thoughts had got nowhere; he had solved no production problems, and there seemed little point in going back over the argument from where he was now, wherever that was. He would only get lost again. Indeed, the more he thought things through, the less able he became.

Anyway, he was out of it: lunch hours, pickling plant and all. He could write his novel now. Or could he? Did creation require dirt and lunch hours – a mucky routine – even persecution? At college, for instance, with its freedom, he had almost faded away. The freedom had got to him and only his excitement at sharing love with Cas – that fierce, bare-boned, early love – had rescued him. Recognising this, he had applied for a practical job. It had taken abysmal steel to make him think again: an argument in favour of tyranny perhaps?

But other thoughts overtook him now, cynical and weary ones: why ever should he care? What did anything matter? We were all to die. This was all that counted. Camus might have taken such a line. Or would he? Camus was not only French, but dead. This morning, he had needed to be away, to be in Worcestershire, and indeed it was good to be here. But it was not so easy to escape his thoughts, or to escape death for that matter.

8

Lois could see the street lights through the curtains. She had taken a mug of cocoa to bed with her and leaned against the headboard in the dark. Those streets were her mother's world too. Her mother had always been with her in Birmingham, at the centre. Now, she was at the fringes, on the coast. Lois could only phone her each day. She put down the empty cocoa mug on the bedside table, slid down the bed and lay back on the pillow. She turned away from the curtains towards the rest of the bed where Jack usually lay, beside her dressing table, its mirror reflected the street lights through the curtains, the light blurring as in distant galaxies. There was a rumble of traffic like waves breaking at the seashore.

*

William had not escaped death. Cas missed his challenge to her, stretching back to those first hesitant or decisive embraces, and his intelligence. He had listened to her always, and especially when he disagreed with her or when he had other things on his mind. No one else had ever listened to her with the same concentration, not even her history of art lecturers who, up to a point, could listen and observe quite well, their gaze trustworthy if also sometimes amorous. The sea did not allow self-pity, however, nor was self-pity in her nature. She had never bent to anyone, but she was weak too. William's weakness was to never be affronted. Her weakness was to always be affronted. Together, they had tempered each other and come through. Birmingham had much to recommend it, even battened down with the virus like everywhere else, but never a view like this. It was a mostly blue sky with tinges of purple in a few clouds above the horizon, and there were a few streaks of purple and white above the headland. The sea was far out and calm. Like a curtain drawn back, it revealed the wide beach, water saturated in patches, with a hint of purple; the beach appeared to stretch all the way to the headland. The high dunes in the distance beside the beach were mostly in shadow but the headland was in sunshine, the green or brown fields saturated with sunlight.

*

One of the things that the papacy had taught him, he now realised as he leaned on the smooth, round, stainless-steel support at the edge of the balcony above St Martin's – a contrast with the soft, purple and white drapery of his sleeve – was not to be afraid of his own thoughts. There was no sea view here, but to compare the Vatican with the steelworks did not require a sea view. The Vatican had a more advanced management style than Sidney. It allowed William to have his own ideas and put them into practice. In his hands, it had become a relatively flat organisation, devoid of pomp and ceremony, or so he liked to think. Sidney, on the other hand, had ruled with a rod of iron. He had a distinguished war record and what he said, went. In the Vatican City, William could think the unthinkable and put it into practice; the logical conclusion of Thatcherite economics. With Sidney, he could think the unthinkable, but had ended up thinking the unthinkable without a job. The pope, by contrast, was an enlightened leader.

Anyone looking at William would not know anything about his thoughts. Thoughts were free, free as the ocean. They would see a man in an old coat, with all his possessions in two plastic carrier bags. They might wish that he did not spoil their view and that he did not trouble their conscience by trying to sell them *The Big Issue*. They were spared this as his search continued. He paced to the left towards Selfridges where there was a Birmingham City Council rubbish bin that he needed to investigate. It was possible that the meaning of his life was contained there. He thrust his right hand deep into the bin up to his armpit. Hands could be used to save goals and to pick up letters too. There was a smell of rotting tea bags. His mother had had a way with tea, but there were no other revelations to write home about. As the bin did not seem to contain the answer to his search, he turned round and walked in the other direction towards the stairs down to St Martin's. There was more than one way to skin a cat, after all. He could plan his own strategy. He was a free spirit. He had job satisfaction at last.

The stairs above St Martin's were not unlike the stairs outside the White House or the steps of the Senate where Roman oratory could be heard. Why were there no contemporary orators? People varied their register to suit the occasion: there was speech and there was speech; there was thought and there was thought. This balcony above St Martin's could have been a Roman amphitheatre and an appropriate location, therefore, to consider the difference between speaking and thinking.

Speech and thought, while requiring words, were also hidebound by them. Pacing back and forth between the bin and the stairs, with St Martin's and the markets down below on one side and the statue of Nelson on the other enabled him to distinguish falsehood from truth, even though methodical argument was dead in the water on the streets of Birmingham. He must seize the moment. This apparently haphazard following of instinct in the arrangement of words was in line with the texting going on in the streets on this Saturday morning, as well as with the philosophy of associationism that gathered strength during the eighteenth century and could be said to have its roots in John Locke and its flowering in the Romantic poetry at the turn of the century. The hanging baskets all over the city were another example of this flowering, though they were past their best now.

As he continued to pace between the stairs and the bin, a group of gospel singers could be heard below in the area between the markets and St Martin's. We might draw a parallel here, William thought, with the developments in music during the period from punk to rap and from baroque to classical orchestration where, with the arrival of Haydn and Mozart, or, in Birmingham, Simon Rattle, the exploitation of each instrument's particular sound and texture – in the case of rap it was the human voice – became desirable. From this viewpoint, William's imaginative behaviour could only be judged by reference to his own life. At the risk of sounding pompous, his own jumbled syntax was better suited to thought than speech, for it had a freedom of movement that speech did not allow him. The movement of speech was open to public censure; the movement of thought need only be licensed from within.

That William did not talk much now had therefore enabled him to develop beyond his circle of friends; it had given him the space and freedom to think outside the box in a Thatcherite way. Strictly speaking, this could not be captured either on paper or in discussion with others, it could only be alluded to. The judgements in his head could not now be conveyed accurately to anyone else, not even to Nelson on his plinth. No one could be expected to understand the intricacies of his position. An example of this kind of thinking could be found in *Tristram Shandy*: Trim dropped his hat to demonstrate the concept of mortality. William had no hat to drop, but no amount of written explanation could express this idea as touchingly. And the innovations of syntax, as well as such illustrations, could be seen in this light, as a reminder that language was contrivance, not always adequate to the task in hand and could be put together and broken up in an infinite number of ways, whereas the path of God was steadfast and invariable, much like that of Concorde.

Maria would have been proud of his radical heart now. Maria, in any case, had always been steadfast. He remembered her at her door later that Saturday, rosy-cheeked and orange-haired.

*

'Stephen dropped me off,' she said. 'He sends his apologies. He's Christmas shopping. Look, I'm starving!' she added. 'You will be too, with your journey and all.' It wasn't as far as flying to the States, William thought confusingly. 'I'll see if I can rustle up something!' she said.

Her dialogue was rather dull, William realised; his wife's insults were a whole lot easier on the ear for him. Anyone who had worked in a factory could not handle much kindness: kindness was a damned nuisance in fact.

He followed Maria into the kitchen. In a boat, it would have been the bows, the galley, where the fisherman had boiled the syrupy tea. There was a sink at the far end with another tiny leaded window facing the back garden and a faded Japanese print beside it. He could make out a few straggly rose plants, a herb garden and a patch of grass. But the mist still cushioned the hedge, and the sky was blotted out completely.

'You can do the soup, if you like,' she said. She judged him well. He knew about soup, though he sometimes wished that it was possible to buy fresh soup in the supermarkets, not just soup in tins. He could open the tin and stir with a wooden spoon. Stirring the soup, like walking the gravel path, kept him in touch with the world. In such ways he took control of life. He stirred the soup. He wondered then if instead of opening the soup, he had deposited the tin in the bank and opened it in the next century, would it have tasted much the same? Would his life have been much the same? Would he have been nearer to God or further from God? Nearer to his family or further from his family? Perhaps he would not even be alive; perhaps the bank would be gone; perhaps the soup in its tin would be the survivor. This was not quite the same philosophical problem as trying to establish in what sense the Quality Street that he had known as a child was the same Quality Street that he tasted as an adult. But again, it was the difference in him that was of interest rather than the difference in the brand. At least, this was his interest – he wasn't a marketing man.

Maria was now back in the cabin in front of the fire and

deftly laying the table. And now she was back with him in the galley, chopping onions, adding herbs, breaking eggs, stirring and frying. He was just heating the soup. 'This looks ready,' he said. 'If it isn't, I'll eat my hat!' This avuncular tone was out of keeping with him. He didn't wear hats anyway.

They ate silently in front of the fire – soup, omelettes, bread, cheese and fruit. He washed up with a thick, white dishcloth.

Later, they were sitting down again, a coffee mug each. Had the weekend been a novel, their behaviour might have seemed rather dull. Novels, unlike life, required suspense, murder even, at least a story to keep the reader's interest. She smiled slightly, as if she knew his thought, or could see into the future, or could sense an irony of which he was unaware. She was in her chair beside the fire almost smiling at him.

He stood up and squeezed her knee through the rough tweed.

'I had better get back,' he said.

She waved him off with the same hesitant smile. Waving was the stuff of childhood and of dreams. He noticed the bulbs in their lighted window: corn-on-the-cob bulbs. She looked in place there, in the doorway, the mist already settling along the guttering at the bottom of the slate roof like the haziness in an old photograph.

9

The instructor was half Lois's age and the participants were a good distance from each other, observing social distancing. Stela and Lottie were at the front; Stela in green, Lottie in purple. They whispered to each other, looked round at her, waved and grinned. She waved back, smiling. Lois must have been about their age – how time moved on! – when she had persuaded her father to join this class too, to get over himself. It had failed. Older people were embarrassing enough at the best of times. You could do without them at aerobics. But here she was still and with the youngsters still at the front.

After the class, Stela and Lottie ran up to her.

'Hello auntie!' Stela said.

'That was hard work!' Lois said.

'Not really!' Lottie said. 'We're in the spinning class now.'

'You know how to cheer me up!' Lois said. Stela grinned, her braced teeth showing. They ran off together, both waving back at her.

*

Cas noticed that this slate-grey morning held a finger of light in the cloud above the headland. The sand was glass-like, stretching to the sea at low tide where the foam was busy, white against dark. A strip of foam appeared to head out to sea from the estuary and extended beyond the headland. Bands of pink sky, parallel to the headland, were reflected in the wet sand. Jackdaws, near the terrace, dived recklessly in the still air. The strip of rounded rocks, which appeared to narrow approaching the estuary, divided the wet sand from the soft, green, brown and yellow gradations of the burrows. The burrows reminded her of William's father's spectacles. In spite of rain clouds over the sea, the sun caught the breaking crest of the waves, and the backward spray as the waves broke. The sun also illuminated a few white gulls against the chocolate sea. With William, in Birmingham, she had escaped urbanity, just as the coronavirus – under the microscope it resembled Kandinsky's *Squares with Concentric Circles* of 1913 painted five years before the Spanish flu – was able to dance to its own rhythm in whomever it resided.

*

Several of the cardinals were standing on the balcony beside him at the top of the picture frame overlooking St Martin's, as if looking out to sea. At first, he thought that one of them was praying aloud as he seemed to be talking to himself. He then noticed his hands-free mobile phone. The Vatican had changed during his tenure. He had been a pope to encourage new technology and new ways of reaching out to the faithful.

In fact, he had become quite an expert on new technology. He knew all about flat-screen televisions, DVD recorders and all the different kinds of home entertainment systems. He did not need a home in order to be an expert in these technologies. Dixons had become his favourite refuge on a wet afternoon. This wired and wireless environment was also potentially thought-provoking, he found. Last week, for instance, he had watched attentively as a DVD player was demonstrated. The salesman contrasted it with how the now obsolete video recorder had to be rewound.

When his papacy had begun, video recorders had been new technology in the Vatican. In the call of duty, he had watched postulants and novices from all over the world attending to the needy and the dispossessed. Remembering how the screen had looked as the tape rewound, he had found a moral with which to redirect his cardinals. The moral had become crystal clear to him, as sharp and bright as the new LCD screens. The moral was that if he looked at life backwards and at high speed, he was apt to get a distorted picture. In other words, it was his heavenly duty to look to the future, even when his health failed. The cardinals, needless to say, greatly admired their spiritual father's resolution in the face of his illness and they valued especially his continuing desire to look ahead ... or so they told him. The beauty of being pope was that he was infallible, at least as shepherd and teacher. He had not felt infallible as Concorde's chief test pilot and so he had had to take particular care in that job.

Although there was this intellectual side to his faith, he felt that his main contribution to theological debate rested simply with his belief in God's constant love. He had of course read innumerable religious tracts during his pontificate, but everything boiled down to whether or not he could face up to his God with honesty, integrity and love. What more could anyone ask of a pontiff? Scholars might spend their lives arguing over this or that theological point. William recognised the integrity of their arguments, but his job was to cut to the chase. He knew that their scholarship surpassed his own, but where had their scholarship got them? After all, he was the one who was pope. He had reached the stage of devotion where he simply had to lift his eyes to the sky. Admittedly, it was not so easy to see the sky in Birmingham – this balcony was a rare exception – but just one patch of grey or blue was all he required. No amount of learning could substitute for an emotional relationship with the Almighty, a relationship forged out of the experience of suffering and living life to the full. Life had led him on a paper trail. There was never a shortage of paper in Birmingham, some of it trapped on this balcony and swirling round his feet even though there was a rubbish bin near to hand. Eventually, he had come to discern the writing on that paper that mattered – the fact that love survived everything.

Below, beyond the balcony, some newly planted skeletal trees had shed a few red leaves onto the grey paving slabs, but there were few other signs of autumn. Nevertheless, having given due regard to Sterne already today, it was the turn of Keats to illuminate some of the things that he was trying to establish. He was almost as familiar with Keats as with home entertainment systems. For the urn, unlike MANKIND, achieved a permanent happiness; these boughs could not shed their leaves. This might have been an autumn weekend, but it held a timeless quality in his eyes.

He tasted 'Autumn's red-lipp'd fruitage' even in McDonald's, where the woman who thought she was his daughter always met him on a Sunday morning. The remarkable conjunction of 'harvest-carols' must have been written for this weekend. It enabled the harvest of his life to shake hands with the singing angels in the choir. And there was also here, he felt, a deliberate nonchalance towards the Christian calendar. This fitted nicely with the Greek and Italian setting of the weekend, and the championing of the pagan divinities at the end of the poem.

The poet, in bringing together wholly different kinds of flowers – lilies and primroses – gave the lines an identical rhythmical sweep, as if to show that Fancy could truly marry the disparate: Cas and the papacy; land and sea; *Brookside* and Concorde; suitcases and wheels; Christianity and Islam; mobile phones and cardinals.

Wisdom came both from learning and from experience. His awareness of the need to find something now had been brought about as the result of a lifetime's thought and observation. He was not shooting from the hip but from a monastic life of quiet contemplation and hair shirts. William's task had always been to see things as they were so that when the young woman he met in McDonald's every Sunday morning told him she was his daughter, he had learned to read between the lines and distinguish between what he would have liked to be true and the evidence presented. To have believed her would have made him happy, but it would also have been to deny the evidence.

To die and leave no love behind would not be his fate. He might not have a loving daughter, but he had the Church behind him, to say nothing of the affection and respect with which he was still held by his colleagues at British Airways and by his basketball friends – in particular, Michael Jordan, Scottie Pippen and Dennis Rodman – characters etched in his heart. His gritty dialogue for *Brookside* had also won him many friends. He should count his blessings. How could he feel unloved with such affection and achievement to fall back on and with his eyes on heaven? The denouement of his search might have something of the restrained power of Bach's *St Matthew Passion*, a fitting end for a man who toiled day and night to find answers.

Such was life. Many things changed. Many things stayed the same. With the passing of communist regimes in Eastern Europe, Saddam had provided an alternative shadow and delineation. These had therefore also been the Saddam years, as well as the years of the video recorder and of his papacy – and the years in which it no longer became necessary to carry suitcases. *Brookside* and Concorde, the queen of the skies, had also stretched their wings, taken flight and then drawn to a conclusion. Power and beauty were given, and power and beauty were taken away. Dubai and Palm Jumeirah – the very idea gave William a headache – might be other examples of the transitory in human achievement.

He remembered how, as a young man, he had observed old men at the steering wheel driving slowly. They would be long dead now. He now was such a man, walking away from the balcony above St Martin's, valuing life, stepping forward cautiously, enjoying every moment of being here for as long as this could last; an old man in the street walking along and contributing perhaps to the texture and pace of an English city. Was it too much to hope that his life now had an unhurried quality that in the end would give it stature? He remembered the pavements that he used to walk up and down as a child, avoiding the cracks, and the wooden fence that he used to run his finger along on his way to school. As a child, he had been unsure whether or not the future would be in his favour and now that the future had arrived, the question no longer seemed important. It was the future of mankind that mattered to him. Down at the bottom of the escalator, there was still confusion.

These great issues of life and death had not yet been resolved to his satisfaction.

*

Back in his yellow car returning from Maria – headlights following the bends of the road, dusk and mist closing in – he wondered whether he was not running away, even more than he had been in the morning. It had seemed like an escape then, but back on the motorway again, heading north, darkness settling, headlights flashing, he was returning to the lost job, the family, the uncertainty; these were to be taken on. There was courage in him certainly – Cas was never going to say, *welcome home!* as was the custom in Japan – but wasn't he still running from something else, from those half-smiling eyes, from the flowers and the cottage in the mist and the kindness?

But the gravel under the tyres was salutary. Gravel under the tyres wasn't quite as reassuring as gravel under the feet; it was one remove from reality. But any reminder of the physical world was a comfort; the physical world was unaffected by his state of mind. Bolting the garage door was another example of a physical reality; whatever his inner turmoil, he was still the man who could bolt the garage door.

10

With Jack asleep, Lois walked to Tesco with her canvas shopping bag over her shoulder. She liked to arrive soon after the doors opened in these Covid times. With her mask on, she knew her way around the store just as she knew her patch of Birmingham. Unlike Darren, she had not strayed far. She was rooted here, faithful to Jack and he to her. Carefully, she chose the carrots, the parsnips, a red pepper, a turnip and a few onions for a curry. Jack would make it. She placed brown sugar, syrup and jumbo oats beside the vegetables in the basket. Her father might have asked how jumbo oats were grown, she thought with a smile. There was already enough butter in the fridge for flapjacks. All this was intelligence as far as she was concerned. Jack knew this too. Her mother lacked this intelligence and so did Callie. Everyone to their own kind of intelligence, Lois thought.

Returning home, she turned on a hot oven and greased two trays with butter. She melted the butter and syrup in a large pan and mixed in the brown sugar and oats with a wooden spoon. She spooned the mixture into the trays, cleaning the wooden spoon with a knife. She flattened the mix with the back of a tablespoon so that the corners were filled. The trays were slid into the oven and the pan, scale container and utensils washed up and stacked on the draining board. She knew from the smell and colour when the flapjacks were ready. She removed the trays with a hot cloth and marked out the oblong shapes with a kitchen knife. She allowed them to cool before lifting each one onto a wire tray with a flat knife.

*

It was another dark morning beyond the pitted glass of the Victorian oak window frame. The burrows, estuary, headland, rocks, sand and sea were gathered together in darkness. It reminded Cas of William in hospital when he could remember nothing of his illness or the care that his family had taken of him. He had believed many untruths, such as that his wife had taken a lover. He had been contemporary in that respect as everyone believed untruths now. Two lights from fishing boats flashed out of sync with each other while the sea, sky and headland were still charcoal in colour and indistinguishable. Gradually, above the headland, a patch of lighter sky below the cloud separated land from sky. A lighter tone then spread west above the headland but not yet out to sea where sea and sky were still indivisible. William would have had something to say about that indivisibility. Then she could make out the horizon between sea and sky, the sea a touch darker. The morning's advance was as inevitable as the breaking of the waves on the shoreline, and her feelings had no bearing at all on this dawn of the day.

*

On the streets his practical skills had not left him. The weekend was a search, requiring every resource that he could muster. He wasn't exactly sure what he was searching for, but he would continue the search at the bottom of the wide steps in front of St Martin's.

Here, an old lady in fur cap and coat, pulling a suitcase behind her, crossed in front of him, as if out of a Chekhov play. The suitcase would not have had wheels once, William thought. Two policemen then walked past him, chatting. They would not have been armed at one time either. But he felt cool and competent. After all, no one knew who he was. Did he know who he was, or what he was doing? William may not have known precisely who he was in a metaphysical sense, but he knew his own power, the power that was wrought in him. There might be a big police operation mounting against him; he might be a man on the run, a wanted man, but he felt as safe as houses. He did not need his own house to feel as safe as houses. There lay the beauty of metaphor, the power of imagination. If anyone were to notice him at all, he would be perceived as inconsequential. Perceptions could be flawed. There was a Chinese saying that water was strong but soft. In other words, he could be accommodating but powerful too. His ability to put people at their ease was probably his greatest asset in this search. He could not quite remember what he was looking for, but he was looking for something and that was what mattered. Some people never looked for anything. He was searching because he loved mankind.

At an earlier stage in his life there had been prevarication. He had had difficulty in taking action. Now, he had been released from this to search the streets until the planets were in their alignment. This might take several years. Then, when the auspicious moment arrived, he would find what he was looking for and the sun would then no longer be covered by cloud.

On that pivotal weekend, this long search had been set in train. His new life owed much to the concept of a natural order, fundamental to an eighteenth-century view of the world. The rich patterning of Henry Fielding's *Tom Jones*, with the Inn at Upton at its hub, could be seen in this light too, like Spaghetti Junction at the hub of the motorway network. Such patterning was an acknowledgement of the natural Augustan order: a representation of the providential pattern. McDonald's fulfilled the same function in William's life now. It was his hierophancy and a tribute to the universal Laws of Nature. To have a pure heart was no easier in a McDonald's age, William thought, even if he always cleared the table after eating and placed the waste in the receptacles provided.

Tom Jones, like William, was a good character – he acted charitably – and the hand of providence was shown to be on his side, the working out of the author's plan becoming the working out of God's plan. Needless to say, such virtue brought hardship – it was not always easy to have no bed for the night.

At the bottom of the escalator, he still had a bed for the night, and he was in the thick of family life and taken very much for granted.

*

'Thoughtful of you to call!' Cas said. Her eyes were blazing and she towered over him.

'I couldn't tell you this morning,' he said, taking the bull by the horns. 'They are sacking me, you see.' There was silence. She looked him up and down, more down than up.

'It's high time you were sacked,' she said.' We don't need

your salary anyway. You were crap at your job. Why did they take you on in the first place?'

In passion, how attractive he always found her! And there was something rather satisfactory about this challenging of each other in the panelled hall, the carpeting both muffling the conflict and lending it eroticism. The children would be lying low somewhere, but hearing every word.

'So you just strutted off!' she said. Her lips began to turn up slightly at the edges.

Was her lipstick too harsh a red for her dark complexion? he wondered. Men had little experience in making judgements on lipstick. He did not trust himself on lipstick, or on anything else at that moment.

But then she flung him off and he was standing in the middle of the carpeted hall like a method actor not knowing what to do with his hands. He could see the bottom of the dining room door as if wedged between her stockinged legs.

'You saw Maria!' she said.

By her expression, he would not have known that Cas and Maria were friends, that they had shared rooms at college. Cas was never jealous. She knew her own worth. It was more, he felt, that she was now claiming her rightful share of his distress.

'I came back, didn't I?' he said. He had to say something.

She opened the door into the dining room with her left hand and twisted the knuckles of her right hand into his groin: he could never anticipate her.

Preparing the tea was more routine: she grilled the chops; he cut the bread and butter and made the tea. The children would stack everything in the dishwasher. He had been through the dishwasher today.

11

The flapjacks in her shoulder bag were wrapped in greaseproof paper and foil. There was still a slight warmth to them. She had left a few on the tray for later when she would watch the football with Jack on the TV. Ioanela, with Dorin in her arms and James beside her, came to the door and they stood outside the porch a few yards from her.

'You are good to us,' Ioanela said. 'It is so sad. The pandemic all over. In Sibiu too. My family stuck there. Your father dead. Your mother at seaside. She is a darling but scary. You are good with everyone. Us too. I love the flapjack. Oats are good for you. Where is Stela? She needs to eat more. Too much boys. She needs to be strong. My Dorin is a beauty. Look at him! My hair is a mess. Do you like the purple? There is no time. So many hours to work. I love them all. They like to sing. I teach them my songs. I teach them my dances too ... in their chairs. How is your Jack? He is handsome. My James is handsome too.' She kissed him squarely on the lips and straightened his leather jacket. 'James is my skip man. He knows all skips. Covid is good for skips. Skips are always needed. He is trained in skips. If he is not good, he goes in the skip!' James smiled proudly. It was a shame not to join them inside for a cup of tea.

*

With her hands nursing the mug of tea, Cas could see a strip of red cloud crossing the seashore. It was reflected in the dark sea, creating the illusion of a pathway. If she had been Moses she might have followed it. She would have said as much to William, but William was not here. The division could have been a break between the world before the pandemic, and afterwards. It would have been good to have William pick up on this point and run with it, either in madness or in sanity, as he invariably would – but she could hear him no longer. The constantly changing pattern of light and shade over the sky, sea, sand, estuary, headland and burrows was a reminder that nothing was permanent. She could handle her loss and her loss did not matter in the scheme of things. In any case, much was fractured now. Mondrian, in his paintings with *sea* or *tree* in the titles, painted before or during the First World War, showed nature as both fractured and balanced. Of course, titles in art could be problematic. She might be old, and an accountant, but she knew this much. Occasionally, a herring gull, working hard in the still air, circled or dived. The tide was halfway in and the stretch of sand glistened as if anticipating the approaching sea. Over the headland, the sky was like a stoked wood fire. A painting could only capture one moment while she was keeping pace with this car crash of a morning that was too much to describe, not that she had anyone to describe it to in any case.

*

As the chief test pilot for Concorde, flying in the red cloud, he had had to grab meals at any time of the day or night. When he'd had the respect of his team, he came to almost welcome the irregular hours. Similarly, writing for *Brookside* often involved working late into the night, the ringing kettle by his side, so that the actors had time to learn their lines before filming. It had been different in the Vatican. The domestic arrangements had been more orderly there – so different from living with Cas. However, as pope, he had refused the lavish lifestyle. Nevertheless, the holy office allowed him time for prayer, as well as time to shepherd his Church into the new century. He would of course miss those important responsibilities, but he had accomplished his duties and it was time to move on. He must think of his own soul and the eternal rewards that would follow the completion of his search. He was proud not only of his considerable achievements, but also of his willingness to leave them behind and raise his eyes to heaven.

One of the blueprints for his success had been Michael Jordan of the Chicago Bulls. William had studied him with great care in order to learn some of his techniques. It was best to look across the pond for the best examples of success in our time. He had learned from Michael to dress the part in well-tailored suits or regalia. Michael, Scottie and Dennis knew that appearances mattered. In basketball, as in life, success or failure often involved fine margins, sometimes in the last few seconds of a game. So it was important to consider everything, as well as to always keep going. He had applied Michael's self-belief and the ability to inspire those around him to each of his own situations – the papacy, Concorde, *Brookside* and the WHO. William had been through so much with Michael, Scottie, Steve, Dennis and the coach Phil Jackson that he counted them among his closest friends. Michael lived completely in the present and would never think about missing a shot that he hadn't taken yet. The parallels with William's life were uncanny. Michael had been willing to walk away from basketball after his father's murder to play baseball for the Birmingham Barons, though admittedly this had little to do with Birmingham in England. And Michael was now willing to leave basketball again after this season and no doubt with a sixth NBA Final win. What could be a better example to William of how to retire gracefully once again!

Life was always a matter of interpretation. One of Debenhams' window displays had a print of Mondrian's *Composition with Yellow*, a work of apparent simplicity and harmonious order. Three black horizontal lines and two black vertical lines were simpler than New Street Station, the small rectangle of yellow to the lower right almost an afterthought but necessary nevertheless. Most of the print was the colour of Maria's walls, off-white – even papal white in the bright shop window – and he was happy to compose himself today with the calm balance of Mondrian as his backdrop in contemplating where he stood.

The city itself might have been more like a painting by Grosz, with vivid reds, yellows and blues, even on a dull autumn afternoon. The pursuit of capital had been his dream too in earlier years. He knew only too well that the advertisements and squalid city entertainments were symptoms of a corrupt and class-ridden society. Meanwhile, he had been released to focus on his search. Like the Russian Constructivists, William's position was to reject the inner workings of his mind, as seen so far during this weekend, and to replace expression with production. Cas had told him all about the Constructivists. She was akin to them, she said. In essence, they were accountants too, she said, disingenuously. Accountancy ran counter to collectivism, he said. It was aligned to bourgeois precepts. What do you know? she said. They were indebted to the instruments of construction: ruler and set square, and the building bricks of construction: line, colour, surface and texture. They would have been happy to use calculators. That's how I work too, she said. Cas knew more than he about art – about most things – and she never lost an argument.

William too was now concentrating on finding clarity within his physical surroundings. The class implications of the ruler and set square may not have been evident in a propagandist sense, but they were there nevertheless, like the leaves of an oak table. He had never seen Pillars of Society carrying set squares, or walking around Birmingham with carrier bags for that matter. Geometrical patterns were also more appropriate for him than figurative pieces. William was the proletariat on his way to the factory while the bourgeoisie revelled in food, drink and prostitution, or at least put their hands on each other's arms. Constructivism tended to emphasise proletarian production for the common good, pouring scorn on any flowering of what was regarded as the elitist, artistic imagination. He must concentrate on the job in hand now without being waylaid by an off-the-shoulder imagination.

Constructivism tended to depersonalise the whole process too, and this approach suited him at the moment. He could regard the self-expression of the individual as irrelevant. The fact that he still loved Cas could be put aside. All these years later, Cas still loomed over him.

The print in his mind's eye, Jeanneret's *Still Life with a Pile of Plates* which Cas had hung in the dining room, was associated with his dishwasher marriage and his accountant wife. It was also a lesson in simplicity to him now: the green bottle distilled to its simplest form; the white pile of plates, papal white, simplified into the essence of a pile of plates, the regular, wavy edge on the left and the hollowed top surface indicating the basic structure. The weekend was also being pared down to its essential features, his search for what mattered. For Cas, what mattered were both ideas and numbers.

Dada was not for him. He found the *Mona Lisa* with a moustache distasteful. Surely there were better ways of confronting a fractured Europe? Who could take offence at a man trying to find what he was looking for?

The print of *Two Women Running on the Beach* by Picasso, had been his choice. Cas had said it wasn't sufficiently urban for her taste and that you wouldn't find her by the seaside. It was placed on the same wall as the Jeanneret, though he had not seen either print for many years. The Picasso was Cas and Maria deriving their power from the usurping of a classical form – two solid classical figures grossly distorted. The background figure's right leg and left arm, the one carrying the carrier bag, extended almost to the edge of the panel, creating a sense of spontaneous movement within the classical frame. Was this the weekend's purpose to balance the unrestrained vision and the restraining platonic scheme?

Everywhere in the Bullring – not just Debenhams – stocked expensive items in preparation for Christmas. Christmas wasn't for the dispossessed. But his priority was his search and the best searches were never in a straight line. So he walked away from Debenhams to a bench near the indoor market. He felt tired and hungry. The bench was oblong and concrete with square holes in it. Such geometry satisfied him. It would have satisfied Cas too. Besides, any form of representation of God was blasphemous. He may then have dozed for a while, his search reaching fruition.

That he had not read a book in years was to his advantage. The prevarication of literature was anathema to the purposes of God and to accountancy. He must take the prevarication out of every word he spoke and thought. The politicians, historians, academics, even certain churchmen, had a habit of balancing one argument against another as if there were no absolute truth. He would save Man from all this. He would speak straightforwardly. He would distinguish right from wrong. Never again would a mire of qualification be his fate. Sidney, like an Old Testament prophet, had spoken. Sidney had not suffered from gradations of meaning – he knew black from white – and William was indebted to him for opening his eyes to the need for absolutism.

A period of quiet meditation was always welcome. To sit here on this bench was good enough for him. He did not need to walk around – or, perish the thought, go on a cruise – to be content. He was not a man to stumble at the last hurdle. There was love in his heart. To be energetic, magnanimous, consistent and unswerving in his duty was no more than was expected of him. To think that at one time, before his solitary life of penitence, he had lived mundanely.

*

Cas banged on the banisters, returning him to how things once were.

'Down here, slobs!' she shouted.

The children were quiet. Lois looked slightly pale. James, not unusually, studied his feet. They were young. He tried to act normally.

'You had better wash your hands!' he said to James. 'Lois is too old to be told. Besides, she's always in the bathroom.'

So much talking from him was not normal though. So he tried to smile instead. But he felt foolish smiling, just as a smiling man who had just lost his job might expect to feel. He realised then that his own hands were grimy. He had already cut the bread. Hypocrite. He leaned over his son at the sink; they washed their hands, shared the soap. How protective he felt! He could remember his own father performing this same act with him. Would James ever have a son and wash his son's hands in the same way? A psychiatrist would probably find homosexuality there. Instead, he saw a whole line of fathers and sons leaning over each other into eternity, an image of continuity, like the Marmite jar with a picture of a Marmite pot with Marmite in it – most appropriate for Marmite. No one ever seemed to finish a jar of that either. An earlier example than Marmite was the Chair of Princess Sitamun that Lois and James had run around at the Tutankhamun exhibition in the British Museum ten years ago. Painted on the back of the chair in gold were two pictures, one from each side, of Princess Sitamun sitting in the same, or a similar chair.

It was Wittgenstein who had talked about always needing another instruction to verify a command. However detailed the command, Wittgenstein's argument had gone, a person could always ask how the words were being used. And this would entail another instruction and so on. It was a never-ending predicament, like the mirrors this morning, like pie, like Marmite, like Princess Sitamun's chair and like this line of fathers and sons leaning over each other at the kitchen sink. It was said that anyone's father and his father back to the time of the Norman Conquest would fit in a minibus. But who would be driving? William wondered. And it was like his purposeless thoughts that stretched on and on, unless they happened to come to their senses. He wondered whether, with time, these problems would ever resolve themselves into clarity in his mind. Perhaps one day he would entertain doubt no longer and be able to assert confidently a meaning to his life. He sincerely hoped that this would never be his fate; it was with all his soul that he despised certainty. God! A day like this and his mind still drifted off. Indeed, especially on a day like this it drifted off. Keeping a sense of proportion, getting the balance right, that was his problem. That was life's problem. The Swedish *lagom*, neither too much nor too little, was what he could have done with at the moment.

His wife was saying something. He asked her to repeat it.

'Have you remembered the mask? I said,' she shouted.

Ah, he understood: an allusion to scrubbing up. They ate silently; James with his head down, Lois with a precise use of the knife and fork, a physical sure-footedness that her mother's sprawling intelligence lacked.

12

There was a small office where James worked. Lois sat there, looking out at the big yard behind, framed by a brick wall with barbed wire on top. James was standing in the yard. He wore a yellow high visibility jacket, safety helmet and a mask. He was talking to one of his female apprentices. She was sitting on a red forklift. She looked happy and confident. She was the future, Lois thought. James waved when he saw Lois and came inside to her.

'The burial is sorted,' he said. He took off his helmet and sat down opposite her.

'The police rang me back,' Lois said. 'I knew when she didn't answer the phone. The rabbi is amazing. So kind. They are sorting everything. The transport. The pine coffin. Everything.'

'I know,' James said. 'It all happened so fast. I had to come to work. It'll be good for Stela to be there.'

'Callie will be there too. I'm meeting her at McDonald's. Maria and Stephen will make up the ten. I was never good at maths.' They smiled. 'I can't hug you, James!'

'It's sad she wasn't with us. But we couldn't do anything. She wanted the sea after Dad died. Covid was just bad luck, a bummer.' James looked suddenly exhausted.

Lois was exhausted too. 'I know,' she said. 'It's not our fault.'

'I know,' James said. 'We'll be all right.'

'I know,' Lois said.

*

On this soft morning, light brown clouds against a blue sky were reflected in a brown and blue sea. There was a fascinating science of pandemic that Cas found as mesmerising as the view from her window. It was a delight to her that we were out of Europe and at least to some extent in control of the country's destiny, though she would have loved to still hear William complaining about this. She understood, of course, that the pandemic did not respect borders or the clean line where the high tide reached the dark pebble ridge and then extended up the estuary like a hydra. The sea, unlike the stock market, was tranquil with gradations of blue and brown. The Fed, as always, would find solutions. During the Wall Street Crash, there had been no Fed to pick up the pieces. Naively, perhaps, she trusted both the Fed, and the UK Parliament, but she also missed arguing with William about such things. To do right mattered to her. She would not apologise for following a path and believing in her husband and her family. She believed in God too, even when God was hard on her and even though, in order to exist, God defied all logic. On the horizon, the sky was a slightly lighter tone than the sea with a thin and delicate strip of light brown cloud above, extending thicker over the headland. The only interruption was the kaw, kaw, kaw of a herring gull climbing in a curve against the still air, wings beating fast. It was morning, not dusk, as the sun rose like a Shabbat candle. There was a hint of maroon in the sky above the headland but she would not be crying over any of this.

*

He liked to think that he still had both an enquiring intellect and a certain physical prowess. This might seem a surprising claim to anyone observing him on this bench. But the illusion of being washed-up disguised the fact that he had the resolution for this search.

Besides, at St Chad's, where he often spent his mornings, there had been a small window into a church outhouse. Last spring, a small bird had worn itself out pecking on the glass, knocking itself out against an image of itself day after day. It was clearly a message about the need to work together for a better world. War was fighting yourself. But it was no use for him to just make this observation unless he did something about the problem. William had proved – as pope, as scriptwriter for *Brookside*, as a key player with the Chicago Bulls, and as the chief test pilot for Concorde – that he knew how to see a project through. With this work completed, his search was underway. He was ready. He was calm. He would never shirk his responsibilities.

He had sat on this bench for quite a while while the darkness closed in. He was right to bide his time – slowness came from God, haste from the devil. His daughter, before she was replaced, had moved economically, always with time to spare. The market stalls had shut and shoppers with their bargain joints of meat had gone away. He was still hungry and at dusk he could eat. However, Ma Potter's Chargrill was too expensive. But he knew where he could get chips cheaply and a cup of tea. He walked carefully with his carrier bags past Debenhams again, with its lavish Christmas window displays. The stairway up to Smallbrook Queensway had been revamped in stone, glass and steel. It seemed to circle up to heaven where there were blue neon lights and a yellow halo. There was also a smart lift and he made use of this even though he wasn't now a council tax payer. A voice from the lift told him unnecessarily that he had reached Shopping Level Two.

Slowly, he walked left down Smallbrook Queensway away from the station. There were delicate white Christmas tree lights on the introduced trees. The Finishing Touches beauty salon charged £30, he noticed, for nail extensions. The Caspian Chip Shop now sold tomato soup. He did not mind tomato soup. Fish and chips were only £1.99, however, and he could buy chips for £1.

Joy, like time, was always relative. He knew from an essay that had taken him weeks that Anna and Vronsky's relationship in *Anna Karenina* did not bring them joy, unlike his once happy marriage to Cas. He was walking back now to New Street Station and he remembered writing that the railway had a bearing on Anna and Vronsky's relationship: a man was run down by a train the day they first met; they sealed their love on the train to St Petersburg; and Anna died under train wheels. Such literary knowledge was still with him though it had never been very useful, or changed his life significantly.

Anna and Vronsky's marriage was associated with movement in this geographical sense and in the sense of embracing modern habits. William's marriage had only embraced movement in the sense that Cas had discarded him, moved on to kiss someone else while keeping the house much as it was. The painting of Anna's portrait – it did not have a green streak – could be seen as just one way of trying to keep abreast of society. His own marriage with Cas had resisted such things. He had needed her desperately but she had found someone else.

The painful part was that he would have made any adjustment to keep Cas by his side. He needed her. He was a part of her. At the Vatican, and in his marriage, he had always resisted the leisured ease that was a feature of Anna and Vronsky's life together in Italy, insisting on shaving for himself and tying his own shoe laces, for instance, even when to bend down to kiss the earth of a foreign country or to pray became painful.

*

He had made a fresh pot of tea just for the two of them and had brought it through to Cas in the sitting room, situated down at the bottom of the escalator. They called it the sitting room in his family. This might have been a matter of pedantry or class or even of education. On the other hand, it was a sensible use of language to call the room in which they sat a sitting room; no one talked of 'lounging' nowadays. Wittgenstein had been onto this too. To find the meaning of a word, one had to look to how it was used. But this was no argument for sitting room – most people called it a lounge. If they called it a lounge, a lounge it must be. Hell! Where was he going wrong? It had been a long day. He did not have the inclination to go back over the argument in order to find out, firstly, what he was trying to establish and, secondly, what had gone wrong with the analysis. Lately, his thinking had often ended in this woolly kind of a way. Was he now in the Sufi tradition, perhaps, where forgetting was the first step in becoming who he was? Either he was losing his grip or else he had gone beyond objectivity onto a higher plane of reasoning where the confusion was acceptable, where the search for patterns could proudly end. Perhaps he had thus stumbled onto a new philosophy. *Confusionism*, he would call it. Confusionism, in a nutshell, was being content to live with confusion – a rare gift! Would he always be content to live with confusion?

In any case, William had never had much time for scholarship and regarded all claims to genius in others as no more than smoke and mirrors. The idea of a first-class mind appalled him: the arrogance of such people and the inevitability that such people would be closed to learning. Most educational structures seemed to him to be a part of some grand deception from which he had always been excluded, in spite of scraping together his doctorate during his first job. After all, there might be no ultimate truth for those structures to support.

'I like the Bauhaus strainer!' Cas never smiled when she made a joke. It was effective. He would have liked to learn from her technique, but if he had not learned how to tell a joke in fifteen years of marriage to her, he was unlikely to learn now. He returned the toast rack to the kitchen cupboard and collected the strainer.

The Bauhaus was at least worthy of thought. And it was a pity that, except for the Wagenfeld table lamp with its glass dome, they had nothing from the Bauhaus in their home. He didn't like the Bauhaus much, but he had regretted failing to buy a Marcel Breuer dressing table in the early seventies, in his first job. He had thought it tinny and rather eccentric. The mirrors, he remembered, had looked as if they were supported on an old bicycle frame with metal coat hangers thrown in for good measure, and the drawers were like an office block and crudely painted. Nevertheless, as an investment, he should have known better than to pass it over.

It was a coincidence that Cas should have mentioned the Bauhaus when the Bauhaus had been in his thinking too – a coincidence or else, perhaps, evidence in support of Jungian analysis or the idealist position. If all his experience derived from inside his own Boltzmann brain in the first place, it would not be at all surprising that the Bauhaus should crop up several times both in his own thoughts and in another character's supposed thoughts that were actually William's own. The Bauhaus might just happen to be on his mind. Paradoxically, and in spite of the lack of decisiveness, he had recently felt a growing regard for his own mind as perhaps something more than batteries of cells. That something extra might be put down to language or art or even, on a sunny day when Maria's walls were papal white, to God. If the body was not everything, if behaviourism was not the whole story, then didn't morality have to step forward from the shadows and take charge? After all, his mind and what it came up with, and arguably the gravel drive, were all that he could trust.

But he was not wholly convinced by this argument: as well as the gravel path, there was Cas. Just look at her. She was handsome. She was proud. She sat *on* the chair rather than *in* it. She sat on her nerves. Cas could meet him halfway. This willingness in her to contend made her a distinctly separate, moral being. She had talked about his moral stare, but what about hers? She had given up her first love – art – to support the family. His income had never been secure. Morality was in fact so marked in her that it had frightened him off this morning. It was all her fault in a way. Nevertheless, she was precious to him. It was only through her that he could grapple with himself.

'I'm not working for anyone else!' he said. This sounded more dogmatic than he felt about it, but he often did this with her. He overstated his case. It left her something to contend with.

'You would make a fine entrepreneur,' she said. 'You've got that ruthless streak.'

He knew what she was saying. She was saying that if he couldn't hack it in industry, he would find it tougher in the marketplace. This was an understandable position for an accountant to take, albeit an accountant who had studied art initially, and it was what she always left unsaid that counted the most. She specialised in uncompleted sentences – accountants didn't need many words.

They did not speak any more. They just sat there. At one point, Lois put her head round the door to say that Jack was outside and that she was going out. She had on a scarlet jacket, William noticed. He hoped that she would be all right. Later, James came in for a while and then he went out again.

13

There were a few tables outside and Callie ordered on the app.
This both was and was not the same experience for Lois as with
her father.

'Two fillet of fish meals, a double espresso and a hot
chocolate,' the girl said. 'I'm not allowed to take them out of
the bag. Can I get you anything else?'

'No. Thank you. That's lovely,' Lois said, taking everything
out of the brown paper bag and glancing at Callie's donkey
jacket. 'The others are meeting us there,' she said.

'It doesn't matter what I wear,' Callie said, taking a handful
of warm fries from the red, cardboard container cupped in her
left hand. 'Gran understood me better than you!'

'Where did that come from?' Lois said smiling. 'What did I say?'
The donkey jacket and trousers were fine. 'You would look good
in anything,' she said. 'I'm jealous! You look like Simon Rattle.'

'Who's he? Just kidding!'

'Your grandad loved him. Always in black. Wild hair. Your
grandad and I saw him at the cinema once with his children, like

any other dad. His children were younger than me. The cinema has gone. He's still going strong. She bit into the fish and bun, carefully preventing the sauce inside from spilling. 'You are here. That's what matters. It all happened so fast. You did well to get back. Maria and Stephen have dropped everything too.'

'Not the first time!' Callie said.

Lois smiled. 'Don't be so judgemental,' she said. 'You know nothing about it. Neither do I. It was before your uncle was born. Gran and Maria were best friends.'

'Funny way to show it!' Callie said.

'What do you care anyway? I didn't have you down as a prude!'

Callie smiled. 'I was only thinking of Gran,' she said. 'But Gran could handle most things, I guess.'

When they had finished, Lois collected the packaging of their meal into the brown paper bag and wiped down the table with the paper napkin. She sorted each item into the containers and slid the black tray onto the shelf above. The routine was ingrained.

*

Cas was a city girl, or old lady, used to traffic and lorries, buses and advertising hoardings. Clients had often argued with her, mostly about her pricing, which was always high. After all, she had a family to support and they could always go somewhere else for a poorer service, she would tell them. She enjoyed argument. Argument was necessary to her way of thinking. Here, through the oak window, there was an unfamiliar harmony, broken only by her rasping cough. With first light, a strip of whiteness clung to the sea's edge and a parallel strip of light rested above it in an overcast sky, as if sea and sky were working together. Another lightness followed the headland out to sea and exacerbated a headache between her eyes. Being invisible here did not stop her head from hurting. She had forced the pace all her life, made herself visible. As men had watched her, she had been scathing of them, quick into combat. The children had had to learn manners from the start. William would not teach them anything. She had often been the only adult in the house, other than Lois. In this early morning, the gradations of colour in the burrows were softer and more muted, so she rested her eyes there on the green and brown tinges. The headland was cooperative too, following the estuary up river with the clouds and the burrows on the same trajectory. It was strange to her that no single element shouted for attention. It had not been like this during her life in Birmingham. There had been no holding back then and the shouting for attention had been a normal and welcome part of family and accountancy life.

*

The walk back with his chips to the station involved crossing the road by Debenhams, Debenhams at a higher level than previously. Would he last longer than the two-level Debenhams, even though he only had one level? He would try to get an early night somewhere in the station, in line with two-level game theory. He loved fireworks, but tonight sleep mattered more and the Diwali celebrations might be more muffled in the station. He needed a good night's sleep in order to do justice to the search. His present discomforts were of no consequence.

With five pounds still in his pocket, there would have been no advantage in selling *The Big Issue* today. And he had a good pension from British Airways in any case. To land Concorde was always a joy, although with so many dials to keep his eyes on, it was always more of a pleasure afterwards than at the time, like going for a swim – red armbands on the table afterwards beside the cup of Bovril and the smell of beef and chlorine. The pleasure had mostly been in retrospect with *Brookside* scripts too. The script might have seemed easy and fluent to the viewer as the cast spoke their lines, but he had toiled over every word. He had never enjoyed a basketball game either until the final whistle blew. Needless to say, the rewards of papacy, and of Christianity generally, also tended to be in retrospect. He was frail now. Rewards could only now be subsequent. The still-warm bag of chips represented pleasure postponed too. He could see Leonardo's *Last Supper* in his mind's eye even though these were only chips and the disciples and cardinals were tactfully waiting at a discreet distance. At the bottom of the escalator, with a button to push in case of emergency, he could hear the front door bell distinctly.

*

His brother and Darren waited on the step and the light from the hall glowed on their faces as in an Old Master. If they hadn't been relations, and if it were December, not November, they might have been carol singers, William thought. He ventured out into the cold and dark beside them as if to register the family bond. The sky was overcast, no sign of stars or moon, though the stars and moon would still be there, he guessed, behind the clouds.

Cas made as if to shut the door and Paul grinned. Darren gripped his hand. He was more serious than his father – more like William, perhaps. It was ten years since James had been that age. He remembered James in the swimming pool, his shiny, red armbands, kicking fit to burst.

'Thanks for the card!' William said. It was only this morning that the card had arrived, but it seemed longer, years ago even. 'And how are you, Darren?' William was uncomfortably aware that his speech betrayed him; he was still the caring son of devout parents.

'I caught a prawn,' Darren said.

'Was it blue?' Cas asked.

He shook his head seriously.

William watched them appreciatively. Paul smiled and leaned over his son, ruffling his hair with a hand. William pictured the Marmite jar again. Paul frog-marched his son through the front door and into the sitting room, where they sat together on the blue chaise longue. Cas brought in a packet of crisps for Darren on a Willow-pattern plate.

'What do you say?' William heard Paul ask, and he watched as Paul playfully bounced a cushion on Darren's head. The tableau reminded him of Princess Sitamun with lotus flower ornaments on her headdress and her feet on a low footstool.

'Thank you,' the boy said sincerely, and he laughed a little. His small hands gripped the sides of the plate that rested on his short, grey trousers. His feet did not quite reach the carpet. William had had a similar posture that morning in the car, his feet on the pedals and his stomach touching the steering wheel. Would Darren one day travel the world, marry a foreigner even? The world would be his oyster.

He gazed at the scene before him. It would make an interesting painting, he felt, one of those sentimental Victorian pieces perhaps, though with late twentieth-century additions such as the boy eating from a crisp packet. The boy was wearing grey short trousers and a green T-shirt; the father was in brown trousers and a comfortable, red sweater knitted by his wife.

The husband and wife of the house looked on from matching blue armchairs at each side of the gas fire. The William Morris wallpaper was also blue, although it was called 'Tulips'. He looked at the jagged leaves and the swirling petals. There was no attempt at realism there. He would look for gravel-path wallpaper the next time. For the husband had really lost his job. His wife knew this but his brother and the little boy did not, although that made the news no less real. It would be impossible, however, that a painting could demonstrate all this. His brother's good nature might be shown in the expression of his face, but what of the lost job? William could be painted in tears, but that would be wrong – unrealistic. He was rarely in tears. Indeed, he could come to quite enjoy being made redundant. Of course, the impossibility of conveying the exact situation need not diminish such a painting's charm. Painting, like music, was no stickler for the facts. And it was a comfort, in a way, to know that in the language of the canvas or the symphony, only the mood and not the precise circumstances of his weekend would be registered. Still, painting and music were one thing; life was another. And he did not intend to keep the facts from Paul.

'I've lost my job,' he told him, pleased at the matter-of-fact tone of his voice.

'You haven't, have you?' Paul said.

'We missed bonfire night,' Darren piped up, indifferent to the mood. He had finished the crisps but he still clung to the plate, wriggling against the cushions. His legs were straight out in front of him.

'That's a damn blow!' said Cas, smacking her forehead. 'How will you manage?'

Darren laughed and smacked his own forehead cheerfully. 'Dad says we can have it next weekend,' he said.

'That's if you behave,' Paul said. 'Go and pester your cousins, big mouth.'

'Lois will be under a gooseberry bush,' Cas said. 'If she's not back for ten, she can sleep there.' Paul smiled. 'Pester James, if you like,' Cas said. 'He could do with pestering. You can take the plate with you too, but keep it level – I'm not having the pattern fall off.' They went out of the room together, Darren concentrating hard on the blue patterned plate. The future was in the boy's grasp too.

Paul, by himself on the blue chaise longue, looked slightly awkward. He would not have expected such news, but he did not say anything. Then Cas came back in again carrying a wooden tray with three bottles of beer, three tumblers and a bottle opener. Cas was the only woman William knew who drank stout, and he was married to her. Maria did not drink at all.

Paul gulped his beer. He said that he couldn't stay and left awkwardly, Darren clinging to his hand. Paul often looked awkward. It was one of the things that people rather liked about him.

'You'll be round tomorrow?' William said. Paul nodded and grinned. William walked up the drive with them. The fog had lifted and there was now a gusty wind. He noticed the gravel. Their shoes scraped against it. It was good not to be at sea on a night like this, he thought.

As he turned back after waving them off, he noticed two youngsters under an orange lamp further up the street. They were engrossed in each other. It was all right being young, he thought. Then he noticed that one of them was Lois. It was her jacket, though it didn't look scarlet under the street lamp. Did this mean that it wasn't scarlet any longer? It was hard to let go and turn back to the house again up the gravel drive.

He shut the front door and headed for his study, turning on the light. The phone rang. Cas would answer. He drew the curtains and sat down at the desk. With the phone ringing, he could no longer hear the clock's tick. Cas answered the phone and he could hear the clock again, though the clock must have been ticking all the time. Perception, like joy, was always relative.

There were footsteps on the gravel path, a low whispering and little joyful exclamations. Lois almost sounded like Darren. She certainly did not laugh like that with him any more. She had no reason to. He heard Jack walking back up the gravel and Lois opening the front door. How quietly she could move! And, of course, she remembered to put the latch down. He heard it click. So many small virtues! He almost heard her scurrying upstairs, as if a hamster wheel was turning in another room.

14

With her mother buried, Lois walked with the others through cast-iron gates away from the walled section at the corner of the cemetery into the spacious and unrestricted area with its towering trees. The Victorian city had saved up considerable space to park the dead. Each of their four household bubbles fetched picnics from their cars. They sat on orange, plastic sheets that James had brought from work.

'Nothing like blending into our surroundings,' Stephen said.

It felt strange without her mother, Lois thought. She would have had a reply to Stephen's observation. Now, she was buried.

'He had smiling eyes, the rabbi,' Ioanela said. She had taken her headscarf off. Her hair was green with flecks of red in it.

'Yes,' Stephen said. 'A man of God.'

'You could have brought Dorin, the chubby little chap!' Lois said.

'I know. But he might have screamed,' Ioanela said. 'Maidie offered to have him. Lottie loves poking his cheeks to make him laugh!'

'I will miss her as if she was my sister,' Paul said.

They ate slowly, quietly, and drank steaming coffee from flasks poured into plastic cups. Ioanela had brought orange juice for Stela. Tears ran down Stela's pale face as she drank.

'It's all right darling,' Ioanela said with an arm round her. 'It's all right to cry like Dorin when you are sad. We are all crying inside too. Look, James is crying outside and he's your dad!'

Stela looked at James and they smile-cried together.

*

In bed, the curtains seemed to rise and fall, although Cas had only drunk one can of stout last night. What would William have had to say about these rising and falling curtains? At the window, even with the dressing gown around her shoulders, she felt cold. The beach with a covering of sea water was flat, contrasting with a busy sea, the waves powering in, a cauldron of white surf. William's death was a fact, irrespective of what happened here as she watched a mountain ridge of water in front of the headland and a band of clouds crossing the horizon. With a disturbed sea and sky and a boundary of lightness above the clouds, there was relief in the tortoiseshell gradations of brown, green and yellow on the burrows that reached to the pebble ridge at the edge of the sand. No part of this scene could mean much to her. This was not Birmingham. The action was where the waves were, but she was past action, and anyway this beauty was a foreign land to her.

*

It seemed appropriate to wash before he slept. His mother had taught him to wash before bed. She had also taught him to say his prayers. He would pray too. He prayed almost all the time now, in any case.

After washing in the station, he found a seat in the covered waiting area in the forecourt below the escalators. This area was long overdue for redevelopment. In Singapore, foreign labour would have been employed to transform the city, but these city elders were slow to get anything done. Everything had to go to consultation and there were always so many objections that little was ever achieved. So, as darkness fell and as he prepared himself for sleep, he was aware that this was neither Vatican City nor Singapore.

To experience love on New Street Station, with the escalators moving up and down beside him and the occasional raucous interruptions from groups of revellers enjoying Saturday night on the town and making fools of themselves, might seem perverse, but these catacombs would more than suffice for him.

With the confidence of youth – he was much the same age at that time as the drunken youngsters who passed him now as he sat on this hard chair near the escalators – he had written then that in T.S. Eliot's *Four Quartets*, time is first shown as a chronological sequence where past and present influence the future; time is also seen as eternally present and therefore unchangeable, so that past events can never be redeemed. That essay, like all the essays he had ever written, had lodged in his head unredeemed, whether he liked it or not. There was also what did not happen, *what might have been*, but that only became a possibility if he indulged in speculation. And there was also a religious dimension that, in a sense, overcame human time and saw *what might have been* and *what has been* as one.

The 'timeless' episode in the rose garden was short-lived because its reality, timelessness, was unfamiliar. Birmingham was full of rose gardens, both in reality and in a manner of speaking, though there were no rose gardens here at the bottom of the escalators, except in his imagination. The reality at the bottom of the escalators, near the station entrance, suited him nicely. It was the kind of reality that he could get along with.

This ultimate and timeless condition represented the sort of calm tension that was to be found at New Street Station on a Saturday night near to the escalators. Paradoxically, moments of timelessness, such as this one, could only be remembered and related to other experiences after time had passed, after the one-handed clock had ticked, so that 'Only through time time is conquered'. Hence the need for two weekends.

To be the pope, the scriptwriter for *Brookside*, the chief test pilot for Concorde and one of the insurmountable Chicago Bulls was an honour. He had been welcomed with open arms into these occupations like an air steward greeting Concorde passengers, or the captain himself. He had lived up to all expectations in these jobs and yet the humility that came with failure almost seemed welcome to him now. And to echo Rilke's *Duino Elegies*, only the boy's smile, down at the bottom of the escalator, was worth offering the angels.

*

James was in bed. 'Hi, Dad!' he said, giving him an unusually bold smile.

'Paul's having his bonfire next Saturday,' William replied. But he could hardly expect a fourteen-year-old to care about a bonfire. He would have had to be under ten or over forty for bonfires to be important. William's father had loved bonfires. Whenever William lit a bonfire, he felt near to his father.

'Bit late!' James said. He managed to have his eyes down even in bed. 'It's nearly Christmas,' he added.

William smiled. He was no good at banter; he left that to Cas. His own mind quickly lost interest or forgot what had gone before and he couldn't fake interest any more. So he tended to keep quiet instead, though the long silences that this often caused were sometimes awkward. An easy manner and a relaxed laugh might have got him anywhere, he thought, except perhaps where it mattered.

Eventually, he said, 'Oh well, kid, see you in the morning.'

Then he drew the curtains. They were bright green. There were Airfix models on the windowsill – soon, he thought, only the glue would be of interest – and there would be girls on the walls if not in the bed before long. Life, rightly, had to proceed. He moved the Frisbee off the chair. Both the chair and the Frisbee were dusty. He piled the ramshackle clothes there. That was enough. He wasn't going to fuss over him. He could remember being fourteen himself: it wasn't much of an age to be; neither one thing nor the other – the same as being forty.

He slapped the side of the bed. 'Night, old fellow,' he said, closing the door.

Lois was reading at her desk in pillar-box-red pyjamas and blue bed socks.

'Don't get cold!' he said, caringly. 'Where's your dressing gown?'

It was behind the door, of course, brown and dowdy. She had asked her mother for another one. He put it round her shoulders and noticed, approvingly, that she was reading *Wuthering Heights*. But he had more sense than to ask her about it, or indeed about Jack. Jack had been with her since primary school. They were one and the same. He would have been on safer ground talking about the book's fine structure, but he had no wish to be a killjoy. What would she think of him now, without a job, structureless? Would she still have Kal and Maidie round to giggle, play their records and attempt moonwalking? It would make no difference to Lois and Jack. Their course was already set.

'Watcha, kid!' he said. But that was foolish too, to try to use their words. Those weren't their words anyway. He was hopelessly out of date. He remembered how his mother had talked about 'motorbikes'. They had just been 'bikes' to his generation.

'Ah well! Sleep well, old girl,' he said, stealing out. He felt rather like the lodger.

'Night, Dad!' she said.

They were tolerant children.

When he found Cas in the kitchen, she said, 'That was Maria on the phone. They're coming up tomorrow.'

'That's good!' he said, still slightly breathless from the stairs.

'Yes quite,' she said, 'and why not?'

'I thought you liked them.'

'I do like them. I like Maria too, believe it or not. I shared a room with her, remember? All you did was have it off with her.'

15

With the picnics packed in the cars, they wandered together and apart around the cemetery.

'How are the skips?' Stephen asked James.

'It's busier than ever,' James said, looking down.

'Good for you! Skips are the future!'

Lois knew that Stephen was sincere. He was not making fun of James in any way. James needed his mother to pick up on the point and take it somewhere else. Jack held Lois's right hand and Callie held her left hand. She felt supported.

'Where now?' Callie asked.

'Look! A rainbow!' Stela said, pointing.

Briefly, it arched over the city, setting foot at each end in the suburbs. Lois, looking up, watched it. Jack, Callie, Stela, James, Ioanela, Paul, Ruth, Maria and Stephen stopped walking and watched it too.

*

It was a grey morning at first with heavy clouds over the horizon and a few herringbone clouds above the shoreline. The tide was low and the breaking waves, though erratic, were part of a great curve stepping over the estuary and along the sands to the headland. William had talked once about the paradox of Zeno's arrow. Cas could do philosophy as well as him. She had supported the family through accountancy, but accountants had ideas too. The tide, like the moving arrow, was stationary in each moment, and so it should not move in and out at all. She would have liked to raise this version of the paradox with him. Early on, their entanglements had been hands, mouth and hair. They had always had each other in one way or another. She could be an informed observer only because she had known most things. The estuary, below the headland, was a strip of light and there was a corresponding strip of pink cloud following the estuary. Above the sea, volcanic cloud formations appeared, edged in red, as if her short breaths took visual form.

*

It was unusual to wake up warm, though an interrupted sleep was to be expected living rough. He had been moved from his chair when they had closed the waiting area and he had slept on the floor instead near the escalators. His elevator pitch was ready and the search was on. There were no doubts in his mind this morning – he had not become Concorde's chief test pilot through prevarication. Like Michael Jordan, he would seize the moment. Nevertheless, he would bide his time; have a proper wash to supplement the lick and promise of last night. The task for today required balance and good judgement, as with each *Brookside* script, so that it fitted the actor like a glove. At the same time, the papacy had shown him the need for an unflinching determination: the need to make decisions and to stick by them. No one wanted a pope without moral fibre.

No other pope had died so fully in the public eye. To be brave eventually was not a foregone conclusion. Why have you forsaken me? Every believer who had loved the pope in life would be brought to tears by the manner of his death. Through his death, he would give testimony to the theological principle that life was sacred, that he would hang onto life to the bitter end, irrespective of the suffering and the television cameras capturing that suffering. His Church bore his pain with him and gave him strength.

All those years ago he had not been ready for such a task. He had lacked clarity of thought and action. That Sunday, also, he had woken warm and had thought that it was an indulgence to do so, almost as if he had broken a penance.

*

He seemed to be wrapped in most of the quilt and Cas had followed the warmth of it to his side of the bed. Their two bodies together, she arching over his back, added to the heat. He remembered the evening before when he had leaned over James to wash his own hands. That vision had been full of hope, the handing down from grandfather to father to son. What then was this attitude of hers, his wife, her breasts against his back? This could have held hope too, but he found himself wondering instead whether husbands and wives were buried like this – a surprising thought for this time in the morning from a man of only forty. And the answer was: of course not, never in the same coffin. Besides, cremation was for him. *Snap out of it!* he thought. This was no way to treat a Sunday morning. It was inactivity that led to gloom. The day was just having its cup of tea and starting out, which was more than he was doing.

There was a *thacketa, thacketa, thacketa* outside in the street. The bike roared and, momentarily, its headlamp lit the curtains. Could he smell petrol too?

This lying awake in a dark room, lights flashing onto the curtains, was out of his childhood. He felt his childhood behind him, egging him on. Were there also, as a matter of interest, blue tumbler glasses somewhere in his childhood, a darker blue than the blue on Egyptian statuary? He almost remembered them well. He could certainly remember the strutting cot bars, the patterns of light and shade they made with the plastered wall, the sudden flashing headlights through the cot bars. Those patterns of light and shade were the landscape of the factory too: white urinals against a grey wall, bars, pipes, skips, cylinders, the trains with lit-up windows racing outside, or a huddled group talking cheerily as a uniformed black security guard strode past.

These were flickering, timeless sensations, the school bell and the factory siren sounding as one for him. He could picture the factory fence and see the little boy who, at the school fence, had wanted to run back home. His mother had walked him round the duck pond and given him a sweet on every day that he hadn't cried at school. He remembered how the ducks had been hungry for the crusts and how his love, then, had been as keenly satisfied.

It was only perhaps on the level of imagery that he could still touch that childhood awe, in the rhythmical motion, for instance, of a labourer sweeping the floor with a wide, soft brush, jerking movements across the floor. Those factory movements were black and white, like old memories, the green-blue of the duck pond absent.

Out of the toilet ventilator window the sky looked heavy but there was a small patch of blue. He'd never seen a blue like that in a steelworks other than the welder's blue flame – an exception. Blue overalls, yes. But they were overalls more than they were blue. The white ones were much the same colour. He didn't see a morning sunlight blue: this blue was something to celebrate. 'Let us celebrate that a patch of the sky is blue,' he said quietly in the way that his father might have said, 'Let us pray!'

On his way downstairs he noticed a square of golden light from the glass panel in the front door, the sun shining briefly through the clouds. The light touched one of the pewter plates strung out along the picture rail. They came from the Middle East, Iran or possibly Iraq, and were engraved in Arabic – etched on the banks of the Euphrates, the dealer had told him, containing teachings from the Koran. In which direction was Mecca? he wondered. Did troops know of pewter plates when they talked about not breaking the china? He filled the kettle with cold water. The sound rang in his ears. 'What's the good of an old tin kettle to a woman who hasn't got a chap?' Where had he got that snippet? His mother probably. How could he act like a chap at all these days when there were things like warming the pot and spooning the tea to do? Or, at breakfast, spreading the butter on the toast, then the marmalade. Those little jerky movements were hardly manly. Then there was the planning ahead, the insurance, the making money. They were not manly either. A man should hunt and fight and hold his head up. Who did he think he was? Only Hamlet or Macbeth had the right to ask what it meant to be a man.

The gas central heating lit with a roar. He thought of all those well-cared-for plaques at the crematorium. That wasn't for him. That was tasteless – not that he minded that others had bad taste. It was up to them. In fact, he was attracted to bad taste. He had been attracted to Cas, after all. He remembered Natasha's pink dress and green belt in *The Three Sisters*. From a revolutionary point of view, bad taste was essential. The middle classes, the bourgeoisie, understood taste. It was insightful, therefore, that Natasha's threat should first be seen in her incomprehension of good taste. Good taste made progress almost impossible. Perhaps the USSR required another revolution now that the Politburo had such impeccable taste. Had he not just read that Andropov liked jazz? What better marker of good taste. But back to the plaques. He understood the reason for the plaques, though he felt that to leave no trace was perhaps more correct and more courageous than to leave some mark.

After all, death was death: glass broke, paper burned, man died. 'All of us die and drift into the abyss where kings and princes are no more', wrote one of the French writers. The quotation had been subtitled on a French film that he had seen last week with Cas on BBC 2, but he hadn't caught the writer's name. It was one of those fifties films where the cars looked like fat women and the women wore checked shirts, even in France, and the lipstick would have been gaudy if the film had not been in black and white. In films like that, he had said to Cas, the people always seemed to have dated but the dogs were just the same. 'Just as well you only go for dogs,' she said. The marble slabs and the flowers in the grille could not outwit mortality, and besides, the time must come when the slabs would crack and the flowers would be absent. Better, surely, that the ashes should be scattered to the wind, unlabelled.

This was Sunday morning – a holiday. It was a celebration almost. This making of the tea was a necessary stage in the progress of the day towards this almost celebration. Of course, Sunday had been the big day when he was a boy. He had been happy to be a part of Sunday then. His father had liked Sunday to be free from other duties. On other days he had made the tea, carried the coal, polished his pairs of black shoes with the broguing at the heel and toe, or taken the bucket of kitchen waste to his precious compost heap. But on Sunday, about the house, his father had done nothing. His father, like the ice cream man, had lived for Sunday. And the son, in spite of himself, missed those spiritual childhood Sundays.

Only later, as a parent, had he discovered that such habits of behaviour had to be fought for tooth and nail, that anarchy was always just round the corner. To the boy, Sunday had been as natural as life itself, as hard to suspect as it had been for Galileo. But like Galileo, he had doubted and, looking back on it, he realised that the seeds of doubt had been there early. He had a memory of the dowdy heads of the church choir. He could see them now, dressed in black, sitting in their plain wooden pews. In this early memory, they had seemed to him miserable and nasty. This impression, he now realised, was unfair. Those ageing or dead choir members were, he now felt, both devout and honourable – God's children. But childhood perception was black and white, fascist. It trampled good sense. The young child had looked, disliked what he had seen and doubted God.

Now, he was more or less back with the tone, if not the letter, of his father's faith, much to Cas's amusement. He was now a Sunday man through and through, grateful that the shops would always be closed. He found himself thinking that a spiritual Sunday was no more odd than something like electricity. And he would never have believed in electricity if he had not witnessed a kettle boil. There was little difference, in fact, between faith and doubt.

Must each succeeding generation reject before it could accept? It was wasteful; such a long way round. Instead of building on what his father had told him, he had spent forty years reaching more or less the same position. This was the classical view that human nature did not change, that progress was impossible because of mankind's flaws. He certainly wished that Lois and James might occasionally take on trust what he told them. But as he had never done this himself, why should they? The process seemed doomed to painful misunderstandings. For the discrimination of sense from nonsense, good wood from bad, was a fraught and lifelong journey.

The purpose of all this, he supposed, was to be rid of everything that was obsolete. Perhaps now, like an old rose, he was mostly obsolete himself. Sidney certainly thought so. On this model, educating himself became primarily a matter of pruning out the old wood to let the light in.

Of course, there were certain insights that he would hate to think might die with him before they were passed on, such as that dead leaves – yes, leaves died too – could be kneaded into a wheelbarrow, each leaf knotting together, long after he might have believed that the barrow was full. The Chinese had used wheelbarrows in the first century BC, perhaps a thousand years before their use in Europe. Paper had been invented in the Han dynasty too. Perhaps an ancient Chinese worker in the paddy field would also have noticed that a wheelbarrow might not have been as full as it had seemed and wrote this thought down on a scrap of newly discovered paper. But this feeling that death was a waste, and that it was a waste not to fill the barrow, was perhaps an especially puritan habit of mind rather than an oriental one. This certainly did not fit with the Chinese idea of the scholar and the warrior. For the puritan mind, a man or woman was the sum of the difficulties that he or she had had to contend with. Perhaps both life and death would become easier if he were to give himself up to the order of things. This was the circle of life: the boy who hated tomato soup, the young man who loved it, the old man indifferent to it. After all, people were living and dying all the time. It was how things were. But he could not take comfort from the collective experience. It was his own life and death, his family's life and death, even his pets' life and death that mattered. He had known death first when his hamster had died. He could tell when a hamster was dead because it stopped scurrying round the wheel. Since then, his mother and father had died and he had watched so many people die in Westerns. He should know by now how death was done.

He could not scurry upstairs with the tray, or without it, in the way his hamster had scurried round the wheel. He could only watch each step, just like Darren had concentrated on the Willow-pattern plate last night. He was nearer to death than Darren and, for that matter, the chubby little boy thirty years ago watching his hamster turn the wheel. But he was recognisably the same creature; then, as now, his rebellion had been a mostly silent one. He was never one to stand up and be counted. And in a loving family, there was no wish to cause offence. Perhaps it was the very lovingness of his upbringing that had turned him into this dishonest man of today, the man who talked to himself. Talking to himself wasn't necessarily so bad. It was said to be one of the few habits of mind that Himmler could not rise to. For William, this had been the beginning of an independent mental life, the beginning perhaps of art – something that parents, teachers and friends could know nothing of. Thanks mainly to Cas, Lois and James seemed to have a sounder view of what life was, its corrupt whole. And they were happier for this. Health probably mattered more than art.

He lifted the tea cosy and poured. His unscientific mind suspected that a cosy sapped the heat. The only purpose of the cosy, for him, was the routine that it provided. The value to him of routines such as lifting the cosy and pouring the tea lay in their potential to disrupt and get in the way of thought. Indeed, there was little respite from thought without these routines. Cas perhaps provided the only other escape from himself. She was wide awake and sitting up in bed, disagreeably.

They put down their cups of tea beside the Wagenfeld table lamp on the bedside stand. Strangely appropriate, that positioning of the tea cups there on the mahogany stand, for it was meant for tea – a tea-urn, in fact. The dealer had shown him the ancient slide, pot-marked with heat and hot water. Originally, the slide would have supported a kettle for refilling the urn. The top itself, where the urn would have stood, had since been restored and polished. The two teacups and the lamp's bald pate were reflected in the dark wood. It was a rare piece of furniture. His heart was pumping and he could just see the moulded cabriole legs and the scroll toes. They must be careful not to knock the stand. There was the Wagenfeld to think about – its function over form more erotic than Cas – and spilt tea, whether hot or cold, would destroy the stand's polished surface.

After making love – love, in literature, was often associated with death – he drew back the bedroom curtains. It would be a shame to put the Wagenfeld lamp on. It was really too valuable for everyday use.

'It's raining,' he said.

'Goodie!' she said. 'Let's go to the window and look at the rain! It's something wonderful.'

What did she mean? He didn't always know what she meant. Perhaps she didn't know herself. She wasn't flawless. She was making fun of him, certainly. But he could not quite catch her tone. She wasn't losing interest in him, was she? Still, he didn't mind his puzzlement. Puzzlement showed him something. It showed him, if nothing else, that he could still be puzzled.

His mother had had just the one tone, like Maria. She was always sincere. This was a handicap in many ways, like having a foot off and hopping everywhere.

But his mother, like his father, was dead and he was sorry for this – sorry for himself mostly, for he would have to die too ... sometime in the next century, more than likely. Death was now his turn. Perhaps clapping, as in the Italian tradition, would herald his death. Or would his absence be found more interesting than his presence, as when crowds came to look at the blank space on the wall of the Salon Carré when the *Mona Lisa* had been stolen in 1911? 'Being here's glorious,' were Rilke's words – Rilke in translation, that is – and it was perhaps the worst part about death: leaving behind what was going on here; having to abandon his curiosity; not being in on what was to come; not to mention not knowing what the future would hold for Lois, Jack and James. Cas might even find another lover. Linked with this was the knowledge that life, like the ocean, would carry on without him, that it would be largely unaffected by his going; no one liked to be dispensable. Just to be clear, even though he lived in Birmingham where the ocean was no longer present, he still had every right to use the ocean as a simile. Language need not be hidebound by place even if he was.

It seemed hard that his parents should have known nothing about recent developments. It might not have mattered to them overmuch that Andropov was to succeed Brezhnev.

How long, he wondered, would the Andropov era last? Or to put the question another way, how soon would a novel that mentioned Andropov be out of date? It was still possible to live life in the West as if the USSR did not exist – the *Titanic* and the iceberg, so to speak. It wasn't as if the Wall was coming down or that democracy would suddenly become the vogue in the Politburo. They weren't daft. Perhaps he should not talk as if such political situations were forever. One day, when the USSR was a capitalist society again, Russian entrepreneurs might even own our football teams. The only certainty was that this would not be in William's lifetime. It was as much the little things that he felt sorry his parents could not witness – Channel 4's *Body Show*, for instance. William was not a great advocate of fitness himself, believing that an unhealthy body was a prerequisite for a healthy mind. The Third Reich may have made Cas hate God and everyone else, but for him, it had muddied any blind association of fitness with intelligent thought. Although fitness had been sullied, he could be proud of the smokers – George Sand, Dorothy Parker, Sartre, Picasso, Camus, Anthony Burgess even. Nevertheless, he could see that the *Body Show* would be a winner, that its future was as secure as the Politburo. Not that he was altogether happy about the new channel. An extra channel meant less common experience, less to talk about. Hence a social disintegration related to the number of channels, the diversity of choice. He might say then that for society – no one could question the value of society – the birth of a new channel was a kind of wounding and that cable or satellite television might be its death. His parents had perhaps died in the nick of time, their faith intact.

He looked in the shaving mirror and, in so doing, at the reflected dressing mirror and his rounded buttocks. Could he taste Marmite? This being able to see himself had all sorts of implications, self-consciousness for one. And hadn't he heard that they used to believe that the dead hid in mirrors? Just to show off for a moment – though perhaps he could not show off without an audience – 'speculation' was from the Latin for mirror, and vampires were not meant to show up in mirrors. To his knowledge, William was not a vampire. Nor was he Parmigianino, Vasari or John Ashbery, but his buttocks were as good as any of theirs.

He wondered what his father would have made of throwaway razors. The blades lasted, he found, just as long as ordinary razors and the whole razor was no more expensive. The slight twinge of conscience he felt throwing out the razor with the blade, the baby with the bathwater, could only be put down to a lack of logic in him. His father, William remembered, had had an American razor, but he had always bought British blades – to support the home industry, he would say. No one talked about the 'home industry' any more. There was hardly any industry left, with the exception of where, until this weekend, he had worked. And Britain without empire, without an 'away', could hardly have a home any more.

After shaving and dressing, he drew back the curtains on the landing on his way downstairs. It was still raining. Here he was, a man of forty, staring through the leaded window at the grey rain. Without the mental life within, he was just this man looking through the window. There need be no pattern or explanation or reason for this, though the window was divided by lead into rhomboid panes. But through the steamed-up window and the rain, he could just make out the bus stop and a lady standing there. Where was she going? No one shopped on a Sunday. She had a buffeting raincoat on and a plastic cape over her head. She looked like a seaman. She was a seaman of a woman, he might say. He thought of the old man at the bus stop outside Maria's cottage. Christmas shopping was best done in quick dips, he thought, as with eating an ice cream. And in any case, he thought obscurely, Christmas will up and shake me warmly by the hand if I let it.

16

After the rainbow, the rain followed; solid rain. They stood in the rain together but observing a distance between each family bubble. Out of love for her mother, Lois did not want to leave. Slowly, Ioanela started dancing an unfamiliar movement. She held her right arm around James's waist and put her left hand over her shoulder. She spun him round. Stela followed them, so thin and light as she echoed the rhythm of her mother's steps. Ioanela rocked forwards and backwards. James following, looked up, losing all inhibition in the dark rain. Ioanela called out, her left hand first at her waist, then at her shoulder. The circling speeded up and she stamped in the puddles. She moved away from James and held her hands to her waist before linking hands with Stela and swinging her round. She returned to James, spinning and shouting, her coat lifting and her green hair ablaze. The three of them held hands and swung each other round, deliberately splashing each other. Callie linked arms with her parents and they turned in circles too. Then Paul and Ruth – they seemed suddenly old – swung each other round like young children discovering rain for the first time. Stephen clasped Maria's right hand and they turned in circles too, Maria smiling a little. Eventually, each of them lay down on their backs in the grass, the rain on their faces.

*

The view Cas saw through the oblong window showed the geometry of nature – the sea, the sky, the estuary, the headland and the burrows – almost as if constructed by Medunetsky, Popova, Stepanova or Rodchenko. As the clouds sheltered the headland and hung over the sea, her difficulties and achievements were brought into geometrical clarity. He was dead. She was old and, if her breathing was anything to go by, not very well. She did not matter. She could watch the sea, watch the morning take shape irrespective of her. On this dull day, there were no requirements to look far ahead. The underlying geometry was enough. In Birmingham, this was nearly always how she had felt. She had earned enough to support the family. There had been no need for horizons or headlands. She had known what was necessary and she had gone about her duties accordingly.

*

William washed carefully in the toilet at New Street Station as he did not wish to draw attention to himself by his odour and because he had been taught to wash in childhood. Although there were always church officials to help him with these tasks, he had always tried to do as much as possible for himself. It would be self-evident both to the Christian and secular worlds that he was ailing. Nevertheless, the dignity of office depended to some extent on still being able to do certain things for himself whenever possible.

Today, he could still wash for himself. One day, when death was upon him, he would try to wave to the world from the window of the Gemelli hospital. He would be the first pope to invite the cameras to see his suffering, to watch in on his death as if he were on the cross. He was aware of the precedent of St Benedict who had died erect, supported by his disciples.

After washing he sat down not far from the escalators in the waiting area that had been opened up again for his entourage. With quiet dignity he tucked his regalia under the chair. The gold necklace and cross were barely visible but they were there nevertheless, like a cup of tea or a reduction in the interest rate. He felt a slight disappointment that some of the cardinals were reading the Sunday papers. Senior prelates should have known better. As leader of the Catholic Church, it was certainly his holy duty to devote Sunday to timeless prayer.

Much of William's moral authority as pope, he liked to think, was derived not only from scripture but also from his familiarity with literature and the essays that he could still quote verbatim. In Jane Austen's *Mansfield Park*, for instance, Sir Bertram's gift of a dress to Fanny – it wasn't as fine as the pope's embroidered silks – and his provision of the carriage for her dinner engagement revealed his genuine regard and concern for her, just as William felt concern for the most junior priests as well as the most senior cardinals. And there was the complicated situation of Mary encouraging Fanny to choose the necklace that Henry had given her three years earlier. This illuminated several not altogether consistent aspects of Mary's character: her kindness perhaps, but also a wish to make Fanny feel indebted, and an element of scheming too. His own ecclesiastical necklace and cross were hardly visible at the moment.

William liked to make comparisons and the space he now sat in between the escalators and the station entrance could have been a cathedral. This comparison was unlike the comparison between Mary and Fanny and also quite unlike the comparison between Cas and Maria. How could he compare such comparisons in any case? This would be like having a policy to protect a no-claims bonus – impossible to get his mind round at that time in the morning. He did not need car insurance any more, or house insurance, for that matter. In his Father's house were many mansions, one of which was this cavern outside New Street Station, and these were not covered by an act of God. Not only were Mary's aspirations to the estate compared with Fanny's lack of claim, but there was also a comparison in their attitude to how the estate should be used: Mary's relative disrespect contrasted with Fanny's wish to honour tradition. Was this the reason that in his many years on the streets, he had always taken care not to drop any litter? Property was no big issue for either Cas or Maria. Cas had taken over their house, but property had never been her motivation, nor had bricks and mortar ever meant much to Maria. She was too oceanic for property, just as Birmingham, if looked at in a certain way, was by nature seafaring.

As he sat there in that holy place in his papal robes, he remembered an example to back up these thoughts on the nature of property. Elena, with her disregard for property in Turgenev's *On the Eve*, found an ally in Insarov. Their love involved abandoning property just as William's life on the streets did. He could not explain why Cas had kept everything intact while engaging with someone else. This setting of the young lovers against the backdrop of the material world was seen in dramatic terms when Insarov visited Elena at home.

By looking on finery, the pope's finery perhaps, she turned her back on him. Property was a diversion distracting them from each other. All of this was true of William's relationship with Cas too, of course.

As far as he was concerned, this space he sat in was common land, devoid of ownership. He recognised that this might not in fact be the case. We can believe a falsity, we cannot know a falsity, William remembered. Therefore, it was the truth of the matter that was at stake, nothing less. Take the young lady whom he always met in McDonald's every Sunday morning. He looked forward to those encounters even though she was as mad as a hatter. She thought that she was his daughter. It went without saying that her mental state was not as settled as his, but to infer that she would have behaved differently had she been sane might be an oversimplification. The argument from analogy solved a problem that never existed. If feeling words were only meaningful through being knocked about in the public arena – each mind taking its cue from other minds – then it was clearly quite unnecessary to ask whether or not those minds existed. He had always felt that this problem had something to do with snooker and now he had the evidence in the cue used here, if not in the billiard table. And this, in its turn, must have had something to do with the fact that the English loved to queue. It was what they were best at.

But he had not concluded the argument yet, even though he could not sit on this hard chair for ever. What was said might well suggest the presence of feelings underneath, the language revealing, unwittingly, the state of mind. Such an idea flew in the face of Cartesian analysis with its emphasis on the private mental life as the only certainty. According to Wittgenstein, language was impossible without its social context and it was simply absurd to think of the mind in a vacuum, though modern vacuums, as he had seen in Dixons, often had their own minds.

Where was all this leading? It was clear that his feelings about this search were not the same as the search itself. Feelings and behaviour were not the same thing at all. Something *felt* might not be identical to something *observed*. Nevertheless, something felt and something observed could refer to the same identical thing – in this case, the fact that he was trying to find the truth, even if what was felt and what was observed were distinct. He was sure that Wittgenstein had said something to the effect that to think of words in too strict a manner, with too sharp a boundary between words, was misleading. The boundary between water and land for Neolithic man, as with a boundary for Heidegger, was where the action was, where the escalator moved up and down nearby and from where his own deliverance had begun.

*

The heavy and delivered Sunday paper was lying on the hall carpet in front of the front door when he went downstairs. The whiteness of the paper was in sharp contrast to the red carpet. It was good to be first to the paper on any day, but it was especially good on a Sunday. But this Sunday, as he took out the colour supplement on his way into the study, he felt that even the paper hemmed him in. He turned the pages mechanically, noticing the pictures but passing on. On a good day it would have been straight to a serious article – art before breakfast. Today, however, he was after something more accessible – triteness, titillation, pillage.

Fantasy on this real Sunday morning, and why not? After all, this particular weekend was more than usually a private matter.

It was a romantic weekend – not in the Barbara Cartland sense, of course – but in the sense of a concern with his feeling and thought; relatively free, that is, of external intrusion. *Interiority* was the buzz word used by critics at the moment. Why should world events be allowed in at all? As far as he knew, the weekend would not stand out in history. It was a weekend like any other in world terms. But it was his weekend, it was happening right now and it meant something to him.

So it was with a certain disdain that he gathered together the various sections of the paper, leaving only the finance pages for later. Then he stood up and paused for a moment, relishing the fact that he could not be disturbed here. The study was his room. The children, Cas too, always knocked on the study door. Even if they were bringing him a chocolate, they still knocked. He liked that. It made him feel like a Victorian father. But Cas, the only worker, would have to have the study now. He would move out. It was rectangular and fairly plain, no Victorian fuss, but it was still somewhere to hide. The rest of the house might be cluttered with antiques, but the only features of the study were the one-handed grandfather clock on the wall to the right of the door, and to its left the framed print of Henri Matisse's gaunt *Madame Matisse with a Green Streak*, or a title something like that. He had bought the print because it reminded him of Cas, though admittedly Cas did not have a green streak; she had a nasty one. If he were speaking less impressionistically or if he were making a list for insurance purposes, then the mahogany wing bookcases opposite the clock would need to be acknowledged. And there was also the walnut cabinet along the wall behind him as he stood in front of the mahogany writing desk and looked out through the rhomboid leaded windows onto the front garden and the still misty rain.

For somewhere else to look, he glanced again at the bookcase. It was late eighteenth century and, having its centre drawer fitted as a secretaire, would fetch a good price. But the bookcase was more than an investment. It held his books. And it was sobering to acknowledge that, without those books, he could not have become what he was. He had forgotten some of what he had read but this did not alter the fact that, to be the man he was, he had first to have read those books. There were some in the factory who could not read, who had not been to the seaside for that matter. But his lot had happened to be mixed up with those books, among other things. He had been to the seaside too, as it happened.

17

Callie had the first shower. Lois was next. Jack followed. In dry clothes, they were still smiling. Jack put the kettle on.

'I didn't expect that!' he said.

'It felt right,' Callie said, warming her hands on the mug. 'To shovel the earth too. We needed galoshes. The rabbi understood everything. And all of us too. He was so gentle and sweet. Then afterwards it just happened, after the rainbow, when the rain came. It wasn't disrespectful.'

'It was lovely,' Lois said. 'And that rainbow! That sort of thing only happens in fiction.'

'If it happened in fiction, it would be naff,' Callie said, 'unless it was D. H. Lawrence.'

'Who's he?' Lois said. 'Just kidding! Your grandmother might have shouted at us. She might have told us not to dance on her grave and to respect Shiva. But she would have loved it all the same. She believed in God but none of the rest. I don't know where your grandad stood on all this when he was sane. He never said. He may have believed in God or he may not. He certainly didn't believe in any of the rest of it any more than your grandmother did.'

'We all joined in, following Ioanela,' Jack said. 'The old ones too. I'm a firefighter and I danced too!'

'And we were all soaked through!' Lois said. 'I told you it didn't matter what I wore!'

*

At the seaside, Cas could make out the lighter strip of foam as the waves encountered the dark rocks of the pebble ridge at high tide and extended to the estuary's edge, white against black. The waves caressed the rocks just as her mother smoothed her dark hair in childhood when, as now, she had been unwell. In his illness, William had thought that love solved everything. This alone defined him as mad in her book. But he had a point. Love needed to be in the mix, but it was never the whole story. Hatred had to be there too, and thought, and comedy. Their interactions had headed in all directions and, in William's case, into delusion too. The sky was dulled with cloud but lighter than the sea. No planes flew any more. The sea grew darker as it approached the horizon, with the headland duller still. As the morning progressed, there was a lightness around the clouds above the headland. The waves, invading the estuary too, had an irregularity to them within an overall scheme, as in a Jackson Pollock.

*

How many escalators like this one had he scaled in his British Airways uniform at airports all over the world? Would the others on the escalator have noticed the upright bearing of a man who, until recently, had been Concorde's chief test pilot? In some ways, the shopping centre seemed more like an ocean liner than an airport, he thought. There were no portholes, however, and he could not see the sea. He continued on his way, passing Vision Express and Foot Locker. The Foot Locker was holy ground. A pair of footprints represented the Buddha's presence in the earliest representations and Jesus had once washed the disciples' feet. Like the puritan, the Buddhist gained insight through pain. Gathering the dust off the feet of a holy person was important to some Hindus too. At least Woolworths would go on for ever. He found this comforting. And, as if to complement Foot Locker, it was now possible to buy a foot spa in Woolworths: 'a relaxing, deep vibro massaging, warm water foot bath'. Would this be as good as having Jesus wash your feet? he wondered. William had always held Woolworths in high regard, ever since he had made love to Cas in a Woolworths photo booth. As Ramadan was over and as he still had plenty of money, he would have a McDonald's breakfast. What better way to celebrate Eid.

As if he did not have enough to contend with in facing up to his own problems, his stalker was in McDonald's again, waiting for him. But he did not mind, and he was pleased to see her, composed and elegant on the blue plastic chair. She was not a young woman but she was a woman of distinction and poise. He might be the only person who could sympathise with her mental state and he felt proud to have befriended her. These Sunday meetings were probably her only lifeline, her only contact with reality. The lady thought that she was his daughter, and there was no end to her subtleties. She had imitated Lois's behaviour and her calm good nature. She even called herself Lois. He had reported her to the police once but they had taken her side. The police tended to have a soft spot for a good-looking woman and he wasn't a council tax payer any more, so he didn't call the tune with them. Eventually, he had taken her under his wing, as if she were his daughter. He liked her, in fact. And did it matter so much that she was confused or that she wasn't his daughter? She was loyal and reliable. She was always there in McDonald's on Sunday morning, summer and winter, for him to console.

It was a time that he could set aside for her each week. She brought her daughter with her sometimes – a bright little thing called Callie, who would hug him and kiss him goodbye, throw herself at him on occasions too, her arms outspread. Callie called him 'Granddad'. Perhaps there was no harm in this. He had tried to get them back on their feet. They had become his disciples. She had not brought her daughter this week, sadly.

'Hello, Dad,' she said.

'You must stop calling me that,' he said. 'I'm your spiritual father. I'm not your real father.' She looked saddened by this but calm, as always. He did not want to upset her needlessly. Did it matter so much that she was deluded? He was only trying to set her on the right track, away from this unreality of hers.

'You are impossible!' she said. 'You drive Mum up the wall. Without her job, she would be cracking up. The house is just as it was, you know, but she's a wreck. Why do you think James avoids you now?' She looked at him steadily. Then she smiled. 'But there's good news. Did Paul tell you that Ros is expecting a baby?'

She had done her research. She knew everyone in his family, but she was wrong about Cas. He hadn't seen her in years. Nor had he seen Paul for that matter. 'I love you, Dad,' she said, touching the embroidered hem of his sleeve. 'You don't have to live like this. You can live with us. Jack and I will look after you.'

It was a trap, of course. Cas might have left the house unchanged but she had found someone else to love. It was true, however, that Ros was pregnant and that he hadn't seen James recently. He had not seen his daughter either ever since this lady had taken on her disguise. Now this replacement daughter was trying to modify the truth.

Admittedly, she behaved like his daughter. She was calm like his daughter as if there were no mental turmoil. She held the paper coffee cup with precision, almost with joy, just as his daughter had always made friends with her toys and never got cross with them. In the same way, this lady always collected up the McDonald's breakfast things carefully so that there were no crumbs left on the table. She seemed to be at one with her surroundings in spite of her insanity, taking the tray to the rubbish bin just as Diana had done when she had taken the young princes to McDonald's. If McDonald's had been good enough for a princess, it was good enough for the pope, surely.

'My child,' he said. 'I love you as if you were my own daughter. I want you to know this. But the pope cannot have children. Surely you understand this?'

She smiled again at this. 'You're the pope now?' she said. 'I should have guessed. All those cardinals around you! A likely story when you are in McDonald's every Sunday! Last time you were Concorde's chief test pilot and the time before you had single-handedly cured AIDS while writing for *Brookside*. Only women can multitask, you know! Not many of my friends have polymath fathers, like me! Are you still friends with Michael Jordan, Scottie Pippen and Dennis Rodman? That made me laugh. I would have more chance with them! My friends divide between Scottie and Dennis lovers. Maidie likes Dennis's roughness. She always went for the bad boys at school. Kal is for Scottie but she likes girls better anyway. I'm with Kal.

Maidie thinks Scottie's a whiner. I say, look at his eyes. He's beautiful.'

He did not wish to be unkind to her. She had enough to bear. He would not press the point. The pope saw so much suffering. He loved all his children, especially this poor woman who thought that she was really his daughter. There were no rules, even in the Vatican, for handling this kind of delusion. Compassion was his only guide.

'Listen to me!' he said. 'This world is confusing enough for the young. I was young once, you know. There is something that I have learned that I would like to share with you. I am talking to you as an equal, as a fellow mortal on the road of life.' He had her ear now as she stirred the coffee. It was almost as if the conversation, the spoon, the cup, the steam rising and the stirring were a part of the same process, the same universal truth. 'You think that you are my daughter,' he continued. 'Very well. I cannot persuade you otherwise. But this is more important than that. This is for everyone – for everyone who will hear it.' She watched him from her shiny plastic chair. He wanted to condense all his earthly and heavenly experiences so that they rose from her paper coffee cup and spread throughout the world. 'It's simple really,' he said. 'It's that love matters. That's the answer to everything, you see.'

'All right, Dad,' she said. 'I've got it. You don't need to go on about it. Even if you're pope!'

He had passed on the baton now to the next generation. This child who thought that she was his daughter had heard his words. She was his follower now.

He blessed her as he left and there were both tears and smiles in her eyes. Lois had had brown eyes too. He pushed open the swing doors into the open air with the cardinals in his train, as if they were Diana's wedding dress. He was filled with a sense of wonder that life, for all its hardship, should be so simple, that love could change everything.

His breakfast this morning had not been quite like the breakfasts of old, but a pope had to embrace change as the one-handed grandfather clock struck ten, resonating to the bottom of the escalator.

*

For Thomas Hardy, bats' wings whirred like that. Here, at ten o'clock in the dining room, with Lois preparing breakfast, there was the smell of coffee, a vestige of what Sunday used to be. With Cas, they had stayed with the form of Sunday breakfast that he had known as a child – coffee! It was the only day of the week that they had had coffee, then grapefruit and cornflakes. He always raced Paul to finish the cornflakes first. Then there would be boiled eggs and rolls. But he had not been able to preserve the sense of awe: father at breakfast untucking his white shirt from under his waistcoat to polish his tortoiseshell spectacles and then squinting through them at the carefully handwritten sermon. He had always kept a spare sermon in his waistcoat pocket. William didn't even wear a waistcoat. Then there was the dressing up for Sunday school and, afterwards, Sunday lunch. And his father's relief and happiness at having the morning service under his belt.

It wasn't that his father's sermons had had any interest to the boy once he was too old for Sunday school. In fact, he had rarely listened to them. The only time that William had been to a striptease with some of the other managers from work in his first job, the experience had reminded him of his father's sermons in that the tedium of it all had provoked him into thinking about other things.

It was unhelpful to hark back like this. It was merely a quirk of memory to see the old days as more meaningful. Cas had called it 'a Stradivarius view of life' – the past always better than the present. She had expressed horror at the BBC for bringing back those old radio programmes. William secretly enjoyed such sentiment, although his intellect supported Cas completely. Cas was progressive in the best possible sense: she looked to the future. She believed that the future could be shaped. She believed that if you did not like something then you should change it. Would she apply this to her husband one day? he wondered.

It was his daughter he watched now: green jeans and red wellingtons and the bright yellow sweatshirt with square shoulders to it; the look of a padded American football player. Channel 4 was showing American football. She had a blue earring today and her hair stuck out all over. Lois hadn't quite the confidence to carry all this yet, at least not with her father looking on. 'Take that!' her appearance said, but her expression was more 'Hi, Dad!', the brown eyes lowered slightly.

'You're a perfectionist,' he said, looking at the table. She had remembered the marmalade, the salt and pepper, and she carried the jug of milk in her hand as if she was in a Vermeer. But he knew immediately that this was the worst thing to say. He should have had the sense to leave her out of it, to talk about himself or the economy or the weather. She looked pleased but embarrassed, as if she had been found smiling after the joke had passed. But he had meant what he said. She didn't take after her mother.

Instead of grinning foolishly, he sat down with the colour supplement. He would let her alone, let her put the eggs on. Her mother, by contrast, lived above the routine – sometimes, under it. She was not at one with her surroundings, but she triumphed in other ways and not just as an accountant. Numbers were no problem to her, but nor were most things, other than making breakfast. When he had married Cas, he had needed a girl whom his own mother would disapprove of. He had found one in Cas who didn't mince her words. Cas had challenged him in a way that his mother could never have done. His mother's very goodness had bound him to her. It had seemed at the time that the only way to cut the apron strings was to marry someone like Cas – not that anyone was like Cas – so that the responsibility for the parting with his mother would not have been wholly his. He could not have borne the guilt of the breach single-handed. Cas had shouldered some of the blame – most of it, in fact. And he needed her villainy too. Goodness was a bore. The medieval stonemasons knew that: their triumph was the underworld. Cas might not have lived in sin but she had taught him to sin, to live his own life.

However, here was their daughter stepping into her red wellingtons, 'wellies' she called them, into her grandmother's black galoshes – 'galoshes' was a wonderfully muddy word but it had died along with her grandmother.

On the front of the colour supplement, as if to complicate this observation, there was a picture of the Queen on her Pacific tour. She was wearing a red woolly dress and a red Ascot hat and was drinking tea in long white gloves. Her gloves were similar to those his mother had worn occasionally way back in the fifties. The Queen herself was a grandmother now, and it took little imagination to look forward to when Lois herself would be a grandmother sometime in the next century. In his own daughter of today, watching over the bubbling eggs in the saucepan, he could see the grandmother of tomorrow looking back and laughing at her by then strange teenage fashion. This would have been a happy thought, almost a handshake across time, but for the sudden realisation that he would be out of the frame by then – the picture would be empty of him.

He was not an old man. But at forty he was on the road to old age. And this Sunday morning, he was perhaps old before his time. Kafka wrote somewhere that a man who is dead in his own lifetime may in fact see more than others and be the real survivor. He would not pretend to know what Kafka had meant. Had he meant that our only task here was to contemplate death? William would score highly on this today. Or was it the idea that we needed inactivity, we needed to sit on a bench sometimes – the doing nothing, like the owl waiting for dark, being somehow necessary. In any case, he was ready for breakfast, something to get his talons into.

'Can I start?' he asked Lois.

It was good fathering to make her the boss sometimes. But as she brought in the eggs on the tray, he realised that she was the boss anyway, regardless of him.

'I'll join you,' she said. There was a banging on the stairs and the door opened.

'Hi!' James said, grinning.

'Hi!' William replied and he looked him over but not, he hoped, in an unfriendly way. Adolescents had enough on their plate with puberty and acne to contend with. Lois and James might be youth without much of a reason for itself but at least there was straightforwardness there. And honesty was preferable to the false causes of his own youth. Causes – charismatic leaders too – were dangerous. They trampled truth. Was religion the same? Was it so overwhelming that it allowed no half-hearts? Did it sweep over the individual struggle? James, his head lowered, might lack fervour, and Lois was hardly Joan of Arc, but they both seemed to have the actual world firmly in their grip. Of course, Cas – who arrived at the door now with a scowl – had helped them to keep their balance by tipping them off balance whenever possible.

18

'Be careful, love!' Jack said to Callie on the platform. 'Use the sanitiser!' Wear your mask! Keep your distance!'

'I will keep away from boys too!' Callie said, smiling. She had nothing with her, just a shoulder bag over her donkey jacket that Lois had dried as much as possible in the tumble dryer. Callie jumped on the almost empty train wearing her mask. 'Love you!' she said, looking out through the door.

'Love you too!' Lois said.

They waved as the train pulled out from the cavernous platform of New Street Station. There was still no natural light here, unlike under the new dome over the station precinct that flooded light everywhere. Callie was venturing back to complete her PhD with nothing, Lois thought, and there wasn't even daylight to send her on her way.

'She'll be all right whatever she does,' Jack said. 'But I still worry for her. With only a donkey jacket and shoulder bag. That's just about all she's got.'

'I know,' Lois said. 'But she's got herself.'

*

Cas could appreciate nature's patterns through the window. She believed in God, after all, even though God was a bastard. She had no truck with organised religion: Midrash meant for her that she could believe what she liked, but God had always been there, against all logic. There were some burgeoning charcoal clouds over the headland, increasing in size above the sea. Otherwise, it was an almost clear, navy sky. William would look up at the sky sometimes as if for inspiration. He would have been better keeping his eyes on the road ahead, she would tell him.

At high tide, the estuary was a curve of light, widening as it joined the sea to form a relatively straight edge along the rocks. The sea also tracked the headland before venturing out into the Atlantic and darkening along the horizon in a purple haze. The pattern was too ordered. Only storms could distract her.

*

Turning right out of McDonald's down the ramp, a group of teenagers, bleary-eyed – from their all-night parties perhaps – passed him heading up the ramp in the other direction. He wished he was their age.

'Rena's got her belly button pierced,' one of the girls said.

Such snippets had been a useful source of material when he was scriptwriting for *Brookside*. The soap might now be tiring and not last much longer but the habit of listening in to street culture remained with him.

Turning right into New Street, for a second time this weekend, the *Iron:Man*, out of sight behind him, became his anchor again. He remembered that it had been a tenet of his papacy not to let the pomp and ceremony of the office separate him from everyday life. Some of the cardinals had adapted more quickly than others to these ideas. He had gradually sifted the wheat from the chaff at the Vatican and it now worked in a streamlined and effective manner, and it was also as familiar to him as every paving slab of the pedestrianised New Street. Each crack between the paving slabs had to be stepped over so that his search could continue uninterrupted. The Vatican was his home, with New Street running through it. He would prefer to die here than at the Gemelli. It did not fall on many to call the Vatican their home but for him, dying at home meant dying in the Vatican, the paving slabs under his feet, the *Iron:Man* behind him, the gravel path within earshot and surrounded by those who would know when to call out his baptismal name three times. Until then, his mission was in the everyday world, searching out fellow sinners. Needless to say, the prisons and the brothels, the back lanes and the street corners were not the only places that required his attention. There was McDonald's too, franchised to the humble and lowly. To take breakfast in McDonald's on a Sunday was to enter holy ground, he always felt.

As he made his slow way up New Street towards the new Bullring, a war veteran was making his way in the other direction for the Armistice service. The medals glistened as if they reflected the sun. William liked to think that he had served his country too in other ways. As the old man passed by, William recognised him as Sidney. Sidney was still his touchstone, though older, less tall and thinner; the medals, strung out absurdly across his chest like pewter plates on a picture rail, were too wide for his frame. The factory had gone but Sidney remained. They said nothing but shook hands. They went on their way along New Street in opposite directions, like glancing billiard balls.

There was a theory called 'inflation' to explain what had happened just before the Big Bang. Did this also have sexual and financial connotations? Within a fraction of a second the preliminary universe enlarged from the size of less than an atom to the size not just of a billiard ball but of a grapefruit, not that billiard balls or grapefruit were around at the time for comparison. There was considerable sexual prowess involved in that enlargement, and it was perhaps more feminine than masculine so that this nascent grapefruit universe could already be said to be mocking masculinity – nothing new there! This was a rate of inflation that even economists and philanderers would have to take their hats off to.

Just as primitive ages sang of love and more recent ages of tumult, so he 'will sing war when this matter of a girl is exhausted'. That was how Ezra Pound had viewed fighting for your country in *Propertius*; William had included references to *Propertius* in his dissertation. As he had pointed out, the pun on 'exhausted' was one of many in the poem, Pound being Elizabethan in this respect. Comically, he had to persuade his soul to put on a timely vigour, a sure sign that his enthusiasm was only lukewarm. The presence of an alternative sexual rendering here reminded the reader that, for the time being anyway, his concerns were with Cynthia, just as William's concerns remained with Cas. Cas had found another lover but kept his possessions in place. Pound elaborated his argument by saying that Callimachus, in whose grove he would like to walk, had managed very well without Caesar's example to follow and without using any of Homer's legendary men of war, escalading fortified walls and so on. The parallel with the centre of Birmingham was inescapable – this was a peaceful grove too, once you made your home here.

The idea that art should strive to imitate and improve on nature had its precedent in Renaissance philosophy, and there could be little doubt that the centre of Birmingham had both imitated and improved on nature. If nature was an imperfect reflection of God's intention, it was the artist's duty to create the beauty that nature would possess but for the fallibility of matter. Whether or not he accepted Vasari's belief in the steady rise of Tuscan art from Giotto to Michelangelo, he now had to recognise the centre of Birmingham as the fulfilment of the Renaissance project.

In the same discussion of Pound, William had identified the willingness to travel for the sake of friendship as a constant theme of *Exile's Letter*. He would have followed Cas anywhere, through the landscape and climate of China even. Sea, mountain and river, rain, wind and snow lent concrete substance to this and could be seen as an extension of the imagist method, using things to speak for themselves. Wheelbarrows would be another example, and so would round coins with square holes in them.

It would be meaningless, as Wittgenstein showed, to speak of babies having hope. Nevertheless, there was hope here in Birmingham on Armistice Day. If anyone wanted to deny it, he would meet them outside the factory gates. Wittgenstein's argument was that even if he were to say 'Go this way', then this invited the further question of how 'this way' was being used. It was a kind of infinite regress, just like Marmite. This was not to say that the grammar of language was the same as the vocabulary of language, or that it was subject to, if not explained by, the same kind of rule. Wittgenstein accepted the presence of rules, but never in every instance and not as the last word, and always with the proviso that they were seen to accommodate to each new situation.

He was reaching the heart of the matter: Locke's view that if William threw a stone in the air, it must of necessity fall – like the Fall of Man – and that stuff happened whatever he might think about it. Let him that is without sin cast the first stone. There was also Zeno's paradox that if an arrow is always in a now moment, the flying arrow is motionless. A person may have observed in the past that whenever something was thrown in the air, it was always followed by the same object coming down again, but there was no necessity in such conjunctions. Michael Jordan, after all, had defied gravity on occasions. To put this another way, blue glass did not have to be blue – it did not have to be the colour of his mother's eyes – and it did not have to be brittle. His mother was not brittle. Nor did it have to hold water in the way that an argument should always be watertight.

It was a contingent truth that blue glass was no match for a falling stone because alternatives were conceivable; a veteran with medals might be brave or cowardly, after all. Nor could William be sure that the sun would rise for him tomorrow. This was not necessarily true any more than Goldbach's conjecture. William's state of mind made him comfortable with Hume's assertion that whatever was, may not be, but he would nevertheless uphold the teachings of the Church come hell or high water. He owed this to the blue of his mother's eyes, the blue of Egyptian sculpture and to the blue tumbler glasses that he almost remembered distinctly.

William was aware that his present search could only be described as an action if his consciousness was involved and this required an exploration of his intention. Surely William was a being with special knowledge and control over what he did. Otherwise he must be an object that events happened to, and he didn't like the sound of that. A man must hold his head up and take responsibility for his actions. To have piloted Concorde required just this sense of responsibility. Try telling an air steward that all actions were events; if you did, you wouldn't get sugar in your coffee, or a kiss on the cheek for that matter. He had always liked to think that his personality and decision-making were at the centre of the discussion rather than reduced to the status of any other object in the determined universe. Surely he was not imagining the emotions of gratitude, resentment, forgiveness and absolution? A world of mere events did not explain these. Surely to be conscious and to be able to act on his thoughts was an essential part of being human; it was this that explained his continuing search. Like Sartre, he wanted to put his feelings at the centre of the debate. He believed in freedom, and freedom had to involve more than logical possibility. Freedom meant that he could have acted differently but chose not to. He could still choose not to continue the search.

Each time he made this journey up New Street, he saw the city landscape slightly differently. He noticed this time the three mast-like sculptures in red, yellow and blue; the blue of his childhood. From his flying days, he knew that he had to be careful to avoid masts like that.

*

Of course, his life had not always been so full of action and achievement. On the earlier Sunday, his career with British Airways had not taken off, so to speak. He had simply returned to his study after breakfast with the impression that his family, too, thought him washed-up, if he could be described as 'washed-up', living in Birmingham where there was no sea any longer. Quite recently, they had walked together as a family to see the Silurian coral reef at the Wren's Nest in Dudley. The ripple marks made from the sea's action now formed an almost vertical sea. Lois and James had seemed mostly bored, but Cas had said that it would have been one of the Seven Wonders of the World if it hadn't been in Dudley. She might even have meant this.

The managing director already knew of William's failings. Sidney had not said a word about the letter when William met him in the washroom on Friday. However, now that William thought about it, Sidney, at the urinal, had avoided his eye. Even if it hadn't been Sidney, he probably wouldn't have mentioned Duchamp. Cas had been writing an essay on Duchamp's *Fountain* on the day they first met. She had channelled his love ever since. Sidney certainly had feelings. He was limited in many ways but he knew what he felt. It was in fact Sidney's limitations that had made his promotion possible; his shortcomings had made him suitable for the top job.

Earlier that year, William, egged on by Lois, had gone to an aerobics class. It had been a mistake. He had never felt more out of place. He was much more at home sitting in his study with the one-handed clock ticking. If the Olympics ever returned to London, he would hardly be a contender. But during that class he had noticed that the best students were at the front whereas in life, the fools always seemed to be at the front. The explanation, of course, was that in aerobics incompetence was immediately apparent, whereas in the workplace or in public life, incompetence need never be revealed.

William in fact valued Sidney as a reference point. He could look at him and be fairly confident that he himself was not that person. This was a trick that he had learned from philosophical analysis. William was sitting in his study, his books within reach. But if he did not know where he was in a metaphysical sense, and he never did know this, he might progress by finding where he was not. William was not where Sidney was, any more than he was where the street preachers were who could usually be found on the streets of Birmingham most weekends and who, like Sidney, evoked in him a mixture of sympathy and contempt. For this reason, he felt justified in thinking about Sidney, even after breakfast on Sunday, for to define Sidney, or to define the street preacher, was to define himself to some extent. Their two existences were separate, like the Worcestershire lanes and the steelworks, and yet through their opposition they had a bearing on each other. This was perhaps a Humean picture – no link – separate billiard balls flying about the table and yet strangely united in their confrontations. Whatever William was, was something of a mystery to him at that moment, sitting at his desk in the study, but he could be clear that he was not Sidney and that he would also never stand up in the street and preach God's word to the people!

19

'Shall we have a coffee?' Jack said.

'Why not!' Lois said. 'We always used to. You've got the day off. I've got the week off. She was my mother, not yours.'

It was good to sit together over the blue and pink plastic table under the huge glass dome with darkness above. She was proud of the city elders for developing this whole area outside the station, albeit with European money. She could hardly remember how it used to be outside the station: a barren area with escalators. The coffee was served at the table by a young man who was also wearing a mask. Having this coffee with Jack felt almost normal again. They did not say much but they looked at each other full on, as they always had done.

*

Cas had chosen isolation of her own accord in order to watch the sea, not to avoid the virus. Lois, who still phoned her every day after work, said that the schools had closed and that the elderly were advised to isolate. This hardly mattered any longer to Cas. Before he died, William had talked about experiencing in his lifetime both the mechanical age and the attention age. *What about your delusional age?* she had said, and he had smiled. Anyway, she would not be giving her attention to anyone else at the moment, any more than anyone else would be giving their attention to her, thank God. She had done enough of that in Birmingham. Her attention was a resource that she would only share with the sea, sky, burrows and headland.

Looking through the high window of this Victorian terraced flat was not the same as looking at a painting because the view always altered. It was more like video art, listening to music or reading a book. Early in the day, there was a high tide and light cloud over the sea and headland, with waves touching the black strip of boulders and reaching a well-defined obtuse angle at the junction of the estuary and the sea. At high tide, the estuary was clearly visible, catching the light as it spread and widened inland. The cloud above the estuary and the headland had a silver streak of light capping it that extended above the sea. At the estuary's mouth there was a circle of light, a mixture of mist and the sea's movement. There was also a narrow strip of darker sea reaching from the tip of the headland across the horizon. Later in the day, the picture was different. The colours had changed and the cloud had dissipated. With the sea far out and the wide sand seeming to stretch all the way to the headland, the estuary was barely discernible. William might have made the point – how obsessive he was about certain ideas! – that it was there nevertheless and that she should not venture onto the mudflats to be swallowed by quicksand. He had always cared for her. The rocks in front of the sand were more grey than black and the burrows a dappled yellow, green and brown, picking up the colours of the headland.

*

He would not say much to the thronging crowds who were
there for him this morning in front of St Martin in the Bullring
in St Peter's Square. He had given the Sunday blessing for the
last quarter of a century and he wasn't about to disappoint
them now. They knew as well as he did that the pope was not
as robust as he had once been. He had suffered many things
as pope, including being shot. The bullet had passed through
him as if testing his resolve. He had been a keen football
player in his youth. He now blessed all those, young and old,
who had turned out for him and he raised his right hand for
their benefit; the same right hand that had picked up letters or
newspapers from the carpet, and saved numerous goals when
he could throw himself about without the responsibilities of
office. Now his job was to save souls. This smallest gesture from
him would always remind them of this important moment in
their lives when the pope had acknowledged them as fellow
sufferers. Marlon Brando had spent many hours in William's
presence, and he had learned from Marlon that less was more
and that the smallest movements were the most telling. Nor,
to Brando, would it have mattered that he may have mumbled
his words to the crowd below and that he may have been barely
audible. William talked to them about the different sorts of sin:
the sin bearing down on the individual and the sin that affected
other people. He concluded with the doctrinal thought that
perhaps both sorts of sin were in fact the same sin, for a sin that
changed an individual changed a society too. It was an idea that
might well have been lost on some of his devotees, but he had
never believed in talking down to anyone, and he was respected
in the Vatican for his uncompromising theological arguments.

On this balcony, with Selfridges to his left and St Martin's and the markets below, he compared the reception with his last visit to England, just before the Falklands War, when the sun had shone all week. The open-air masses had been moving and joyful. He had not come to Birmingham then, but in Coventry he had made it clear that war was completely unacceptable. In Liverpool, he had talked about football. But underlying his witness to faith had always been the idea that morals were absolute and that no compromise was possible. He had a Jewish wife, after all, and friends who had died in the Holocaust. Auschwitz was not far from Krakow. He had trained as a priest in secret under the Nazis and fought the tyrannies both of the Third Reich and of communist Poland. Indeed, the light had always seemed the brightest when the darkness was the deepest.

The people who called him Holy Father this morning in Birmingham valued his steady witness to hope and his endurance of suffering. He believed that it was God's hand that had enabled him to escape car crashes in his youth, as well as a shooting, and to face his declining health with courage. When his death came, would they remember to break the fisherman's ring? Could he rely on those around him to repeat his baptismal name three times and would they remember to seal his apartments? In the old days, he would have been tapped on the head with a hammer and this too would have been an appropriate action to bestow on a one-time steelworker from Birmingham.

He explained carefully to those who gathered around him that a pontiff's death was like anyone else's death really. He knew all too well that to be a pontiff was still to be mortal. He was no First Emperor determined not to die and to continue ruling forever over a terracotta army. His witness was to show his suffering to the world and to face death in the same way that he had faced life, with robustness and grace. The papacy was more than a desk job and carried more responsibility than he could ever have known at the bottom of the escalator with a job in industry.

*

It occurred to William now, sitting at his solid desk, that Sidney had something of the deckchair about him, just as a preacher had something of the soapbox. William wasn't altogether happy about these metaphors, but insofar as things could represent people, a deckchair and a soapbox could safely be said not to represent William. But the deckchair certainly wasn't quite right for Sidney either. There was nothing collapsible about him. Indeed, if the firm had been a car, which admittedly it was not, Sidney would have been its brakes, for the first answer that he gave to any question was always 'no'. And this answer did not change, even after he had had time to think about the question. The convenor had used this to his advantage at a recent meeting between the board and the shop stewards. He had asked for the managing director's reaction to any pay rise of less than £20 a week. 'You can't have it,' Sidney had said, 'and that's final. We aren't running a charity.'

So how was the analysis going? William wasn't Sidney and he wasn't a street preacher. This much had been established. But the clarification hardly helped his predicament, for Sidney was what a steelworks needed. Recognising this, William felt little animosity towards him. Moreover, there was delight in bumping up against a contrary – contraries kept a man alive. William feared that he was capable of tolerating anyone: just where would he have drawn the line? He pictured Maria kneeling at the fire. Was tolerance necessarily a virtue?

But Sidney's characteristics were not exhausted yet. Sidney also had survival skills. He had survived in the same factory for forty years after he was demobbed at the end of the war. Would Sidney live forever? Then there was the fact that Sidney, while he would never back down, had a vulnerable side that William found almost endearing. Last August, for instance, in the corridor, Sidney had placed his lean left hand on William's right shoulder. This gesture, William had thought at the time, was an amalgam of the big buddy shop-floor arm over the shoulder and the big-business hand on the arm. Sidney, in his wisdom, had split the difference. 'I bet you didn't know I slept starkers,' Sidney had said. And he had been right. William did not know this. Nor, until that moment, had it been a burning issue. Sidney had then explained that his wife had made him beautiful pyjamas when they were first married but that these had been taboo in the army and so he had never used them. 'Let that be a lesson to you!' Sidney had said, winking at him heavily. William wasn't quite sure what the lesson was meant to be and he suspected that Sidney wasn't quite sure either, but this intimacy had touched his heart. He could not dislike someone who had taken the trouble to mention such a thing to him.

Their exchanges had always seemed awkward to William. Sidney had asked him into his office eighteen months ago.

'You're an egg-head, Bill,' he had said. 'Do we need this multiphase press? They're two million a fucking time from Japan.'

'Well, we aren't using the presses we've got to more than forty per cent capacity as it is,' William had said. 'We could cope with an increase in demand as we are if maintenance did their job.'

William had to admit now that he had been wrong. Sidney had, of course, taken no notice of his opinion and the press was installed. It was rather good – foolproof, clean, massive and gentle – the sort of press that might found a religion. Japan was certainly in the ascendancy. America had had its day, William felt sure. But all the same, Sidney had been impressed by William's response. The idea of maintenance doing their job had struck a chord with him.

'Damned maintenance!' Sidney had said. 'The presses down all the fucking time and they still want more money. We won't get much profit out of that bastard lot.' Then he had thought a moment and added, 'If they weren't so damned idle, we could use the presses day and night; the full fifty per cent.' It seemed unlikely that Sidney did not know what fifty per cent meant. Perhaps he was joking. He was certainly a good managing director.

It wasn't that a steelworks didn't provide food for the imagination, it was just that, for effectiveness, William was better to ignore it. The art of a steelworks consisted in such things as horseplay: a press operator who could mime a massive masturbation; a ten-foot penis – Greek art at its best. Another operator would bellow out, 'Everyone's a winner!' It was his one exclamation. 'Everyone's a winner!' would ring out above the thunder of the presses as the hot, shiny, newly shaped components were flung into the bins; 'donkey pricks' was the metaphor used for those bevel-pinions and main shafts. And they weren't called 'bins' either. The factory was not without sensitivity to language. To call them 'bins' would have been akin to William calling the sitting room, the *lounge*. He had learned the right words eventually. For a year or two he had called them *bins* himself. Then he had graduated to *skips*. Only last week had he discovered the ultimate word – used by the most seasoned shop stewards and by the convenor himself: *stillages*.

Pressing on with this subject of art as revealed in industry, there was Amir Baz – the saw doctor – lean and intelligent. He had once been a tailor in Lahore. He claimed to have been able to look at a man and make a suit for him without measurement. William believed this. No one could sharpen a saw blade as well as Amir so that it cut steel like cheese and glistened like an aeroplane catching the sun on a bright morning. Amir Baz was indisputably an artist. He had once borrowed William's paper and, on returning it, had said sadly, 'I bring your paper back, man! Too much trouble in the world, man. Whole world, too much trouble. Very nutty world, man.' William could not have conveyed the state of the world more succinctly.

He considered also the Jamaican truck driver who brought in vegetables as gifts from his allotment and who drove the truck too fast. The safety committee had reported him and then, later, he had driven over the carpenter's foot. In spite of steel toecaps, the foot had been a mess. But what was art if it was not present in Pencil's love of speed, his cheery wave and his temper?

Pencil had once knocked out a furnace man for calling him a black bastard. 'Yes, man, that's what he called me,' Pencil had said. 'I heard it with mine own ears. I ask you this man ... when a black man looks at a photograph of his family, is a black man any less jiggered than a white man? No, he ain't!' Had Pencil seen *The Merchant of Venice*? William wondered.

'One day soon, man,' Pencil had added, 'there will be a black American president.' He had said this with conviction, almost as if he believed it.

William had said, 'Next time, old son, wait till you're outside the factory gates!' The talk had ended with some frantic but heart-warming revelations. How, for instance, when Pencil had first come to Britain, he had expected a Christmas card landscape – reindeer, little rabbits, Christmas trees, country cottages, perhaps like Maria's – instead, Birmingham! And how, in Jamaica, there was a house, around it some land, then another house on the next plot and so on, so that when the taxi had dropped him at his brother's terraced house, he had thought the driver had made a mistake and had left him at the factory instead – a great long building with smoking chimneys.

What William did not seem to have grasped lately was that a steelworks needed to make money. Instead, for him, it had acquired a human interest, a philosophical interest even, quite beyond its commercial purpose. Unlike Sidney, he had taken his eye off the ball. The lead into his own dismissal was an example of his lack of focus on the job in hand. It had been no surprise that Horace had refused to empty the acid tank. The preparation manager had cut his overtime. Stan, the foreman, had told Horace to clear the tank. The operator had knocked a beer can against the wrong button and had emptied the basket.

'No!' Horace had said. 'I'm sorry this has happened on your shift, mate. It's nothing against you, but the answer's no. I'd get as much stacking shelves in the Tesco.'

'I'm sorry this has happened too, mate,' Stan had said, 'but I'll send you home, if you haven't changed your mind, that is.'

'No,' Horace had said. 'It's dangerous in there. The fumes rot your teeth terrible. I've got to keep the plant running while the operators stand and watch me or push the wrong fucking buttons. It's marvellous when the labourer has to show them what to do. They're only glorified labourers themselves and they earn twice what I get.'

William had come in on the case rather late when Horace and the preparation manager and the shop steward had been unable to reach any sort of conclusion. William had spent several hours listening to every aspect of the case and eventually had reported it all to Sidney. Sidney had told him to sack the man.

'What the fuck else is there to do if he won't clear the tanks?' he had said.

'He seemed happy enough as long as he got his overtime,' William had pointed out, belligerently.

William hadn't sacked him. He had often listened to Horace talking about this and that. And he couldn't very well listen to him and then sack him. Besides, he liked the man. William had been sacked as a result, and quite properly: a steelworks could not be run on sentiment.

20

Her mother had only wanted the sea view. The sea view could stay here, Lois thought. The rest of her mother's things – a few clothes, a mug, a radio and the garish lipsticks – she bundled into the car in black bags. She would take most of them to the Birmingham tip where there was one of the best collections of garden gnomes that she had ever seen. The gnomes summed up rather well the heathenism and humour of Birmingham that she loved so much. Callie, James and Jack had wanted to help her clear the flat. She had refused their offers, preferring to go alone as she felt it would give her the space and time to take on board her mother's death.

It would not change her life that her parents were dead. She had done what she could for them. She had loved them. She had her own grown-up daughter. It had been good to have Callie at home during the first lockdown, piecing together parts of her PhD at home. Everyone said that Callie was like her grandmother. Lois had talked with Callie at last. Not so much as mother and daughter. It was more as she used to talk and still talked with Kal and Maidie, irreverently about anything under the sun, about boys, for instance, or girls in Kal's case. There had never been any secrets between the three of them, but it was new for Lois to talk this way with Callie too, no longer guiding her. Callie needed no guidance now. She had her own trajectory. Not once had she cooked anything or cleaned the house. Jack had done more than she about the house and he was working. This was no resentment for Lois or Jack. This was Callie, their daughter, and they were proud of her.

*

The morning held a cloudy sky merging with a cloudy sea. The headland was blotted out. The sand, saturated with water, reached glossily to a barely distinguishable ridge of white waves at the sea's edge. Even with little visible, this was a richness of view never experienced in Birmingham, though the illuminated red lettering of the Tesco sign could have been found there too. The art she was attracted to was urban or architectural. There was no sky or greenery in Grosz's mostly red *The Funeral*. Jeanneret's paintings and architecture were of objects and concrete. Popova, Stepanova and Rodchenko constructed work from pattern and line. They did not need the seaside. For her, there was nowhere to go with art after Malevich's *Black Square*. After this, she could be an accountant. As the light increased, the sea's horizon became clearer, with the sky a lighter grey than the sea. She could also make out the end of the headland, though most of it, above the estuary, was still in cloud. Was there a tinge of red in the brown and green strips of the burrows that followed the estuary's flow, or was this only a visual echo of the Tesco lettering or the result of her throbbing head? The red was the colour of the lipstick she might have worn if William had been there to notice it on her lips.

*

Above St Martin's, William sat down under Nelson's statue. He could just make out the square concrete outline of the factory where he had once worked before he became pope. It was now a distribution centre with a Tesco store beside it. Sentiment alone could not keep manufacturing alive. Even *Brookside* had not survived until now on sentiment only. As scriptwriter, William had spent his time removing sentimental language. Writing for a soap was not unlike running a steelworks – he had had to cut back ruthlessly. A good use of language was always a tightrope between the specific and the general. He had had to get down to brass tacks but he had also needed to let the ideas flow. Medicine was the same. As the chief research scientist for the World Health Organization, he had played an important part in developing a series of treatments for AIDS. The problem, as with scriptwriting and botanical drawing, had been balancing specifics with generalisation. The solution had been to immunise for specific cases. It had not yet been possible to apply these specific remedies to AIDS in general.

Nelson, whose statue looked out proudly above him, was an example of a man who had also done his duty. Like Nelson, he could rest on his laurels now, for William's testing work in science and television was nearly done. Nevertheless, glancing up at Nelson again, he realised that Nelson's example and achievement could be interpreted in different ways. Some people might even think that Nelson was no more than a poser with his medals, his wife and his mistress. Looking back on his own life from this angle, with Nelson in view, William could see that worldly achievements did not matter at all. The only actions that mattered were the small kindnesses that he had shown to other people, and there were precious few of those. If only he had known when he set out that those small considerations were the only things that counted, he could have saved himself a whole lot of trouble and heartache. Was that the truth he had been searching for all weekend?

In Birmingham, at least, few knew who Nelson was or what he had achieved. He probably wasn't in the national curriculum in any case. Birmingham was not a maritime city. Nelson had been so busy making his way in the world and risking all, both in battle and in love, that he could not possibly have paid enough attention to those who suffered at his hands, however caring an admiral he was thought to be. Perhaps a great leader should not be judged in this way, but it was in the acknowledgement of suffering and the extent to which we suffered ourselves that we could look God squarely in the face – give God facetime, as the Americans would say.

The visual arrangement of the Bullring laid out in front of him as he sat on Nelson's plinth lent itself beautifully to the idea of man pulled in different directions by good and evil, as in *The Castle of Perseverance* – St Martin's on one side, commerce on the other. The characters took great care to explain who they were and what they were doing. It was to the credit of the dramatist that he had made the antagonists so colourful and entertaining, because that could easily have undermined William's moral purpose. Selfridges must be sufficiently splendid for mankind to be attracted there. Otherwise, this would seem unconvincing and mankind peculiarly gullible. At the same time, the playwright could not let the Deadly Sins triumph in the end, and needed to show that they care nothing for mankind's soul, or so he had written in an early essay. So this theatre space with Nelson, Selfridges and St Martin's near the markets contained the message at the heart of his weekend's journey. Indeed, the Deadly Sins openly admitted that their influence was only of worldly use and of no benefit after death. There was a precision about the climax that would have pleased a naval strategist like Nelson, each confrontation following a similar pattern: a reply to the antagonist, a biblical quote, a reference to Jesus's example, and defeat for the sin. Who could have expected Birmingham's city elders to have promoted Meekness, Patience, Charity, Chastity and Industry in so convincing a manner? William was almost ashamed that he no longer paid his council tax.

Although he recognised how much he had achieved since that earlier weekend when hardly anything had happened, he took no lasting pride in these achievements. Then, as now, his interest in worldly matters had been misguided. He could remember sitting in his study then, waiting for his brother's family to arrive and concentrating on how he might remember the weekend in the future as the time when the new *Brookside* serial had started.

*

This had led him on to the question of realism in art. In literature and in the soaps, what mattered was whether or not the readers or viewers were swept off their feet – sewage disposal worked on the same principle – and such involvement might occur, realism or not. It was remarkable what a novel or soap could achieve if the reader or viewer continued to eat from the writer's hand. Olivier, in his Shakespeare films, had recognised this. He had made the settings deliberately ham just so that the language would seem that much more real and carry the day ... or the sewage.

The producers of *Brookside* had taken a different approach. They had bought a housing estate. He hoped that they could afford the mortgages. Would the programme still be running in the next century when the mortgages were paid off? He could not tell which aspects of his own times were making history. But a soap seemed an appropriate choice of marker to him: history was now made as much on the television screen as in Parliament. Popular culture now had an academic and historical credibility and it was only right that he should register this in any future remembrance of the weekend.

Of course, if he scoured today's paper, he might be able to identify something that would prove to be of true significance to mankind, rather than a mere fictional soap. For instance, tucked away at the bottom of page 25 of *The Review*, there was an article on 'Health in America', about a mystifying epidemic of cancers and parasitic infections that in eighteen months had been diagnosed in 600 patients. It appeared to be some kind of gay disease, although some cases had also been reported among haemophiliacs and Haitian immigrants to the United States. There were even twenty cases in Europe. What if this was to become some kind of epidemic involving thousands of people? There was no need to be melodramatic, William reminded himself. Only 250 people had died from the disease and there were only a handful of British cases. But there was always a possibility that this could become a serious health problem. Then the weekend might more usefully be marked out as the weekend when this disease had first come to William's notice rather than as the time when *Brookside* had been incubated.

Paul's red minivan splashed to a halt beyond the hedge. The

drizzle had stopped but the road was still wet. William watched from his study as Ruth, Darren and Paul walked together up the drive, a happy family, chatting away amongst themselves. He went to open the door.

'Come on in,' he said.

They were all smiling. Ruth was smiling a little too much, he felt. Paul would have told her about his lost job of course. But Ruth was all right. No one could take offence at Ruth.

'Enjoy your holiday?' he asked her.

'Yes, thank you,' she said, grinning.

Wasn't she just great, he thought? She could have married anyone, even Sidney. The idea pleased him.

Lois and James jumped out at Darren from behind the dining room door. Just occasionally, at such moments, they were recognisably brother and sister.

'Hi, Lois! Hi, James!' Ruth said. She had a special voice that she kept for when she talked to children and to dogs. *La-de-dah*, it went, *la-de-dah-de-dah*. But Lois and James didn't mind. They knew their aunt. They liked her. Everyone liked her.

'Did you have a good holiday?' Lois asked. Adolescent girls had such an unsmiling directness. They couldn't laugh at themselves. But then not many people could. William rarely could.

'Yes thank you,' Ruth said. She was still grinning as they all went through into the dining room.

It was a happy throng, and in his house, too. It was an honour to have a happy throng in his house.

Cas scowled at them from the kitchen. Ruth pecked her on the cheek. William studied Cas. Even on a bad day her authority was invincible. Still, she would need and welcome Ruth's help with the lunch. Ruth had the edge on her in that respect only.

'So you all want coffee now?' Cas said. 'Make it yourselves then!' She ran a hand through Darren's hair. 'Just checking there's no elephants there,' she said.

'Let me get out of these shoes,' Ruth said, 'then I'll make it.' She added in a thoughtful tone, 'It makes you think.'

'Why don't you wear the comfortable shoes in the first place?' Paul said, smiling. 'We don't need to stand on ceremony here.'

William helped Ruth with the coffee and carried the tray through to the others in the dining room. As Ruth handed round the cups, he rested the tray on top of the television. They restricted the television to the dining room, just as members of his father's congregation would insist that the minister be ushered into the sitting room. It was a matter of pride. Then Ruth produced some Penguin biscuits from her bag. He hadn't had one since he was a child. It was interesting that something perishable – Penguin biscuits or Quality Street – could help to give his family life continuity.

There was a sense in which a brand was not permanent, of course. The biscuit, or the chocolates, had been eaten innumerable times, but they were dependably available. People, by contrast, might move away or, like his parents, die. And if he went to find one person or place, he couldn't go to another person or place at the same time. He had discovered this yesterday when he had upset Cas by visiting Maria. Penguin biscuits or Quality Street, on the other hand, could be found wherever he went and at any period in his life so far.

Places puzzled William too. He resided in a particular place – Birmingham. But there were other places too. Places never seemed to move, except astronomically. They stayed in one place forever. He could only occupy one of them at a time.

What were all the other places doing while he was occupying the particular place that he had chosen to occupy or that he had been landed with? All this was in the nature of things and William felt it appropriate to dwell on the nature of things from time to time, if not all the time. It marked him out both as a sage and as a nutcase.

21

Lois was a safe driver – deliberate, observant, eyes on the mirrors and the traffic ahead – as she drove north on the M5; the rhythm of driving encouraged her to take stock. The flat was cleared and the landlord paid. Her mother could not intervene any longer. She had been a good mother, always loving her and looking out for her, though she hadn't always welcomed the battles when she was a teenager. Her mother had made her stand on her own feet. This had freed her from her parents' obsessions. She was comfortable where she was now, driving along. It had always been this way for her. She had trained as a nurse before it became a graduate profession. She had not been to university. Neither had James or Jack. Nurses didn't need to know about Malevich. You did not need to know about Rilke to run your own skip business or to be a firefighter. She had imagined marrying a firefighter from when she was a little girl – the black and yellow uniforms, now with red shoulders like American football players. Her dream had come to pass.

*

Cas spent most of each day in bed but the foot of the bed faced the window, so her view might still be considered an improvement on a Birmingham vista. There were charcoal clouds above the sea and headland, with blue sky above the clouds, dabbed with red. Eventually, the morning sky was pink and blue as the high tide worried at the rocks, allowing little room for the waves to break. The burrows were consistently brown, green and yellow with the sandy path between the burrows and the rocks reflecting the sun's light. Their Japanese guide in Fukuoka City had said that the sun was always watching her. The light from the sun came indoors into this north-facing bedroom, even into bed with her. She would have explored this idea with William. It was the kind of idiocy he relished. If she could not be serious now, when could she be serious? It was a comfort to have reserved her plot in Witton, not that God would care where or how she ended up. The young rabbi had been gentle and funny about it all. Of course, to believe in God was to deny the scientific evidence. It was to be no better than those who would not accept the evidence for a greenhouse effect or listen to the scientists over the behaviour of viruses. The evidence pointed to no God, but she was content to keep God in bed with her, although not too close, even if only as a hunch. The waves were busier at the estuary's edge and also in the distance at the far end of the sands in front of the headland, where the white surf also caught the light. The sun bathed the headland and the burrows, finding an amber flapjack brown in each, and glowing at the sea's edge. Gradations of red and green stretched out to sea, or was this only in her feverish mind's eye?

*

He was above domesticity now and Sunday was no longer for the family. It was now a shopping day like any other. Years ago, Sundays were still Sundays. But he was a man at home in a changing world and content to rest here a little among his friends in the warmth and good humour of his home city. He loved every brick and every stone of Krakow. Searching could never be strictly chronological and he had been so wrapped up in his thoughts today that he hardly remembered retracing his steps from the balcony and entering the Bullring where the steaming bull still stood on guard at the entrance. In any case, a thorough search required him to backtrack in bloodhound fashion so that he missed no scent. On this occasion, as often on Concorde, he had resorted to autopilot, though Concorde, unlike his search, usually only had the one trajectory. The Bullring in any case was where he always ended up each day, however he got there. And he was happy to spend most of this special day among his young admirers on one seat or another in this vibrant new shopping centre. The Bullring was as much his home as the Vatican. To empty his mind of thought wherever he found himself was a gift that had come to him late in life.

Only those with the courage to be alone could stop the movement of the mind and find their innocence, forgetting their bodily needs. If he were to die now, his sins would be absolved and he would find Nirvana. Many pilgrims to the Kumbh sought death, sought to be released from the cycle of birth, the cycle that might require them to be born again as an insect or a ghost. To die now, with a basil leaf in his mouth, would be to go straight to heaven, for now was a sacred time. All the gods would be present; Maria and Cas would no longer need to worry about his soul. He too could be a part of Ganga's ever-changing, ever-flowing sameness.

He ventured into the fresh air once and the sun came out briefly. Many of the shoppers might not have noticed the sun. He knew, however, that this was a sign from God and an indication that his search was near to conclusion. He had had another clue last night when the man on the television screen in the shop window had smiled at him. The newsreader had been subtle about this. Only William would have known the significance of the smile that had been directed at him alone. And after breakfast, were more proof needed, there was a yellow sign over his head – 'Pedestrians Keep Left' – which of course was to indicate that he was to sit at God's right hand, washing God's feet even.

To be a witness to hope and to the dignity of human life through his own suffering was a rare privilege. He was a witness to the value of life as well as to the suffering of the cross. He would teach the most beautiful lesson of all: how to die serenely. The Holy Father dying was like anyone else dying in many ways. Could he be given the last rites more than once? he wondered, and was this the same thing as communion for the dying? And how could a conclave of one hundred and twenty cardinals know how to proceed without his direction? He had appointed nearly all of them. Was not it natural to wish to die in the Bullring or at home in the Vatican, rather than in an antiseptic hospital, smelling of chlorine? These were profound theological questions to be resolved before his apartments were sealed. Meanwhile, at the bottom of the escalator, he could come and go as he pleased.

*

William closed the front door as he went out. Cas and Ruth wouldn't want him under their feet, and Paul would understand. Paul would play with Darren, lay the table or help lift the roasting pan from the oven to baste the chicken and potatoes. Paul would know how to make himself useful just as William knew when he wasn't needed. He wasn't needed quite a lot these days and he knew only too well that Cas earned enough to support the family without him.

But the gravel was supporting; it had its own rhythm, its own swish under his feet. He was in his drive but he could equally well have been on the deck of a boat. Although his thoughts could roam, he was still rooted to deck. The factory had its own rhythms too. The iambic beat of the cropping machine, for instance. That was bad poetry, no variety. He could almost learn to sleep through that, if it didn't shake the foundations so much. He could catnap in his study through the grandfather clock's tick, after all. Now, he could escape from the factory, its rhythms and images and characters. He must let Cas have the study too, now that she was the only worker.

He would walk round the park. Where else? He crossed the road and entered the park through the Victorian wrought-iron gates. He would walk round the pond first. He always did. This was a fine pond. It could have been a monastery pool had there been a monastery attached. Perhaps there were age-old carp in it. What, in Birmingham?

There had been something in the paper this morning about a monastery. No, there wasn't. He had thought about a monastery instead. He had been reading about Tavaré's dead-bat 89. That was class. And what a foil he had made for Randall! William had thought that perhaps Tavaré, because of his abstinence, would take his vows when he left cricket. That was the monastery connection. It was a connection – or loose connection – within William's own head, nowhere else. Those ugly scenes in the Perth heat and the grim determination of the English team – 400 was no mean score – had no actual monastic link. But it helped the analogy that these were honourable men who had not been on the rebel tour to South Africa and had not supported an apartheid system that seemed to be every bit as solid as Tavaré's innings, or the Berlin Wall. Was it comic or tragic that Nelson Mandela had lost out to Princess Anne as Chancellor of London University, the so-called arch-Marxist pipped to the post by a hardworking royal. In a novel, it might be wiser at this stage not to mention the cricket series at all, certainly not in such glowing terms. The tour could still flop. Such tours often did. Australia might still win back the Ashes. This morning, in particular, ashes seemed almost worth fighting over. It then occurred to him that a wicket in cricket was not something tangible at all. It was more like a journey or a search; it was something to remember years later, something to look forward to even, like a cruise. In any case, cricket had no actual connection with this pond. It had no more connection with this pond than, for instance, the factory. However, a monastery – which, as he had already established, happened not to be attached to this pond – might have much in common with the factory. In fact the factory was a monastery in a manner of speaking. Inside his head, all sorts of neurones were now tying the concept 'factory' to the concept 'monastery'.

No sooner was this link established, however, than his attention was taken up with all sorts of haphazard factory imagery: the welder with his methodical manner, his cylinders and tubes and the coral blue flame. There were also the furnaces, their boxes of red-hot components, like beds of tulips. And, for a moment, he remembered again the plaques in the crematorium. Were they marble or imitation marble? And what was marble anyway? Was it the thought of tulips that made him remember the crematorium or just the thought of furnaces – or a mixture of the two? Even his own thoughts were unknown to him on occasions.

So he turned from his thoughts to the world before his eyes, ears and nose to see a boy fishing on his own, concentrating hard. William stepped round him. There was a smell of rotting wood and leaves, and the sound of a police siren in the distance. And suddenly he was comparing the factory siren – what a howl that made! – with the school bell. He remembered how the teachers had rung it twice. The first time you had to stand stock-still. The second time you had to get into line by form and height. He had always enjoyed that, especially as, being somewhere in the middle of the queue, he felt safe and unnoticed. He had enjoyed it because he was good at being good, at doing what he was told. But not, it seemed, any more. Even the factory siren was a thing of the past for him now.

But the factory siren was a thing of the past in a wider sense than just for him personally. He had been aware recently of being at the end of something there. It was the end of the mechanical age; the end of mostly male workplaces; the end of the shop-floor age. We were all to be middle-class now, perish the thought. He was embarking on the attention age when everyone was after his attention. He had said as much to Cas, though he might not have had her attention. Perhaps such awareness as this – standing back to see the direction of travel – was the artist's peculiar responsibility. Was this an even more important role than ensuring that the presses were used to capacity, or appreciating the difference between annealing and quenching? An inspector had returned a quenched component into production recently, causing a grand smash on their biggest single point press. It had been a day to keep out of Sidney's way! But he felt confident at this moment that art and ideas and history also had their place, even when they couldn't prevent things being smashed up and even when they went no further than his own head.

A dark wisp of a girl ran up to him. She was carrying a giant teddy bear. 'I'm cold!' she said and ran back to her parents.

He thought of the furnaces again, then what one of the furnace men had said: 'Er must be in by six thirty. And if er ay, then er knows er's in trouble.' He also remembered Harry Beasley, who had come in drunk one day and gone round the factory, cloth cap in hand, collecting for his new baby. And why not?

William's interest in such things was genuine, born of admiration if not patronisation. And as if to test out this tendency, he noticed four gangly West-Indian boys kicking a red plastic football on the green turf. They looked happy and carefree to William in a way that he had perhaps never been. It would be a boy like this, growing up in Georgia or Hawaii, who would be the next president of the United States, or so Pencil imagined. Then he remembered what another man had told him: 'It's a pansy's game today! Now a lace-up leather ball – that took some kicking when it got wet. Stanley Matthews could cross a ball the lace away, so that it didn't hurt the forward's head, and Bill Shankly said that Tom Finney could play in an overcoat. Nobby Stiles asked Alf Ramsey if he should mark Eusébio for the match or for life.'

This man, as much a philosopher as any he had met, had also said, 'The time just seems to go now. I was at the bus stop.

I looked at my watch. Then I looked at the bastard again and five minutes had gone. God knows where that went!' Wasn't this sentiment as much to the point as any winged chariot, and bang up to date too? It would have gone unheard if William had not been there to hear it. He suddenly seemed to himself rather important.

'The girls,' the man had continued, 'you see them in their party dresses and the next thing you know, hey presto, they're fully developed like, pushing a pram.' A pram pushed by a woman was more filmic than literary, William felt. He could also possibly come to terms with time more easily in film than in literature. He could see his father's generation as young men, for instance. He could see Jackie Kennedy as young and dazzling and could compare this with the fact that she was now old – although not yet dead, as John F. Kennedy was dead, and William's father and mother.

The girl who passed him smiling wasn't pushing a pram; about twenty, she would have been. An old lady followed her, a grey old lady walking with a certain grace and determination, like an elderly poodle. Could the old lady have been like the girl once? he wondered. He thought of his mother and immediately set his mother down on the factory floor. He wondered if the factory and his mother could ever have mixed. Were they chalk and cheese, land and sea, irreconcilable? The factory workers he knew were not without sensitivity:

'I dig up the potatoes first crop, and the little ones' – the setter had bent his thumb and forefinger into a circle to show the size – 'get half-boiled and go into the freezer for Christmas Day. Just the job!' The setter had smiled at the remembered happiness and curled his thumb and forefinger again, this time to indicate perfection.

But there was Sidney too. The setter was the setter. Sidney was Sidney. Sidney was vulnerable but you could not call him sensitive. He was in fact the least sensitive man that William knew, except perhaps at the urinal. And no one could say that Sidney was not of the factory. Sidney was the factory and Sidney was, therefore, quite right to get rid of him. Somebody had to.

Such realisations as this – that he was more or less irrelevant to the factory and even to his family – were unsettling. The tall trees, planted in Victorian times, arched above and, in spite of a wonderful smell of cooking spices from a house nearby, there was something about this walk that was fighting him into a corner. It was bringing to him clarity of mind and this, just now, was unwelcome. He could really only bear up to a weekend like this with his mind addled. Still, the clear thinking would be temporary – no more than hunger. He anticipated the chicken that Cas, Ruth and Lois would be roasting, perhaps with basting by Paul. What would Sunday be without a roast?

James would be helping out too in every way he could. Times were changing. And here he was just walking along. He must head back. It would be rude not to be there when Maria and Stephen arrived. They were his guests. Rude! That was a quaint old word and quite obsolete, like 'galoshes'. But the word 'rude' was obsolete for a different reason. Galoshes had more or less disappeared, so they didn't need a word. The word 'rude', on the other hand, was dead because rudeness was everywhere. Rudeness had become so much a part of life that you no longer needed to draw attention to it – rudeness was life, just as Sidney was the factory.

22

Lois climbed the wooden steps onto the boardwalk beside the skip with the last of the bags. There were often similar boardwalks at the seaside but the recycling centre was not at the seaside. It was in Birmingham. She carefully swung the shiny black bag into the rusting skip. Both her parents had carried baggage. She had loved them for it but chosen differently. She had lived a good life with Jack, but without the black bags, she liked to think. Callie, as ever, would make her own choices. Lois's mother had insisted on being alone with the sea eventually. Lois had understood her mother's wish. She had phoned her each day but left her to her privacy, no face or lipstick to put on.

*

There was a storm for Cas to watch with banks of clouds sweeping in to the seashore from far out at sea, the wind shaking the window frame at her feet. A herring gull, high up, braced itself against the wind and was cast backwards. There were dark clouds over the headland and lighter clouds over the sea. Disarmingly, there were also patches of blue sky between the clouds. William had always avoided storm and confrontation. He could never see things as they were. He was European in every way. He loved Ibsen, Brecht, Pirandello and Chekhov. When he wasn't crazy, he liked to work with people. He saw good in everyone, even tyrants. She knew, however, that evil had to be confronted, that you should not even try to go on a picnic with depravity. For her, parliamentary debate was everything. At the same time, with the wind at the windows and the waves attacking, the differences and similarities between her and her husband, who was dead, no longer mattered.

*

It was dark outside when he eventually returned to the balcony above the wide steps with the yellow, blue and pink water sculptures beside him. Rome was such a pleasing city.

He had often wondered whether to abdicate at the turn of the century. Would he have fulfilled his mission as pontiff once he had taken the Church into the new millennium? The argument was a strong one. But popes didn't abdicate. All Catholics, the pope included, believed in the value of a good death. Morphine didn't match up. Indeed, for the Catholic, the purpose of life was death. He was not a Holy Father to refuse that last glorious hurdle. It had been his wish to have no hiding away, no drawing of the veil on his death; his last gift would be to share his last hours with the faithful of the world.

William was happy to take a few paces, biding his time for as long as his energy lasted. There were no factory sirens, school bells or other deadlines on the streets. He sat down with his plastic bags in the garden area halfway down the steps. There were three pines from the Middle East and a hedge. This must be the Garden of Gethsemane, he thought. He was safe here. Paradise was a walled garden like this, possibly with serpentine walls. There was also the wonderful sharp smell of citrus in the air from the lemon grove.

Sitting in this garden area, smelling the lemons, he was aware that Genesius, the actor, had mocked the Christian baptism. He had always felt close to Genesius. In Krakow, in his youth, he had wished to be an actor too. No wonder that he had seen eye to eye with Marlon Brando recently. His papacy, however, had been for real. It had had nothing of pretence about it. It had been method acting at its best, opening up his inner soul to scrutiny – not that he was giving much away, sitting here with his carrier bags beside him.

He recognised puritan influences from his childhood, too, that he had put to good use in cleaning up the World Health Organization so that it could cope more efficiently with AIDS. His success with the Chicago Bears – only Michael Jordan had worked harder – as screenwriter for *Brookside* and as chief test pilot for Concorde was also in part to do with his upbringing, that constant requirement to do his best at everything. His mind had never been sharper and he was now beginning to embrace the true complexity of life, he felt, as he sat with St Martin's church not far below.

Did drama sometimes venture where prose feared to tread? The significance of Natasha's little excursion in Protopopov's troika in *Three Sisters*, for instance, was not obvious immediately, any more than William's excursion into Worcestershire. However, Chekhov drew attention to this first with the sound of the Troika bells, equivalent to gravel under the wheels, then with the doorbell ringing and, finally, at the end of the act, with Natasha crossing the ballroom in fur coat and cap. Natasha had no gravel path to wear. It was also worth noting how Protopopov was always in the background. He never appeared, but his presence was felt throughout the play, just like Sidney. William looked around carefully, as he sat in this garden, to make sure that neither Sidney nor Protopopov were in view. One of the ways that Natasha was made to seem threatening was through her habit of appearing at moments of tension. For instance, she entered carrying a candle just after Soliony had made his threat, later carried out, to kill any rival for Irena's affections. Cas's lover, by way of contrast, could do as he liked as far as William was concerned. It was clear that the sisters' Moscow would never be realised, just as William's factory no longer existed.

William, although seated quietly at the moment, was on a dramatic roll. He remembered a few paragraphs on *Peer Gynt* from his dissertation, by which time he was married. William had made the point that Peer was a misfit, someone the other characters could gang up against and taunt cruelly; a Norwegian Heathcliff. William, too, was sensitive to criticism. Following Peer's departure from Solveig, it left him without ties in Norway and free to go seawards and walk around Birmingham city centre as many times as necessary in order to find what he was looking for. But he could also find what he was looking for by sitting here and going nowhere.

The resolution he was finding here by simply sitting down in the garden also called to mind the *Brome Mystery Play*, from the same chapter of his dissertation. The play's integration of entertainment and teaching was related to its simple form. His life had been simpler then too, just before Lois was born. The usual four stress lines accommodated the speech of Abraham,

Isaac and God, and the persistent though irregular rhyme pattern allowed father and son to pass the rhyme from one to the other, just as William had taken the wheel from his father, underlining the blood bond. One reason that this roughness worked so well in the cycle play was that the story was already familiar. This was not true of William's story. Even William could not be certain how everything would pan out even at this late stage in the weekend. Would an angel show up for him too, he wondered, if he was constant in obeying God's will?

Sitting here, as if in the theatre, enabled him to continue to pursue this dramatic vein as far as he could take it, and to an admittedly absurd degree. Gloucester's blindness had a bearing on Lear's madness. They were both routes to an eventual clear sight. William had achieved clarity without either blindness or madness. While Lear came to face up to his flawed judgement, Cordelia's judgement was true throughout. This was not the same as William's situation. William saw things clearly already, and he no longer had a daughter, other than the woman whom he had taken under his wing out of sympathy for her mental plight. The pattern of Lear's development in the play was from blindness to clarity, and the cathartic storm, as well as his own madness, were necessary elements in this education. This weekend had no storms, only drizzle, but it had the same redemptive spirit with the eventual triumph of love and clear sight.

Finally, to exhaust nearly everything he had ever written about drama and to purge it all from his mind as he sat inactive above St Martin's church, he recalled Pirandello's *Six Characters in Search of an Author*. The characters were understood neither by the other characters nor by the actors and producer. The father and stepdaughter were locked in mutual attraction and disgust, like William and his supposed daughter. And yet they came near to being united in horror at the ineptitude of the leading man and lady at representing their situation. Marlon Brando, in spite of his weight, would not have made that mistake. The play ended with a sequence of light changes. The colours of the water sculpture might have been yellow, blue and pink rather than green and blue, but the Garden of Gethsemane would suffice for the foyer while the wide steps were the stepdaughter, of course, laughing quietly to herself.

His weekend was being rounded off nicely as if it were the theatre. Marlon would have loved to witness all this. Pirandello also knew Rome well. It was fortunate that William had kept a sense of proportion in spite of all this complexity. He knew what to do and the search was on.

*

He moved some of the coats from the coat rack as if he was preparing to perform family charades, hanging them instead on the hooks beside the front door. An antique should not be strained. At the same time, it pleased him to have a full house.

'Hi, Dad!' James said, clumping down the stairs with two chairs. He looked so young, so keen to keep things on an even keel, to make a success of the day.

William smiled at him and went through the dining room to the kitchen. He owed this much to Cas. She seemed to be at ease. With Ruth, Paul and Lois to help, everything was in hand. The table was fully laid and the smell was good. Ruth was stirring hot fat and flour in the meat pan to make gravy. She always got on with the job without any fuss. Cas, on the other hand, tended to give every impression of speed without actually moving fast. But then she had an active mind. He had married her for her active mind, not for her skill with gravy.

'Everything all right?' he asked. It was one of those foolish things that a sacked director might be expected to say, but Cas only grimaced.

'Did you put salt in the cabbage water?' Lois asked Cas.

'Does it matter?' Cas said.

'I can smell you did,' said Ruth.

Smell the cabbage had salt? What a miracle Ruth was! She was pouring a little of the cabbage water into the meat pan. It hissed and the steam rose. She stirred fast but still with time to spare. Lois watched her intently, learning, for Ruth seemed to be aware of the gravy and the heat as one. She adjusted the gas instinctively. As with mind and body, religion and philosophy, William thought, the heat and the gravy could not be disentangled. But he left them. They could do without his observations.

In the sitting room, Darren was on his knees concentrating hard not on a Willow-pattern plate this time, but in trying to position a piece of jigsaw that he was turning in his hand like a rosary. James was helping him, though a little self-consciously. Stephen and Maria smiled.

23

Lois drove home from the tip through familiar streets, quieter than usual. It had been a long day. She savoured the moment, driving with care as always. Her life was especially precious with her parents absent. This was the only life, and she knew her worth in it. It resided with Jack and Callie and in her work and friendships. She liked to plan things out and make good moves at the right time. Jack was the same. He was just Jack, displaying some of the ordinariness her parents had never mastered. He could do most things in the house and out of it. She could rely on him and him on her. He would take stock before entering a burning building. He was strong but not the kind of man who would pick up the hammer and tongs before thinking.

*

As the white surf stormed in from the mountainous sea and the wind shook the window pane, Cas missed him. The sea was dark and the headland darker. A cold air enveloped her. She could not get warm. The wind and sea were up. She had always been strong but she was retreating into this nature now; this nature that was not Birmingham. She acted strong. Someone had to. She had given birth to the children, suckled them, shaped them. From the beginning, she had loved William in every way. She did not need to agree with him to love him. He talked about little Englanders. She talked about Parliament. She loved confrontation. He hated confrontation. It was why he was a useless director. He could not state the obvious. He would always understand her, and everyone else, quite unreasonably. Now, the sea, sky and headland were variations of grey, and a churning, white foam reached almost to the horizon.

*

He walked slowly, reverentially even, carrying his bags into the church. He sat down towards the front in a pew not far from the choir stalls. He was also within sight of the Burne-Jones window. This made him feel almost as much at home as viewing the William Morris wallpaper that had once been in their sitting room. He turned the order of service in his hand as if it were a rosary.

He was early and the choir was practising with an elderly, bearded choirmaster who resembled those depictions of God in Sunday school books. They all wore casual clothes. The choir then dispersed and the organ began to play. He had seen jazz players do the same; warm up their instruments and leave the stage. Andropov, long gone, had liked jazz. The candles were lit and William found the occasion atmospheric with the darkness outside and the candles inside. Even in the centre of Birmingham, this was a cosy feeling, like being on a boat. A lady warden said 'hello' to him. Another lady shook his hand.

It must have been a rarity for the pope to visit St Martin's and they clearly appreciated his communion with them.

The choir then came in again dressed in white vestments. These were surely the angels; heralding the end of his search.

The other worshippers, and even the choir members, would not have been aware that he had arranged the music for the introit himself, nor indeed that the girl with dark hair in the choir stalls was deeply in love with him. It was a secret between the two of them: the kind of yearning that had existed between Leopold Bloom and Gerty MacDowell in *Ulysses*, and just as romantic on his part. The fact that the candle beside her was exactly the same height as the candle beside him was proof, if proof were needed, of their undying passion.

He was proud to have financed the new Bullring himself, but he preferred that this generosity should remain anonymous. The city elders had not been able to persuade him to declare his hand; the fact that he had found love was far more important to him in any case. The Beatles had been right – money couldn't buy you love. It was just unfortunate that a convicted murderer was pretending to be the rector at St Martin's and ruining all the good work. Moreover, he was Cas's new lover. What would Martin, the Hungarian soldier who had given his cloak to a half-naked beggar, have thought of this impostor? It was his responsibility to reveal the fraud of this adulterer, who behaved as if he had taken holy orders and was justified in wearing the holy vestments and preaching to sinners.

William was still turning the order of service in his hand as he sat alone in his pew. He was not fooled by the rector's garb and his kindly manner. The fact that there were bars on some of the stained glass was evidence that this sham officer of the church should have been in prison. Moreover, the hymn number was the impersonator's prison number. The other worshippers would not have noticed these details, but his powers of observation surpassed theirs. No wonder he was on first-name terms with Elizabeth Taylor. Only last week, he had spent the day with Elizabeth and, true to form, she had showed up late. It was important that stars supported each other in times of need. He could smell incense – or was this Elizabeth's exotic perfume? – for the time was auspicious and the stars were aligned in the firmament. He might talk to Elizabeth Taylor, but Elizabeth I of England would be excommunicated if he had his way.

As he looked over the pew in front towards the choir and as the service continued, he remembered that the handling of time in eighteenth-century novels reflected a change in the perception of time during the eighteenth century, or so he had argued in his dissertation. Until this period, for example, the Aristotelian unity of time – the action of a tragedy to take up no more than twenty-four hours – remained the dominant characteristic of Western drama and demonstrated the interest in timeless universals rather than in linear change through time. William's weekend broke this mould. It extended not only over two days, but also over many years. The only serious quarrel with Aristotle seemed to have been over his belief in the eternity of time that ran counter to Christian doctrine. For instance, that time is eternal was one of the doctrines that had been suppressed by Archbishop Tempier in 1277. At William's instigation, there was a young researcher looking into the problem of the eternity of time at the Vatican. She had spent many years on the task already and was now a little less youthful than when she started. The eighteenth-century fascination with juggling chronologies and the difficulties encountered in this respect by Pascal, Bousset and, later, Darwin, among others, were largely due to the fixed nature of the Christian timescale. Tristram was humorously exact about the moment of his conception. It was fixed by reference to the winding of the house clock and its coincidence with 'some other little family concernments' that might equally well have taken place in a Woolworths' photo booth.

The groundwork of Copernicus, Kepler, Galileo, Huygens, Hooke and Newton gave time free rein, like the reign of Elizabeth Taylor, whom time had barely touched at all thanks to her plastic surgeon. Moreover, the philosophy of John Locke had encouraged time's subjective experience, as if William did not have enough on his plate at the moment, as the service proceeded along established lines, without bringing in the unreliability of his perception of time.

To sit quietly in church had always been an opportunity for William to think about anything other than the subject in hand. But the nature of time did in fact have a bearing on the nature of God – something that he would have expected churches to have an interest in – so he was not entirely off track on this occasion. William had never written many letters even before he took to the streets, but the epistolary form tended to be a continual reminder of chronology. Each letter, for instance, was headed by the date, if not by the time of day as well. And letters, by their very nature, tended to account for how time passed or was passing. Moreover, letters were punctuated with such phrases as 'when the meal was over' that mark out for us a daily timetable, not that he had had lunch today.

Even without the letter form, this climax in William's life seemed to slow down time. This was partly because the moment required an explanation that delayed the action with its attendant detail, narrative time, as a consequence, passing more slowly. It was also that he liked it here in this church and it seemed a shame to move on. We sit up and take notice because the normal narrative succession – one event following on the heels of another, like the hamster placing one foot in front of the other on the wheel – has been interrupted. It was as if William had had to wait for lunch.

*

They sat round the same four-part table made of mahogany. Each part was a table in its own right, though laid side to side. The end supports of each small table were crossed diagonals with a central floral motif of Elizabethan style and this made it hard for his guests to find room for their legs along the side of the assembled table. But he was at the end of it, Cas at the other end, so he had leg room, his belly resting on the cold wood like the touch of a church floor, or the steering wheel of yesterday. He liked to be at the end of the table, and not just because of the leg room. He carved, loading the plates with chicken. Cas and Ruth spooned out the carrots and the broccoli.

They ate happily, silently. It wasn't what was said that was special about family meals, it was more the accumulated togetherness of them – the fact that they stretched back through time, father at one end, mother at the other.

He smiled and took another mouthful of chicken. Well now, this was better. He needed food and company round a table. He had been worked up lately. He hadn't seen straight. It had been as it was for him in school biology – he had been obsessed by detail. Instead of surveying the whole, he had been absorbed with just the frog's leg. In the presence of that frog's leg, the teenager William had had a feeling of absolute failure to grasp even the smallest detail. In another adolescent this might have led to faith. In him, it had helped to establish his doubt. He had felt no less hopeless recently, quite paralysed. But with good company, a plate of hot food and a glass of cider, he could see his error: he had even been examining the words he used. What did it matter the words that were used?

Ruth, Paul, Darren, Maria, Stephen, Cas, Lois and James were helping him back to sanity. Balance, that was what mattered. With them around him, he realised that he was just one of them too. What did ideas or thoughts count for beside humanity, beside just sharing a meal? Pretension wilted here. Meals like this were just meals like this – people together. Was this the point, for the Christian, of the Last Supper?

'Leave it if you're full,' Ruth said to Darren.

'I've tried, haven't I!' Darren said.

'Haven't you bloody well just!' Cas said.

Love knows no boundaries, William thought drunkenly. He was relaxing and quite content with clichés. Love only happens, he thought quite absurdly. When all is said and done, it was worth being nice and good and kind and helpful. This was it. This was the end of him. He was soft in the head but he did not care.

'I know nothing,' Paul said. 'Nothing at all.' The cider was getting to Paul too.

'You don't mean that,' said Stephen.

This was the kind of conversation that William felt that he could get along with.

'Do you remember when I was in hospital with pneumonia and this nurse asked me to mend her car?' Stephen said to Maria. 'And I said "Here I am! I'm in hospital. How can I mend your car when I'm in hospital?"'

Everyone laughed but this was a good point. You could not be in two places at once. Humour was a matter of confidence. If the storyteller had confidence, they could get away with anything. It did not even need to be funny. He wished he could entertain like Cas or Stephen. He felt like being the life and soul of the party right now, but that, as always, was out of the question.

Ruth's apple pie was handed round, with cream. Splendid! He would have quite liked to put his feet up on the table.

'You know something,' Paul said. He looked tipsy. 'We adults are middle-aged now, but it doesn't seem any time to me since I was your age, James.'

James grinned.

William could remember being James's age too. He used to rush around the stone-flagged yard at the back of the manse on roller skates. He had kept that boy's shortcomings ever since and more than likely rolled some of them to his smiling son.

'I love you, James,' Cas said, 'but if you don't stop grinning, I'll put you through a Bar Mitzvah. But you're right,' she added, looking at Paul, 'alphabetically speaking, we're on P or Q by now.'

'We had better mind our Ps and Qs then,' said Stephen inevitably. But his faltering delivery made any joke hold. He faltered with confidence, a winger wrong-footing the goalkeeper even with his coat on.

She's found her match here, William thought, studying his wife. But why, then, Maria for Stephen and why he, William, for Cas? It was an illogical world. But that was how it was. He could not argue with how things were. Or could he?

'We're sounding like our parents used to,' Paul said. He spoke to Lois. 'They used to rave about two black singers – I don't know their names – and about Leighton and Johnson who were just names to us. And they used to go on about the music halls. They had both seen this illusionist on a church outing. "The bird was chirping and flapping around one minute," our father used to say, "and the next minute it was gone!"'

24

Lois parked in their street and walked to the house. Maidie was walking towards her in the other direction. She wore an orange fleece and held a pie. What a good friend! With the restrictions, Lois could not invite her in. Maidie talked in the street about things other than Lois's mother.

'Jack said you would be along any minute. Stela and Lottie are in the same bubble at school now, thank goodness. They prat about, bless them, just as we used to do with Kal. At weekends, they wear make-up. They dress goth sometimes. Good for them, I say!'

Lois smiled and took the pie. 'Thank you,' she said.

She opened the front door. Why was she crying? In the kitchen, she put down the pie. Jack held her in a long, strong fireman's hug.

*

There was drizzle and grey mist over the sea. If Cas half-closed her eyes, which was comforting, this could almost be Birmingham. She was under no illusion that coming here had changed anything. William was dead. She was old. Lois and James were still in Birmingham, but it had been important for her to be by the sea as the sea had no interest in her and no pity. In Birmingham, there were expectations, even in old age. She was conspicuous there, someone who was turned to, an authority figure even. She had had her fill of matriarchy.

The cloud, sea, sand, burrows and headland were a grey harmony with the mist rising. Her hair was now more white than grey. She had never been sentimental; to age was in the order of things. In nature, or in Birmingham, nothing ever stood out for long. She was absorbed into all this with her once black hair. Nature smoothed the rough edges. She had stood out for a while and fought always – for her family and for William. In old age, they had both accepted how things were and they had had each other too, until now.

With the mist everywhere, little that was distinctive remained, but she was all right with this. It wasn't even sad. It was just how life was, and death too.

*

The prisoner's vestments were clean and sculptural, not unlike those of the coloured masts and the coloured water sculptures but in red, black and white, like an oystercatcher. But their cleanliness did not fool William. Such purity was only skin-deep. This man was an adulterer.

One of the characteristics common to saints – not that he would presume to be a saint, of course; the sin of presumption was not in his nature – was that they could identify fraud. They could see through sham. Knowing the truth themselves, they expected truth from others. A man who had grown up in Nazi Poland and cut his liturgical teeth under the communists had a sixth sense for baloney. With four decades of ministry in Krakow behind him, even before he became the Holy Father, humbug was immediately apparent to him.

To resolve these questions in his head was a matter of urgency and to seize the moment, a matter of both judgement and integrity. The question still to be formulated, even when the solution to all the other questions had been found, was at what point in a life of the faith did the call to action become a necessity? How did he gauge the moment to leave his books on the desk and walk out into the garden with its crinkle-crankle walls and in open confrontation with a serpentine world? Often, the saints were hallowed because faith and action were one and the same gravy train in them; part of the same brew stirred together, the steam rising like incense into a church where sin was dispersed naturally.

As he watched Cas's lover in his ecclesiastical garments and listened to his all-too-convincing words, there was much to consider in this dark church. He was glad of this opportunity to sit in the south transept and to think about everything. He still had his faith and a simple life. On the streets of Birmingham, there were no dishwashers, no self-referential art on the walls, or sons and daughters playing chess. But he could hold his head up here and look deep into the eyes of the next woman or man, for goodness resided everywhere, even in Birmingham. He knew where his priorities lay. They lay with the washing of feet, not with the washing-up machine. He could now be kind to everyone. He could say, 'Hello!' He could say, 'I love you!' He had time to play his records and to dance in the street unimpeded by pillar-shaped earrings.

*

With the pans washed and the dishwasher loaded, the smell of coffee was everywhere. Maria counted the red saucers onto the tray. She was wearing delicate pillar-shaped enamel earrings in flaming yellow as if she were a basilica. Seeing this delicate jewellery, it occurred to him that art was never wholly free of science. In fact, it could only live by science's leave. But this was old ground. It was another patch that he was trampling for a second time this weekend – the rosewood bedroom chair and its contrast with Chippendale had occasioned a similar train of thought.

By way of diversion he looked from Maria, who was placing the red cups on the red saucers, to the calendar above the kitchen table that had Jackson Pollock's *Autumn Rhythm* as November's print. It had been painted in 1950 when William was still in short trousers. The painting, like Cas, did not belong in England. It was from New York. And it had more life in it than Maria. The lines danced in front of his eyes, stealing Maria's limelight. Cas, on the other hand, might eat *Autumn Rhythm* for breakfast, like scrambled eggs.

Autumn Rhythm, one could argue, was an example of purity. It was concerned with flatness, form and the boundaries of a canvas. The areas of splashed white paint might be said to move forward from the kitchen wall, but this was in the context of an all-over pattern so that he could not speak meaningfully of depth in any one area of the canvas or, in this instance, *print*. Maria's eyes, on the other hand, were as deep as an ocean bed. Although *Autumn Rhythm* always related back to its own colour, shape and the distribution of pigment, Maria's eyes related to something that never touched ground. *Autumn Rhythm* was pure because it was concerned with painting itself. Maria was a different kettle of fish. She was not what his eyes saw. Unlike *Autumn Rhythm*, her subject matter was beyond herself.

'Will the children have coffee?' Maria asked.

'Lois and James, not Darren,' he said, grateful for the intermission. He rubbed his hand on her shoulder and, at that moment, he could not help but be reminded of Sidney.

Plato talked about impressions on the mind, Descartes of wax and seals. Sidney, if nothing else, was an impression on William's mind, the seal stamping his wax. Cas was this too, though as his lover, she might be a less reliable example of causal theory. If there was a physical basis to perception, then Sidney was it, he felt. He was veridical, unavoidable and clear evidence in support of representational theory, more was the pity. Sidney abided by the Laws of Nature, if not by the Laws of Decency, and it was therefore more than likely that he coincided with reality. This was bad luck to say the least. He would sooner that Lois existed than Sidney. He loved Lois as a father loved a daughter – unconditionally. He did not love Sidney. But Sidney had to be the one individual in his life to demonstrate incontrovertible causality. He could only hope that what he saw in Sidney was perhaps not exactly what was examined. The best he could hope was that Sidney was of a slightly different hue to the hue with which William perceived him. He felt sure that what he saw of Sidney bore some relation to how Sidney was, but it was possible that there was a haziness around the edges of Sidney, as in an old photograph, that had failed to register in William's mind's eye.

For all this, there might come a time when Sidney, the gravel path and perhaps Cas, too, were no longer a part of his life, or he of theirs. Then he might be cast adrift in a sea of relativism and with no touchstone on reality. At that point, he would not wish to be held accountable for his opinions or actions. Sidney, Cas and the gravel path were helping him to keep on level ground.

As for Maria, she was an excellent example of the theological relativism that was becoming less attractive to him. In the summer, just before the Falklands War, William had taken Lois and James to hear John Paul II in Coventry. William had gone because it was a sunny day and because it might be his only opportunity to hear a pope – and because he had not yet taken out life insurance on Lois and James. The pope had impressed William with his certainty and with his good sense. The pope was now taking up a position in William's life beside Sidney, Cas and the gravel path.

It was an accident of fate that rubbing Maria's shoulder should have reminded him of Sidney. Maria was poles apart from Sidney, and under phenomenalism the connection made no sense. Nevertheless, the connection brought to mind again Hume's billiard table and with it the memory of a chance remark by the patrol inspector: 'Those pockets were like flower pots! The jaws stuck out like chapel hat pegs.' And then William saw the patrol inspector in imagery, as a bird, an oystercatcher over rocks. Did images have any point, he wondered, or were they just what they were, whatever that was?

25

Jack had turned on the dishwasher and left her a geranium leaf shower gel on the kitchen table. It was in an ornate glass bottle. Where had he bought that? Lois showered with the unfamiliar smell and texture and dried carefully, dressing for bed even though it was only early evening. In her dressing gown and slippers, she piled the washing into the washing machine and set it to sixty degrees. This would remove any micro-organisms from her work uniform. Science was her friend but it wasn't everything. The washing machine and dishwasher worked beside each other to their own rhythms, like Jack and herself. She placed Maidie's pie in the oven, made a cup of peppermint tea, settled into her armchair and closed her eyes.

*

Cas noticed the dark shoreline rocks, the silver estuary, rain clouds high in the sky, creative in shape, and a furious sea. She was frail in this landscape with the wind taunting her. But she had not lost her poise in old age. Even in bed, she had a certain ascendancy, her eyes on the horizon. She remembered William before his death, frail and thin but restrained, though the morphine had helped. There was no reason not to be sure-footed now, at least in bed. A flock of jackdaws battled the wind, swooping low in front of the window and climbing back to the woodland behind the terrace. The mouth of each wave enlarged and darkened before breaking, and white spray floated across the top of the wave, the foam then spreading wildly as it approached land. She was almost that spray above the breaking waves.

*

After the hymn, the confession, the absolution, the Lord's Prayer, the responses, the Psalm, the reading from Luke, the Magnificat – another arrangement of his – the Apostles' Creed, the responses, collects, the anthem, the intercessions and the hymn, the pretend rector stood up to deliver a few words of his own. William realised that he could not allow this to continue any longer. He therefore stood up, walked to the altar table and placed one of his carrier bags on top of the candle. The blue flame was not as blue as the welder's blue flame. His search was over. Like his father, who was in heaven, William loved fireworks and garden bonfires too. And why should he not be allowed to celebrate Diwali? As the flame burned, one of the churchwardens jumped on top of him; William's head struck the stone floor. Was it apocryphal that a cardinal would hit the pope on the head with a hammer in due course?

A church floor was like a red carpet in many ways except that it was hard and also cold to the touch. It was not red either, and this implied no special dispensation to saint or sinner. There were a few drops of blood on the stone floor from where he had struck his head, as if it wished to give him the red carpet treatment and to turn water into wine. He remembered tipping the boiled water away as if it were his father's lifeblood.

To give life to faith had been his mission, but it had often seemed impossible, like squeezing water out of stone. Had Cardinal Wolsey, the son of a butcher, and *Legate a latere* felt the same? Could he not have countenanced a divorce from Catherine of Aragon when Cas had not divorced him?

Lightning never struck twice, it was said. This was a falsehood. It struck just as many times as it struck, and what about the sea receding? Matthew Arnold had spoken of its melancholy, long, withdrawing roar. He worried greatly about the sea receding. When the sea receded, it was time to run as fast as possible in search of high ground. He worried about his hair receding too. It had been buoyant and wavy in his youth – shiny, too, with Brylcreem. When hair receded, death was already on the horizon, inescapably bearing down like a massive, glinting wave in the morning sun.

But he was among friends here in the church. There was no cause for alarm. It was no more unlikely that a gardener should become a patron saint to sailors in the Aegean than that a man from Krakow should find his way to the Vatican. There was still time to resolve all this. The blood escaped no faster than the communion wine. Should he not welcome the transubstantiation, the Corpus Christi, even the impanation? After all, Man could not live by bread alone.

It befitted a man to hold his head up high and never to be weighed down by the duties of office. Here in this church, he could reach conclusion. His life had been a simple one, befitting a monk. He might have been the bastard child of a girl at Sykeon, but his own character and behaviour remained unblemished. He could rest in peace, God bless his soul. The interregnum was approaching. *Sede vacante*, he might say, or to put it another way, his head hurt.

*

'I had this friend,' Stephen said. There was no hint of a smile. Maria had handed round the coffee and each of them, Darren too, listened to Stephen attentively. 'He never used to fill in the coupons because he said you were more likely to be struck by lightning.' Stephen looked puzzled, as if genuinely unsure what to say next. 'I had news of him the other day,' he continued. He took a sip of coffee, then looked up at the ceiling. 'He was right, you know.' He took another sip of coffee. There was an expectant silence. 'He had been struck by lightning!'

This laughter among his friends and family cheered William to the bone.

He remembered the chocolates. Lois and James had given them to him last week for his birthday: his fortieth birthday. The chocolates were in the study, inside the bookcase's secretaire. He went to fetch them and noticed the paper's financial pages still on the desk. He was happy to leave them there. The family mattered more. In his student days, the financial pages would have been flung straight in the bin as a matter of course. He had had to revise his view when Cas, after college, had trained as an accountant. As a result, the family was financially secure, whatever direction his life took. But, anyway, finance was a part of life and he felt that he should not be cut off from anything. He wasn't quite sure where this progression was taking him. Perhaps he would be embracing religion next. It was a gloomy thought. At any rate, he could see hypocrisy in the idealism of his youth; each grin and smile and protest a small lie. It was perhaps a little sad that certain things should cease to be issues in his life. It was the pattern of history too – so much effort for nothing.

But it was worthwhile fetching the chocolates because Lois and James looked pleased. He remembered how neatly Lois had wrapped them in the birthday paper. The card had read *Happy Birthday, Dad – Love from Lois and James*, and there were crosses for kisses. Left to himself, he readily embraced sentimentality. Still, no one could deny that unwrapping parcels was one of life's remaining pleasures, along with opening a new tin of coffee or feeding shoe polish into dry leather – his father again.

He had known that it was Lois who had wrapped the parcel because boys couldn't wrap parcels. An ability to wrap parcels must be something in the female blood. And with this ability went that loping clumsiness of womanhood too, that ungainliness in running or throwing snowballs. It was as if God had thrown in these small handicaps to make men feel better about the fact that women were otherwise so much more beautiful, intelligent and practical than them. The ability to wrap parcels, he felt sure, was the first sign of women inheriting the Earth, whatever the Vatican might think. This might not happen in his lifetime, but eventually society would realise that men were a handicap and that life would be better without them.

'Mine's lovely,' Ruth said to James. James smiled but looked away. 'Makes you think,' she added. Darren was on her knee.

James collected the coffee cups and took them out. William watched him. He remembered his own self-consciousness at that age. It was still there sometimes.

'So you're forty too?' Maria said.

'No – forty,' Lois said.

'I love you but shut your face!' Cas said. 'It's Stephen and me who make jokes around here.' William smiled.

'Just think,' Stephen said, 'twenty years back it never occurred to us that we were in utopia, the world of our dreams. Why not, do you think?'

'Because we weren't,' said Cas. 'It really wasn't what we wanted at all.'

It never is, William thought. What did she want? he wondered. Perhaps he would never know. Did she want success? Did she even want him?

Then he remembered the girl who had passed him in the park that morning preceding the old lady. She had been wearing a badge with 'I love Jesus' on it. There was no harm in that, William now thought. Perhaps he would love Jesus one day too. Better to love Jesus than nuclear arms or motorbikes. Motorbikes? Did he mean *bikes*? No, in this context, a motorbike was better. It had a better ring to it, even though it risked him sounding like his mother. And there was a distinction between this usage here and that of his mother's. In his mother's case, it had been unfamiliarity with youth culture, a galoshes orientation; in his own case, he trusted that it was more a matter of poetic sensitivity, an awareness of rhythm.

Such a tedious concern in him with the particulars of language was, he knew, a hallmark of neurosis. It was also a sign of boredom, a lack of other concerns. Indeed, perhaps this was why the girl's badge had stood out for him. Those with anything to believe in were indeed something special. This was not to say that such people were justified in their belief. They might equally well be deluded. But good luck to the girl in the park! If only she could hold on to her youth and her beauty too.

Ruth stood up. 'We should be getting back, eh Paul? It's nearly dark already.'

Maria stood up too. 'We can't stay much longer either,' she said. 'Thank you for your cooking. That pie was a treat.'

The steelworks were no more absurd than polite conversation, William thought. Paul was shaking hands with Stephen. Strange thing, this shaking of hands; it was like a great river, lapping and reassuring, like a gravel path. Then Paul picked up Darren.

'We'd better get this tadpole home,' he said. 'See you at the bonfire!'

'Right,' William replied, grinning.

At that moment they were the two little boys again. He waved them off from the front door. A windy dusk was around.

26

Lois took a paper mask out of the box on the hall table. She would need this on the train tomorrow. She also had a spare one in her bag, just as her grandfather, apparently, always had a spare sermon in his waistcoat pocket.

In the kitchen, she smelt lemons. She cut into Maidie's pie neatly with a sharp knife. It would last them several days. Jack would enjoy a slice in the morning after work. It was delicious: chicken and lemon. She had not heard of that, or geranium leaf shower gel either. When Maidie's mother had died, Maidie had come to their house with Lottie. Lottie had worn the West Bromwich yellow and green scarf. Jack had said the Baggies should spend money on good strikers now that they were in the Premier League. Lottie had said, with a tooth-brace grin, that she liked them going down again. They had always done this, she said, ever since she could remember. That was why she loved them. Jack had chuckled – that open, warm smile. They would be better off without a goalkeeper too in that case, he had said. They had all laughed together in their sadness. It had been a rare discussion for them, Lois realised afterwards; it was the kind of discussion her parents would have had, almost moral and religious. She and Jack tended to take one day at a time, he attending car crashes or house fires, she restoring health when that was possible. She and Jack would also still hold hands sometimes.

*

The view – sea, headland, burrows, sand and sky – was untroubled by her loss. There were a few people on the beach, like flies on the window pane, but they did not know Cas, or she them. Even in his illness, William had loved her and listened to her. She had loved him by arguing with him. The grey city of concrete, noise and fumes that she had known with him had been the impartial setting for their disagreements. He would have welcomed the kindnesses and neighbourliness that the pandemic had thrown up. He was a sucker for such things. She would have reminded him that accountable government was a greater necessity now that nationalism, bigotry and false information was contagious too. Without him to argue with, where was she? There was a delicate pink and charcoal cloud formation over the headland, softening inland. At the mouth of the estuary, a patch of sea mist looked like sea spray and she was happy for her eyes to settle there.

*

A display of fire and smoke spread over the church pews and the heads of the sparse congregation like the spray above a breaking wave. Afterwards, he could still hear people talking faintly. He felt privileged to be entering the Kingdom of God. The angels in their white vestments were lined up facing each other as if at a barn dance. They joined hands and lifted their arms high to form a tunnel. This was a tunnel of purity by which his entry into heaven would be blessed. He had always kept his feet on the ground. He was not a man comfortable with displays of emotion, but he could feel the tears on his cheeks, like spiders at play.

But there were still one or two questions to be resolved from this stone floor of the church that held him close. Why ever was William not lined up with the angels? This was surely a gross error of judgement. It was as bad as allowing a quenched component back on the presses. And another problem: how had a tea trolley found its way into a steelworks? A tea trolley was associated with polite conversation – scones, jam and a teapot that never ran dry, which in its turn was like the faith of the foundress, Katherine of Bologna, Maid of Honour at the Ducal Court of Nicholas. He never found polite conversation in a steelworks.

*

He looked across at Maria. Her shock of hair showed up brightly against the blue chair, but she looked as calm as ever. In her, above all else, was dependability. There was a constancy in her that Cas could not match, nor had she tried to. Maria was more dependable even than his mother, and, in a changing world, it was comforting to meet up with permanence from time to time. It was as if the twentieth century had waved to her and let her alone. But at the same time, he found the lack of panic in her unsettling. Should she not panic sometimes in the face of life, with a print of *The Great Wave off Kanagawa* by Hokusai beside the kitchen window in her cottage?

Cas was never serene. She changed all the time. She lived almost to change. She claimed to have neither religion nor art.

She was wrong about art. She had art all right, even if she had accountancy as well. Just as the steelworks had art, without knowing that it had it, without even knowing what art was.

What was art? Was it so different from religion? Did art and religion overlap? Indeed, were they the same thing? He thought of the Venn diagrams that James had been drawing in maths, better by half than tables or geometry. Wherever had geometry gone? He hadn't had sight nor sound of geometry since his school days. Had geometry gone the way of galoshes, the way of all flesh?

Anyway, to get back to the question in hand, was the intersection – yes, that was the word used – between art and religion an empty set? Was that really the question? And how did he ask if there was anything in the bit of the circles that didn't overlap? If there wasn't, would that mean that art and religion were the same or different? Even if he could get the questions right, there would be no obvious solutions. He couldn't reduce life to maths any more than he could reduce life to art or religion. What a mess this weekend was! A playwright would have simplified it all, used his red pen.

He must try to stick to facts. Margaret Thatcher, like many Romans, was practical. She wasn't for aesthetics or humour. The artist, on the other hand, did not want to know why Canada geese flew over every day, wings beating the air and calling out. The artist was merely content that they did so. There was his father too. His father had had God and, for the sake of argument, William was prepared to say that his father had been too sincere for art. Ah, he was getting somewhere. So his father was inside the God circle, but not inside the art circle. The terms 'God circle' and 'art circle' were unfortunate, but he couldn't help that. Yes, there was something in religion that didn't intersect with art – his father for a start, except that his father was dead, but there would be others like his father. William was like his father. So when he, William, finally stepped into his religious father's shoes – it could happen any day – there might be even less hope for him. He would be stuck with God. Wasn't that enough? God and a family of his own were enough of an undertaking for anyone.

Not that God seemed to need him any more than his family did, unless God needed him in the sense of needing someone to love. James and Lois would still play chess whether William was there or not. Chess was a good game: black and white, solid, like a steelworks. His only function had been to provide the games table and that was already provided – oblong, rosewood and inset with marble squares, not plaques. It had a hefty pedestal column and a solid base. The base was similar in shape to the oblong top, but with big God-like bites out of each side. It had bitten into his pocket too, but then it was from the 1820s and in mint condition. Lois had pulled the piano stool to the other side of the games table and she leaned on her knees studying James's slight embarrassment as he made his move. There was no danger whatever of Lois either losing or her damaging the stool; its carved walnut stem and cumbersome tripod base would have supported five men as heavy as him, fifty girls as wispy as her.

He knew, without looking, that the seventeenth-century wedding chest was behind his chair. On it were carved the two lovers and they too were playing chess. Paradoxically, perhaps, the stringent etiquette of the game was congenial to flirtation. His two children, however, were not lovers. Ah, but there was the subconscious. Yes, but the subconscious, by definition, was unknown to them.

The subconscious existed, if anywhere, in imagery. The factory had been rich in imagery. For instance, he had an abiding image of a tool setter removing a roll of paper towel from the container in the toilet block and placing it in his locker so that he could be sure of being able to dry himself after his shower at the end of the shift. Not a godly action but visually powerful: a roll of paper taken from a container and hidden in a locker.

So, while his father had God, the steelworks had imagery. Wasn't maths neat! Factory dialogue was another example of the artistic spirit. A Geordie had told him about waiting for the middle slice of the stottie cake and about how no one would work on at least five days of the year up there.

'Want to work Christmas Day? Fuck off!' he had said. 'Want to work Boxing Day? Fuck off! Want to work Good Friday? Fuck off! Want to work Easter Day? Fuck off! Even the atheists will tell you Good Friday, that's the Lord's Day!' He had added with a smirk, 'Longest day of the year that is, like a Sunday – nothing bleeding open.'

Today was a Sunday but, with Cas and Maria pushing in the tea trolley, it did not matter that nothing was open. There was a trolley in the Final View not unlike this trolley. There were things expected in a steelworks: endless lies to be seen through and put up with; girders, cylinders, acid tanks. Even, in the shadows, seven-foot-tall men with raincoats and flat caps would have been less surprising than that trolley. But unlike William, it had a purpose – it was used to wheel around the measuring instruments.

James lifted out the nest of tables from under the half-moon top of the walnut card table to the right of the gas fire. The other card table in the pair was to the left of the fire with the mahogany quartetto tables underneath it, but these were too valuable to use for tea. William cast his eye over the table that James had placed in front of him. It was high – no muscle on the tall legs – with tulip carving around the top surface and a heart-shaped pewter plaque inlaid in the centre: vintage art nouveau and rather ugly.

27

Lois watched the street from the sitting room window, the house still smelling of lemons. A couple walked along the pavement, their shadows shortening and lengthening as they passed the lamp post. She had courted Jack around these streets and, since then, they had never let go of each other. Her parents had not interfered. They had mostly known when to keep out of it. Jack wasn't for negotiation anyway. He had sat at the next desk in primary school. At sixteen, their minds were made up, their lives were settled.

*

There was a towering sea, and the headland was obscured by rain. There had been days like this for Cas in Birmingham during William's illness, the difficulties endless and no end in sight. Nevertheless, his love and his ideas, mad as they were sometimes, had been worth the trouble. Now, the sea was mesmerising but it did not replace him. He was beautiful in mind, always refining his thoughts, always surprising her, even when he was embroidering his own fantasies. After university, she had known what had to be done for William and the family. She was the breadwinner. She would always cope. She had left some of the thinking to William but had matched him every step of the way. He wasn't good for much other than loving her. It was timely that he had died before Brexit with the country at a watershed. He was European to his fingertips. Nothing upset him more than patriotism or populism. For her, Parliament and her family, were what mattered. Now, she attended only to her breathing, the headland, the estuary, the burrows and the sea spray.

*

A lady said, 'He's gashed his head.'

'He's all right,' a man said.

'Let's pray for him,' another man said.

William remembered that, many years ago, a young man had climbed into the lion's den at London Zoo. That young man had been wise beyond his years, William thought, and what a wonderful example, holding hands with the Christian martyrs!

Under the weight of all this love, the kindness was hard to bear. Could he ask them to leave him alone or provide him with an *exeunt omnes*? Or would that be pushing his luck, presuming too much? A cardinal with aspirations to be pope would end up a cardinal, or so the saying went.

To join the Roman martyrology was no mean feat for a recluse. The gift of prophecy was of little use without a proper suit. What was the point in keeping your eyes on Mount Athos if your feet needed washing at the Foot Locker? This was the question to be answered by the church elders. He wished they would stop talking about him and let him read the Sunday paper. What had the patrol inspector been up to, an oystercatcher among the rocks? It was too late to put things right once the components had been shipped: it was like using contraceptives when the baby was on the way. He knew of no rule to prevent the pope from reading the paper on the stone floor of a church. Why couldn't they leave him alone? If they wanted to pick an argument with the Holy Father, why didn't they meet him outside the factory gates? Other than one or two remaining discrepancies, he was ready to be called to account. His investments were appreciating by the day and his affairs were resolved, lined up neatly in order of value when the school bell tolled.

William felt nothing but contentment as his strength seeped away among the candles and the cardinals, who were visibly upset at his condition. The prayers and love of his Church all over the world gave him deep solace.

There was a sense of completion, of a job well done and of a life fulfilled. He could see that the shape of his life had been worthwhile, if not symmetrical. His message – that love mattered; indeed, that love was the only thing that mattered – had gone out to the furthest corners of the curia.

He was a modest man. He had merely set the ship on its course. It would be for others to assess his achievements and monitor the ship's progress. He was content to leave the deck and to let go of the wheel. The wheel did not turn once the hamster had belly-flopped.

With his brogues still on, he climbed the pulpit steps as if they were a ladder, *la scala*, leading up to heaven. He could see on the hallway ceiling a small crescent moon where the hall light had been reflected by one of the pewter plates on the picture rail. And it was with great joy that he encountered the angels ascending and descending the escalator, his eyes settling on solid earth.

*

In his study, the grandfather clock ticked and the financial pages lay over the desktop. The dealers would call the bends on the desk's front *serpentine*. It was a rich word, reminiscent of Original Sin and the Garden of Eden. Serpentine walls for growing fruit were a later invention. It was appropriate, too, that the financial pages should droop over the serpentine bends. For him, making money was a sinful, lonely activity, full of contradictions. For Cas, it was a necessity and nothing to get worked up about. She took making money in her stride; making breakfast was more problematic for her. By contrast, he wondered why, for instance, with unemployment at three and a half million – three and a half million and one to be precise – shares should reach new peaks. Surprisingly, he now compared this in his mind with the way his thinking flourished when his body sagged, his best ideas coming to him when he was fat. If he ever lost weight, it would be a sure sign that he was bereft of ideas.

He glanced again at the paper. He should have read it. He was considering a move out of Gilts. Gilts had had a good run. They had increased by about forty per cent in the twelve months he had held them. This was probably the time to sell. But where could he put the money instead? There was something rather sad about having more money than he knew what to do with, and Cas continued to make money at an increasing rate. It would certainly be worth increasing his life insurance contributions to make full use of the tax concessions, not that he was planning on dying – possibly take out a policy for the children too. Lois was already sixteen. Not that this would account for much of the excess. Certain sections of the antique market were undervalued at the moment too. He might be well advised to increase their furniture stocks, for instance. He was attracted again to gold, even though the pound was likely to fall in the run-up to the election; a stake in the American market should take care of that. He saw investment relatively clearly considering that his other thoughts were so confused. Perhaps making money was more art than science. Perhaps it was the only remaining art. There was a grim thought!

But it hadn't been a grim day. To sit at his desk, the angles carved with rococo ornament, the rain tapping the dark windows divided into rhomboid panes, the paper before him, the clock mindlessly ticking, was not to imply that the day had gone badly. It was only to countenance a slackening off of a weekend that, in actual fact, had never been taut. William went south out of the city and came back; his friends came north into the city and returned. Not exactly a stunning structure, though perhaps more interesting than walking around the city centre a couple of times. In a novel or play, he would have had to consider the critics, and critics, for some reason, were peculiarly sensitive to structure. Now if the weekend had contained irony, that might have provided appeasement; dogs salivated at food, critics at irony. Dramatic irony would have pleased them even more. They loved to have something to recognise. But dramatic irony, by its very nature and like the subconscious, would have to be unknown to him.

Happily, this was just a weekend. He could take it as he found it. He might return to the sitting room in a while. They might get round to a game or two. Cas might put a record on and there would be a mug of tea, or just quietly to bed.

28

The phone was ringing in the hallway.

'How are you, Mum?' Callie said.

'I'm fine!' Lois said.

'Have you cleared the flat? I wanted to help.'

'I know. There wasn't much there. I wanted to do it on my own. A mother and daughter sort of thing.'

'Well done! We are mother and daughter!'

'You know what I mean.'

'Not really!'

'How are you doing? All those students around!'

'I'm fine. There are more than a thousand with Covid. Not many of them are isolating.'

'Wow! Take care! Love you!'

'Love you too!'

Callie would always find a way through. She was like her grandmother: a force of nature.

*

A low cloud and a gentle rain inland cushioned most of the headland but Cas could also see a strip of blue sky without cloud above the horizon at sea. As hurrying waves approached shore, white foam along the beach and especially at the mouth of the estuary attracted her attention. With a coolness around the window frame, the dark, grey gradations of the sky were reflected in the dark, grey gradations of the headland, burrows, beach and sea. She could have been here in bed or else far out at sea.

*

He stared at the empty picture frame on the hospital wall. It was rectangular, like a swimming pool, and it did not move up and down like an escalator. This empty frame connected nicely with where his life had ended up and where things seemed to be beyond the hospital walls. The canvas was ready for repainting and for new ideas and new ways of viewing.

As for his own position, he was also ready to begin, adding dabs of colour here and there. With his sanity at least partly restored, he knew that Cas had rarely left his side during those years while her accountancy practice prospered, not that he could remember her there beside him.

The bang on his head from St Martin's stone floor might have done him almost as much good as the treatments that Dr Derrington had conjured up in his crucible recently. Through one remedy or another, he seemed to have found a resolution and happiness again.

Lois, Jack and Callie would soon arrive to take him to their home, at least until he found his feet and settled into his saner life. Lois had even sent him a text – it was better than birdsong – suggesting that he pack his case. Through the hospital window, there were patches of blue sky among the winter clouds, and the car park from which he would be collected was as attractive to him as any romantic sunset could have been.

But Cas came instead to take him home. He watched her through his hospital window rising to her full height from the passenger seat, as tall and proud to his eyes as ever. A diagonal shaft of sun lit her briefly from an otherwise cloudy sky casting a long shadow over the gravel and grass where the snowdrops, like stars in the sky, provided context. Her hair was cut short and it was no longer dark but grey in the transitory sunlight. James was as big as an ox, looking down at the grass on the car park's verge – if James were to throw himself at him, as he used to do once, he would knock him over. Could he smell Bovril infused with chlorine?

He could hear their feet on the gravel leading to the hospital entrance. She walked into his hospital room without knocking, glanced at his case and looked at him squarely. He loved that uncompromising intelligence and those curiously unbending dark eyes.

'Where's the straitjacket?' she said.

James grinned and, head down, picked up the case. He was too strong to bother with its wheels. William stretched out a hand to touch her and was gladdened that there was no hint of a smile either in the creases at the edges of her eyes or around her too red lips.

29

Lois could smell the coal tar soap and feel Jack's warm weight beside her. He had left a mug of steaming tea beside the empty cocoa mug from last night.'

'Great pie!' he said. 'Maidie's my kind of girl!'

'I'm your geranium girl!' she said. 'Where did you find it?'

'Debenhams.'

'That's closing.'

'I know. You were my first choice, but Maidie would have been next!' She dug her elbow into his chest.

'Callie phoned,' she said. 'They have a thousand cases. They aren't all isolating.'

'Idiots!' That's students for you,' he said. 'It had lemon in it. I've never heard of that.'

'What do firefighters know about anything?' she said.

'There's a new American president and there's a vaccine,' he said. 'I know that much!'

'Both of them had to end sometime,' she said.

'Maybe. Or maybe not,' he said. 'Some fires, you think they're out and then they ignite somewhere else.'

*

Cas could see at her window the domed sky and the sea united in a delicate pink and blue. There were also strips of grey in the sky, and an earthy green and brown in the burrows. From the burrows, she heard a solitary curlew, quietly at first but escalating its liquid call as it lifted in an arc away from her towards the estuary and floated in wind as the sound unravelled. Water on the sand reflected the pink hue of the sky, and the sea was turquoise with touches of ruffled white waves at the shoreline. A flock of jackdaws swooped down erratically in front of the window, like clothes in the wind on a clothes line.

*

His retired life with Cas had seemed relatively straightforward to him by comparison with what had gone before. The cruise had been a continuation of this, albeit on the move and over water. Although it was accurate to speak of *retirement* for Cas, retirement had never been quite the right word in his case as he had not retired from useful employment, nor from employment of any kind. But he was more than retired. As the stairs had become too difficult for him, even with banisters, Cas had moved their bed downstairs, with James's help, and the Wagenfeld lamp, too, into the study in view of the rococo desk and within earshot of the one-handed grandfather clock. Long before she retired, Cas had rightly taken over the study. 'The end of paternalism,' she had said. Now, it served as their bedroom. The bed was immediately under the print of *Madame*

Matisse with a Green Streak, if that was the correct title, not that he ever needed reminding of Cas, so it did not matter that he could not see the print or remember the exact title. The William Morris wallpaper was in the next room and Cas slept beside him, though she often woke early as if to a baby's crying. This marriage had had much abstinence, and yet it seemed to him to have known most things and to have found resolution now. Was there also a sense that among this room's clutter, his mind was uncluttered at last? He was in love with her still and content with her touches.

He recalled some of the patterns of recent years, though the morphine played tricks on the chronology of these events and compressed time, not that he had ever been a stickler for the facts, and with disinformation abounding, this lack of accuracy was contemporary. Everyone else was under a morphine cloud too. During this period, though not any longer, he would bring Cas a cup of tea in bed as he had always done and had learned some cooking and made porridge for her, served with yoghurt, to start the day healthily. Making porridge wasn't so difficult either: a cup of oats in the pan with one and a half cups of water, and then he would stir with a wooden spoon as the steam rose so that his thoughts and the steam were indistinguishable. It meant that each day began constructively for him, with his ideas rooted in activity, his feet on the gravel path so to speak, even if the steam rose. With Cas, he often spent an hour or two over breakfast, the smell of coffee lingering too. They were content with each other, even when they had little to say.

James's marriage day to Ioanela some years ago had been a happy affair at the registry office, with dancing in the church hall afterwards. William had delighted in Ioanela's braided hair and ribbons, elaborately woven like gros point needlework in red, brown and green. James had broken the glass to Cas's instructions just as William had done at his own wedding.

On another occasion, he had walked with Cas through the Edward Burne-Jones room in the museum to the Staffordshire Hoard. Cas had liked the folded cross. Were crosses not meant to be folded? she had asked perversely. And as bombs killed twelve in Baghdad and two soldiers in Afghanistan, they had walked together to the Oratory to see the pope wave to them and look sideways at them in a way that managed not to look shifty. From a retired accountant's perspective, Cas said that the Fed Chair mattered more than the papacy. This acknowledgement of the pope, she said, was only an insurance, in case she had overlooked anything. This was a different pope admittedly to the one William had heard in Coventry before the Falkland's War. But like Quality Street, Penguin biscuits and McDonald's, the brand had not changed much. This pope had studied Cardinal Newman in his youth and had beatified him for his habit of prayer, his intellectual training and his moral discipline, among other reasons. In what sense, William wondered, was seeing the pope the same experience when it was a different pope? He might need to see two popes together to help clarify this question, something that had not been possible until now, except by studying the paintings of Francis Bacon perhaps. That was until the new pope had stepped down so that popes could be seen side by side in *The Two Popes*, courtesy of Netflix. There was a philosophical and religious treatise, William felt, to be written around the question of what it was to see a pope. It would involve thinking about the bridge between heaven and earth and the guillotine, so to speak, that made Cardinal Ratzinger's head spin before Michelangelo's frescoes in the conclave. It would involve thinking about the nature of journeying and arriving at a different place to where he started: the sort of thing that the best novels were taken up with and that had been a part of their cruise from Genoa to Shanghai – their swansong together.

Now perhaps was the right time for conclusion, with Britain no longer to be a part of the European Union. Instead, though it was no compensation, the new library of Birmingham was a folded cross, unfolding perhaps before his child's eyes, its contemplation room, used mostly for Muslim prayer, heart-warming. This library's realisation had been every bit as good as its prospect, unlike cups of tea or reductions in the interest rate. The Higgs boson was on the verge of discovery, if not confirmed, Windows 10 was in full flow and there was an interest in the Internet of Things. The children's hospital was a casino and, with Cas, he had had a wonderful Mughlai meal at the church in Sparkhill, now a restaurant, where William's father had once been a minister. It was good to see the building well used and alcohol still discouraged, even if the non-conformist distrust of flamboyance had not been entirely honoured. Unusually, they had chosen the same starter, fish pakora. 'Have you gone soft in the head?' she had said. 'Can't you think for yourself?' But they had diverted as usual for the next courses, Cas with haleem then rasmalai, he with nihari then halwa. He had said that the garnishes – ginger, green chillies, coriander and lime – were identical, so they hadn't gone their own way that much. 'Similar, not identical,' she had said, her lipstick smeared. 'Don't go sentimental on me,' she had added. During the meal, when they hadn't been talking, William had been able to imagine the organ playing and the choir in black walking from the vestry, now the toilets, to take their seats in sight of the pulpit.

The European Cup, Rio Olympics and World Cup were

over, with the Zika virus and doping as backdrop. Gareth Southgate's waistcoats might have pleased William's father, with or without a sermon. The London Olympics could have been yesterday in morphine time, demonstrating to William, among other things, that kindness could still be found. The Jamaican team had chosen Birmingham as their base and it had been good to watch Usain Bolt on the TV, relaxed but focused, striking gold three times and glancing sideways at the same time in the 200 metres, like the retired pope tended to do too, but without seeming in any way unreliable, or as if he was about to throw in the towel. Now, with the triple triple at Rio, Usain had joined William, and one of the popes, in retirement.

Greta Thunberg, with one or two long plaits, was already an icon and fully justified in her anger. William's third pope was securely in place and, reassuringly for William, having no truck with hell – and a third Fed Chair had replaced Janet Yellen and Ben Bernanke: all safe pairs of hands compared to the papacy, Cas said. In Japan, the tsunami and Fukushima disaster had made William weep. But there was yet another Olympic Games, after Rio, for Japan to focus on, and the three arrows of Abenomics would have to land somewhere, Zeno permitting. Indeed, he had visited Japan with Cas recently, the sun catching her bleached hair, and the Japanese Prime Minister, with supersymmetry, had visited Donald Trump, black hair and fair hair, before and after he took office. There was a picture in William's head of Akie and Shinzō, framed by Melania and Donald, arriving at Palm Beach at the top of the Air Force One steps, the steps looking like an escalator through the morphine.

The world, like an escalator, had moved on, as it always did, leaving William behind. And when he half-closed his eyes, he sometimes thought he could make out the contrasting black and white silhouettes of Sidney and Donald marching together away from him as if in a Laurel and Hardy film, or maybe even a Leni Riefenstahl documentary.

At the same time, Marlon Brando was long dead and Amy Winehouse too; her high heels and exaggerated beehive captured by a bronze statue in Camden Market, but to hear her voice, William still had to turn to his iPod. Steve Jobs, influenced by the Bauhaus, was also dead. And Michael Jackson was no longer moonwalking. Tom Finney had died, in or out of his overcoat, and Elizabeth Taylor had arranged with her agent to be late for her own funeral. Norman Wisdom was dead too. He had been an unlikely star in Albania long before William's first weekend and before Enver Hoxha's gold leaf statue had been pulled down and the head carried to the hunger strikers at Tirana University, signalling the end of the last Marxist dictatorship in Eastern Europe and providing powerful visual imagery.

Carrying the head of a statue was one thing; beheadings by the Islamic State were quite another. William had lived too long and could do nothing about any of this, nor was he best placed to moralise on any subject. Besides, more than ever, he did not know where his ideas should settle with so much fake news abounding. But even such uncertainties held the stirrings of birdsong. There was the wonderful discovery that unfished marine reserves could help to save the oceans. Perhaps there might always be fish in the sea after all. Malala Yousafzai, while studying in Birmingham, had shared the Nobel Peace Prize with Kailash Satyarthi. They had invited Narendra Modi and Nawaz Sharif to the ceremony, he recalled, or was the morphine playing tricks on his memory? And Mirga, with a conjurer's intense gaze and delicate, hand, arm and body movement, was living precisely in the moment, like Michael Jordan, still, stately, decisive, solemn, warm or energetic, wings lifted to her fingertips, teasing out the music even in Birmingham for all who could hear it.

He stared at a crescent moon of light on the ceiling from the Wagenfeld lamp and, like a lunatic, remembered other snippets of news through the morphine state. Kate and William were married with a child prince, a toddler princess and another baby prince. Colonel Gaddafi had been found in a drainage pipe many years earlier, akin perhaps to the hole where Saddam Hussain had been discovered. While William still cried over Ukraine, Syria, Gaza, Iraq and Afghanistan, as he had cried over Fukushima, Pope John Paul II had been beatified and Osama Bin Laden killed in Abbottabad at some point. And no, there was no connection between abbots and Abbottabad, except in William's morphine-clouded head. Also, Nelson Mandela was dead, Winnie too, mandala-like in the shape and pattern of his life.

To breathe in and out required William's concentration and thought. This was no way to carry on. But he did not wish to die, and death was too trite an ending to a life. Besides, being here was wonderful, as Rilke had said, and he had done death already, and failed in the task. The Sufi notion of dying before death was about moving beyond self-importance so that when he was eventually shrouded in a white cloth – off-white would do – this would indicate his equality with others in death. For now, perhaps, sleep was less presumptuous. It left open the possibility that he might wake up. Heidegger said that death was the only thing no one else could do for you, not that it had occurred to him to contract this out in the way that everything else was contracted out nowadays.

There was also a sense of completing the circle, though the morphine made it a less than perfect circle. He had watched on the BBC news channel one time – there were many channels now and cloud-computing was taking hold – Barack Obama in Vietnam and hugging an atomic bomb survivor in Hiroshima. Some years earlier, well before his cruise with Cas, Camilla had glistened in a dark blue dress, the blue from somewhere in William's childhood, and she had worn a tiara borrowed from the Queen. And just when he thought the supersymmetry was completed and the royal family was back to form, Meghan, refreshingly and with a winning smile, had tapped into and helped to reset the social order and the royal household – Netflix again, in *The Crown*, with the last laugh. Of course none of this was set in stone and the saga would continue without him. And such surprises kept the morphine at bay for him a little longer. The Obamas at that time, rather than this time, had visited Dublin, Buckingham Palace and Westminster Hall. Michelle Obama had worn a stunning white dress – off-white perhaps – with matching gloves to above her elbows, but he knew too that what she stood for as a beacon to the downtrodden mattered more than her look. Those gloves were similar to the gloves that the Queen had once worn on her Pacific tour many years before and that William's mother had worn once or twice back in the fifties. Michelle Obama looked like a goddess; the wide dress straps crossing her breasts and shoulders magnificently; not a folded cross this time but certainly an angled cross. William approved of crosses, folded or angled, as well as libraries unfolding like butterflies, and clocks with one hand that could only be approximate about time. This softened the message in the same way that the flags of Jasper Johns and the distorted and squealing whammy bar versions of the 'Star Spangled Banner' by Jimi Hendrix, or Lizzo's 'Truth Hurts', had magnificently tempered and enhanced the American Dream. The Brexit vote saddened him, whatever Cas might think, because the European Union had always modified our patriotism, making the country more grown-up and less full of itself.

James and Ioanela, Ioanela's hair dyed crimson, had moved in with Stela and baby Dorin for now. Lois and Callie had visited yesterday, bringing a jelly that Lois had made – you wouldn't find Callie in the kitchen – but that William had not been able to eat. He had, however, drunk a murky cup of tea that tasted as if the oxygen were missing.

'Hold the plate still,' Cas had said to Stela, 'or the jelly will wobble and lose its colour.'

Stela had grinned. She was almost a teenager and growing up tall, with sleepovers or parties most weekends. Maidie's daughter, Lottie, was her closest friend and they were forever talking, texting and giggling, according to Ioanela.

'She'll be pushing a pram soon,' Cas had said to Ioanela, referring to Stela.

'As in Chekhov,' William had added huskily.

They had all looked at Ioanela, breastfeeding Dorin, with Stela, thin as ever, at her side. James, standing behind Ioanela's chair, had looked down proudly at his family. Both James and Ioanela had been smiling.

Stela was more self-conscious than Callie at that age, though she had still hugged William. You could not hug someone in the cloud. His legs were as thin as her legs, he had observed, though his legs were not in ribbed, blue tights, akin to the tight-knit, ribbed cardigans that girls had worn in the sixties – nor had his legs belonged to her, though reassuringly there would have been some genetic carry-over, Higgs boson permitting.

Maria and Stephen had visited him the day before. Maria's hair was no longer orange but her hazel eyes were still steady.

Now that they were both retired, they liked to see their friends more often, Maria had said evasively. Her conversation was still dull, but it was good to see her hesitant smile again.

He had seen Darren, Ros and Carmi in the summer, and Ruth and Paul had flown back with them to Raleigh. Ruth and Paul were back home again and often in the house, disturbing the gravel each time and partly obscuring the clock's tick. There would be no gravel path in the cloud.

'Carmi is a graduate now,' Paul said. 'We saw the photos. When she used to sit in a chair, her feet stuck out like chapel hat pegs. Now she has that confident, American smile – all the teeth perfect.'

'It makes you think,' Ruth added.

Cas kissed him on the forehead, partly obscuring the light from the Wagenfeld lamp, and he noticed that his feet were marginally out of alignment. He could see why Seneca had said that you should look at death and comedy with the same countenance.

'I love you, but the trouble you've caused,' she said.

She did not always need to complete sentences. She was imprinted without haziness, dark and distinguished in his mind's eye like a photographic negative, when he closed his eyes to rest. He let her go for the time being so that he could no longer hear the hamster wheel turning or the one-handed clock's tick.

Acknowledgements

Stephen Edmed, Stan Barstow, Roy Tuckey, Ashley Stokes, Clare Harris, Sara Maitland, Holly Ainley, Gale Winskill, Lee Dickinson and Averill Buchanan.

About the author

Andrew Budden has worked in industry and has studied the eighteenth-century novel, among other subjects. He lives in Devon in the UK. This is his first novel.

9 781739 739102